In her room, she felt...antsy.

Settling in to read or watching TV held little appeal.

Sarah thought of the gorgeous pool downstairs. Last night, she'd enjoyed her swim even if she'd also felt it would be wiser to stick to her room.

Because of Maddox. Because sometimes, a woman was better off to steer clear of potential trouble, no matter how green his eyes might be or how charming his smile.

But seriously. She would be working here five days a week for several weeks, anyway. Treating herself to the pool now and then was just good sense. Swimming was a great form of therapy—stress relieving and also good exercise.

And Maddox lived here, after all. She couldn't just turn tail and run every time she caught sight of him. Plus, he'd made it very clear that she was welcome to use the pool any time the mood struck.

Sarah picked up the remote and turned off the flat screen on the wall across the room.

Because the mood?

It had definitely struck.

She grabbed her suit, cover-up and monitor, and headed for the pool.

Dear Reader,

Sarah Bravo is twenty-four and single, an RN who plans to spend her life serving people who need care but can't afford hefty medical bills. And Maddox Hale? He's forty and divorced with two children. A hard-charging executive at a big New York real estate firm, Maddox enjoys making money, closing deals—and living well.

These two might have grown up on neighboring ranches, but other than that, they have nothing in common—aside from an instant and sizzling attraction that won't seem to go away no matter how hard they both try to ignore it.

Now she's living in his big, fancy ranch house, looking after his injured father. She needs the money and his dad needs the care. All Sarah and Maddox have to do is avoid each other until his father is back on his feet. It shouldn't be a problem. The house is enormous, and when Christmas comes, they'll be miles apart.

But even in a big house, the rules of attraction can't help but apply. As Sarah and Maddox get to know each other, they find it harder and harder to deny what they feel.

I hope this story reminds you that love really does triumph over seemingly impossible odds. And I wish you and yours a beautiful Christmas and a joyous New Year.

Happy reading, everyone.

Christine

WHEN CHRISTMAS COMES

CHRISTINE RIMMER

SPECIAL EDITION

Harlequin®
SPECIAL
EDITION™

Recycling programs for this product may not exist in your area.

ISBN-13: 978-1-335-40204-2

When Christmas Comes

For questions and comments about the quality of this book, please contact us at CustomerService@Harlequin.com.

TM and ® are trademarks of Harlequin Enterprises ULC.

 Harlequin Enterprises ULC
22 Adelaide St. West, 41st Floor
Toronto, Ontario M5H 4E3, Canada
www.Harlequin.com

Printed in Lithuania

MIX
Paper | Supporting
responsible forestry
FSC® C021394

Christine Rimmer came to her profession the long way around. She tried everything from acting to teaching to telephone sales. Now she's finally found work that suits her perfectly. She insists she never had a problem keeping a job—she was merely gaining "life experience" for her future as a novelist. Christine lives with her family in Oregon. Visit her at christinerimmer.com.

Books by Christine Rimmer

Harlequin Special Edition

Bravo Family Ties

Hometown Reunion
Her Best Friend's Wedding
Taking the Long Way Home
When Christmas Comes

Montana Mavericks: The Trail to Tenacity

Redeeming the Maverick

Wild Rose Sisters

The Father of Her Sons
First Comes Baby...
The Christmas Cottage

Montana Mavericks: Brothers & Broncos

Summer Nights with the Maverick

Montana Mavericks: The Real Cowboys of Bronco Heights

The Rancher's Summer Secret

Montana Mavericks: What Happened to Beatrix?

In Search of the Long-Lost Maverick

Montana Mavericks: Six Brides for Six Brothers

Her Favorite Maverick

Visit the Author Profile page
at Harlequin.com for more titles.

This one's for all you fans of the Bravo family stories. I've written more than sixty Bravo stories now and I still have ideas for a whole bunch more. Thank you so much for your thoughtful notes, emails and letters over the years. I love to hear from you. And thank you for loving the Bravos and looking forward to each new installment in the Bravo family saga. Happy reading to you all!

Chapter One

"I'm sure she's a fine nurse," said Fergus Hale as soon as the door closed on the third applicant for the Monday through Friday live-in shift. "But she seems mighty stern. I would be constantly wondering what I did wrong."

"It's okay, Dad." Maddox Hale leaned back in his desk chair in the roomy private office he'd built for himself at the family ranch. It was an office he'd rarely used. Until now. "We've got three more applicants to talk to today. I'm sure one of them will work out for you."

"Turn me back around," Fergus said.

Maddox turned his laptop around so that he could see his dad. Fergus, on Zoom from his hospital bed twenty miles away up in Sheridan, Wyoming, brought his iPad in close to his craggy, white-bearded face and scowled. "Where'd you get these nurses, son?"

"YourNurse.com. It's the top job board for nurses. I found six likely prospects in the area. Once you make your choice, I'll arrange for the final background check myself." As Maddox spoke, his dad was shaking his head. "Okay, Dad. What's the matter now?"

"This is overkill." Fergus had fallen out a second-story window two days ago. By some miracle, he'd broken only his leg. "I don't need a live-in nurse."

"But I want you to have the best home care. An RN can pretty much give you whatever care you might need."

"Son. I've got a few friends who've been laid up. They had home care aides to do the day-to-day stuff. A nurse is expensive. Medicare isn't going to pay for what you're trying to buy."

"I don't expect Medicare to pay. I'll take care of the bill."

"That's just throwing your money around, if you ask me."

"You're worth it, Dad." It was the truth. Fergus Hale might be grumpy right now, but he was still the best dad any man could ask for, bar none. A dad who had always loved and supported him, even when Maddox chased after dreams his father didn't understand.

Fergus had always hoped that his only son would grow up to take over the family ranch. But Maddox had had his own goals. He'd left the ranch at the age of eighteen with a full ride to Harvard as well as his father's unwavering support. And in the twenty-two years since Maddox had headed off to get himself an Ivy League education, his father's respect and affection had never wavered.

"Humph," grumbled Fergus, tipping the iPad so Maddox could see his splinted right leg. "What a mess. It's all swollen up."

"I know, Dad." Once the swelling went down, they would put a full cast on it. And if things went well, the closed tibial fracture would fully heal over the next twelve to sixteen weeks.

"How am I supposed to run the ranch in this condition?" Fergus muttered in disgust.

"You're not. You're taking a break. And the hands will

manage, you'll see. Plus I'm here all summer and I'll keep an eye on things, I promise you."

"You're not supposed to be working. The kids are coming. You're supposed to be on vacation for once in your life."

"It'll all work out, Dad."

"Ugh. I'm sick and tired of this situation already."

"It won't be that long until you're back on both feet again."

"Yeah? So, how come it seems like I've been in this hospital bed forever?"

The old man had always been fit and strong. Now, at seventy, he was still in great physical shape—or he had been until the day before yesterday.

Maddox grinned. "Tell me again how you fell out that window…"

His father granted him a flinty stare. "Told you once. That's enough."

"Right…"

The fall had occurred at a retirement community called Sylvan Acres up in Sheridan. Maddox still didn't really understand how it had happened. So far, the old man had played it way too cagey when it came to sharing the details of the incident. Fergus claimed he was at the facility for the community's regular Friday night Bingo event. But it must have been a really long Bingo game, because Fergus had gone out that window at around eight Saturday morning.

Maddox was just about to razz his dad some more on the nature of his all-night "Bingo" experience at Sylvan Acres when there was a tap on the door.

"It's open," he called.

Alma, Fergus's longtime housekeeper, stuck her head in. "The next one's here." She was smiling. "It's Sarah Bravo from next door."

Maddox had recognized the last name when he got the list from YourNurse.com. The Bravos were a well-known family in Medicine Creek, but he didn't remember any Bravo named Sarah. "I should know her, right?"

His dad was nodding. "She's a sweetheart. Youngest of Nate and Meggie's three." Megan and Nate Bravo owned the Double-K, which shared more than one fence line with the Hale Ranch.

Sarah... Maddox tried to picture her. A vague image of a little girl in pigtails grinning up at him during some summer barbecue years ago floated into his mind.

She was only a kid, wasn't she? The way he remembered it, Meggie's youngest was barely out of diapers when Maddox left for college. She would be too young to be his dad's live-in nurse now, wouldn't she?

Alma was still standing there in the doorway waiting for a word from him.

And Fergus's frown had morphed into a giant, happy smile. "Little Sarah from next door. What do you know? Show her in."

Nodding, Alma ducked back out the door.

Maddox asked, "How old can she be now? I filtered the search for *experienced* local nurses."

Before Fergus could answer, the door opened again and a gorgeous, doe-eyed brunette appeared. She wore trim black pants and a jacket to match with a blue button-down shirt and black boots. Her thick, glossy hair was pinned up.

And he'd been right. She was young. Too young.

"Hello, Sarah," Maddox heard himself say as he pushed back his chair.

Sarah smiled. "Maddox Hale…" She approached the desk. "Life goes by fast, doesn't it?"

"It does indeed."

"We met once," she said. "It was way back in the day. At least that's what my mom tells me. I don't really remember. I was four, maybe five…"

He nodded. "Yeah. It was in July, at a barbecue out at the Double-K." He'd just finished his sophomore year at Harvard and he'd had a summer job right there in Cambridge, but he'd managed to get a week off to go home. "You asked me to hold your snake."

A burst of musical laughter escaped her, one she quickly quelled. "Dickie. He was a garter snake. I loved him." She looked kind of wistful now. Adorably so. "Sadly, garter snakes don't live forever. He died when I was fourteen."

"Sorry for your loss." He said it teasingly. Couldn't help himself. There was something about her that tempted him to…

What? Pull her nonexistent pigtails? Ask her what she was up to this evening?

No. Uh-uh. This was a job interview and he needed to behave in a professional way.

She shrugged. "Thank you. It did kind of break my heart when he passed. Dickie was a sweetie, as garter snakes go."

Time to move things along, he thought. Sarah Bravo was charming and beautiful—too much so. She was all wrong for this job and he already knew he wasn't going to hire her. Beyond her youth, the last thing he needed was to be attracted to his father's live-in nurse.

But for a minute, he just stood there, staring at her. She stared right back, unbothered by the silence or by the way their eyes held.

Finally, he shook himself. "In any case, it's good to see you again." He offered his hand and she took it. Hers felt small, cool and a little rough—from ranch work, no doubt. Her grip was firm.

As for the woman herself, her hand might be cool. But she was hot. Way too damn hot. "Have a seat." He nodded at the guest chair facing his desk. She took it.

"Turn me around," his father groused from the laptop screen.

"Sorry, Dad." With a rueful smile for Sarah, Maddox turned the laptop so that Fergus could see her.

"Sarah!" His dad sounded downright delighted all of a sudden. "Seems like I haven't seen you in years…"

"Well, it has been a while. How are you, Mr.—"

"Oh, now," his dad interrupted her. "No, you don't. Don't make me feel a thousand years old. It's Fergus to you."

"Fergus," she repeated, that glowing smile blooming again. "How are you feeling?"

"Been better, but I'll survive. Someone told me a month ago that you were home. I kept meaning to stop by, say hi."

"It is so good to see you," she said.

"I heard you went off to college, got your degree and moved to… Colorado, wasn't it?"

"That's right. Until a couple of years ago, I was at Ohio State for my BSN." Her gaze shifted to Maddox for a second and then right back to the laptop. She beamed at his dad and continued rattling off her resume. "Once I graduated, I got my nursing license and moved to Denver for my first nursing job."

"You weren't in Denver long, I see…" Maddox had grabbed his phone from the corner of his desk, brought up her resume and started rereading her job history as she spoke.

"I worked in Denver for a year."

Maddox quizzed her on her duties during that time. She answered every question thoroughly and clearly. Then he asked, "So you were doing well there?"

"I was, yes."

"Why did you leave?"

She made a thoughtful little sound. "I realized I wanted… more, I guess. To work where nurses are desperately needed. And to see the world a little. I took an assignment at a rural clinic in Bolivia."

"Whoa," said Maddox. "That would be different."

She nodded. "It was." Maddox couldn't read her expression, but the radiant smile had faded. "Turned out, I was the only nurse for miles around. My Spanish is serviceable, but most of my patients spoke a local dialect. And the overworked traveling doctor assigned to my clinic made it there to treat patients every few weeks at best. It was… challenging. I've been home for a while now, taking a little break from nursing, spending time with the family, helping out on the Double-K."

Maddox studied her expression. She was hiding something. What? He intended to find out. "So you haven't worked as a nurse since returning from South America."

She met his eyes directly. There was steel in her gaze now. "That's correct. I was injured on the job and it took me a while to heal."

"What happened?" His dad asked the question for him.

She hesitated. "I have to tell you, I haven't been looking forward to answering that question."

"But why?" Fergus asked gently.

Sarah Bravo smiled. It was a sad smile, but enchanting, nonetheless. "It's not a pretty story."

"Please tell us," said Fergus, his voice heavy with concern.

She glanced up at Maddox. He gave her a nod. She said, "My injury occurred during a visit from our traveling physician. There was a difficult birth requiring a C-section. In the middle of surgery, the patient's husband showed up. He burst into our improvised OR, despite two of the clinic aides trying to keep him out. He was intoxicated, very upset and incoherent. And he had a knife."

Fergus exclaimed, "Oh, Sarah!"

Maddox said, "He attacked you."

"He was going for the doctor, but I tried to stop him. He stabbed me twice in the abdomen."

"My God!" exclaimed Fergus.

Sarah continued, "About then, the aides got hold of him and subdued him. The rest is kind of a blur for me. But I can happily report that no one else was hurt, the baby was born healthy, the mother survived and, well, clearly, I did, too."

"What about the husband?" Fergus asked. "I hope he got sent up for assault in the first degree."

"Actually, that's another story." Sarah cast a second questioning glance at Maddox.

"Go on," he said.

"Yes, tell us!" Fergus chimed in eagerly.

With a sigh, Sarah nodded. "You see, in Bolivia, there are two systems of justice—the system set up by the state, and the laws of the various Indigenous Peoples. In the village where I worked, the people had their own ways of handling legal disputes, including violent crimes. Later, while I recovered from surgery, I learned that the man who attacked me was sentenced to a public whipping and warned not to do that again."

Fergus let out groan of outrage. "That's it? A whipping and a warning?"

"Yes. And the whipping was severe, or so I was told. Also, according to one of the clinic aides I still correspond with, the husband was killed in a knife fight a month or so after he attacked me. His wife took the baby and moved back in with her mother."

"Well," said Fergus, "It could have been worse. At least the poor woman and the baby got away from that man."

"Yes." Sarah looked at the laptop fondly. "Yes, they did."

"And you?" Fergus asked. "You're fully recovered?"

"I am, yes." She turned those enormous eyes on Maddox. "I'm completely recovered and looking forward to getting back to work."

"I'm just glad you're home and safe," said his dad. And he wasn't done yet. Fergus had more questions—about the Bravo family, about Sarah's sister-in-law, Piper, who, Maddox learned, was pregnant with her second child.

Maddox let his dad and Sarah catch up a little, interjecting interested noises whenever appropriate. In reality, he was only waiting for her to leave so that they could move on to the next applicant.

Yes, she and his dad got along well. And yes, she was ready to go to work right away.

Didn't matter. Sarah was not the one for this job. If he hired her, she would be living right there at the ranch house with the family five days a week. He didn't feel comfortable about that. It wasn't something he needed to examine too closely. It was just a plain fact.

One of the other applicants would be a better fit.

The door had barely closed behind her before Fergus said, "That settles it. Sarah's the one."

Maddox suggested, "How about we get through the other two interviews before we make a final decision?"

"I won't change my mind."

"Let's just talk to them. Okay, Dad?"

"All right, son. Bring 'em on."

Forty-five minutes later, the final prospect left. Her name was Millie Lejardi.

"I like her," said Maddox as soon as Millie was out the door. He turned the laptop around again so he and his father were face-to-face. "She's got a lot of experience and great references. She's calm, too, and down-to-earth."

His dad agreed. "I like Millie just fine—but it's Sarah we're hiring."

It wasn't what Maddox wanted to hear. "Think about it, Dad. Sarah Bravo is too young to—"

"You're wrong, son. By my reckoning, she's twenty-four, maybe twenty-five and that means she's all grown up. We're hiring Sarah."

"But the Lejardi woman has so much more experience. Plus, I did some reading on what to look for in a home nurse."

"Sure you did, son." Wearily, Fergus shook his head and rubbed at his injured leg.

"What I'm trying to say is that in my reading, I learned that it's ill-advised to hire a friend. Your nurse should have no emotional ties to you. A nurse needs to be objective in order to be able to give you the best care."

"Don't you have enough to do running your real estate conglomerate, without wasting time fussing over this choice when I'm perfectly capable of deciding for myself?" Fergus asked with a lift of one silver eyebrow. "You're the one who insisted I would have round-the-clock care. I think it's only fair that I get to make the final choice as to who's giving me that care."

What could Maddox say but, "Of course it's your choice."

"Then, I choose Sarah."

"But Dad, please just think about it. Boundaries matter. Nurses need to be neutral, focused solely on helping you get better, and a friend can't always be counted on to—"

"Oh, for Pete's sake. Yes, I know Sarah. But Maddox, I know everyone for miles around, Millie Lejardi included. Sarah's fully qualified and I've got zero doubt she can be objective when it comes to my damn broken leg if that's what you're worrying about. I trust her. I honestly do. She's a ray of sunshine and I need a little sunshine while I'm laid up. Hire her for me. Please."

At that point, Maddox was fresh out of comebacks. His dad had every right to make the final decision, no matter how much Maddox wished Fergus would choose someone else. "If you're sure…"

"I am—and I hear the lunch cart in the hallway. Love you, son. I'm signing off." The screen went to white with the blue Zoom logo.

Maddox checked the time. He had an online meeting in half an hour and another an hour after that. They were meetings he couldn't postpone. Meetings he should have attended in person.

The original plan was for him to arrive in Wyoming two weeks from now. The idea then had been strictly about finding a way to reconnect with his children. His ex-wife, Alexis, had been after him for a while now about his lack of quality time with the kids. As usual, Alexis was right. He needed to put more effort into being a decent father.

A summer at the family ranch had seemed a good way to begin being a better parent to his thirteen-year-old son and eleven-year-old daughter while also spending more time with his dad.

He'd pictured a lot of swimming in the gorgeous pool he'd had put in a few years back. He'd imagined long horseback rides over the rolling Wyoming land, with his dad along to help him brush up on his parenting skills.

But then Fergus fell out a window, and here he was, two weeks early, taking an endless parade of online meetings with investors, colleagues and coworkers back in New York.

And not only was he here two weeks ahead of schedule, now a too-young and far-too-attractive live-in nurse would be here as well—but that was okay, he reminded himself. He would pivot and adapt to the new situation, just like he always did.

Alma tapped on the office door. She breezed in with a lunch tray and a small carafe of coffee.

The housekeeper had been a fixture at the ranch for a decade and a half now, ever since a month after Maddox's mom died suddenly of a heart attack. He'd been twenty-five at the time, taking on what he could for his dad, who'd refused to come out of his room for weeks after the funeral. Fergus Hale was a one-woman man and it had just about killed him to lose his beloved Mary.

That was a tough time. Mary Hale had been the heart of their three-person family. A year later, when Maddox married Alexis, it had hurt like hell to see his dad sitting alone in the front pew.

Now Maddox gave the housekeeper a grateful smile. "Alma, you're a lifesaver."

"Eat that sandwich and don't work too hard," she scolded as she turned to go.

He ate the sandwich, drank the coffee, took his meetings

on time and tried not to let his mind wander to thoughts of big brown eyes and thick, glossy pinned-up hair that just begged to be let down.

What in the hell was the matter with him? Sarah Bravo had walked in the door and his brain had gone flying out the window.

It bothered him a lot, this sudden ridiculous attraction for someone so much younger. Powerful men got a rep, after all. Maddox had watched it happen over and over. Many of the men in his circle had gone from what they actually called "starter" wives at the beginning of their careers to a series of trophy wives—each of whom was younger than the one before.

That was not going to happen with Maddox. He was never getting married again. Not to some young thing and not to any of the women he'd dated since his divorce. Nowadays he went out with interesting, age-appropriate, sophisticated women who understood that a marriage proposal was never coming out of his mouth.

Bottom line, Sarah Bravo could too easily be distracting. And he had no time for distractions. This summer, he needed to focus on forging a better relationship with his children and looking after his laid-up dad while staying on top of things at Hightower Property Trust.

"Twenty-four…twenty-five!" Sarah called out as she dropped her hands from covering her eyes. "Ready or not, here I come!"

There was silence, which surprised Sarah. Her niece was three and a half and irrepressible. As a rule, if she was awake, Megan Emmaline Bravo was talking or laughing—or both.

Sarah turned slowly in the center of her brother Jason's

rustic great room. "Where *is* Emmy? Hmm… I just don't know. I have no idea…"

A tiny, stifled giggle sounded from behind the sofa.

"What's that I hear? Could that be Emmy?"

Silence. Sarah pictured her red-haired niece, little hands clapped over her mouth, trying so hard not to make a sound.

"I guess I'm going to have to take a real good look around now." She started walking, pausing by the window to give her brother's dog, Kenzo, a scratch on the head. "I'm going to have to go over every inch of this entire room…"

There was a rustling sound coming from behind the sofa—followed by breath-held stillness. Sarah clomped around the great room, making lots of noise, peering under the coffee table and circling every chair, but never once looking behind the sofa.

After a few minutes of that, she flopped into an easy chair. "Oh, I give up," she announced with a heavy sigh.

Laughing gleefully, the little cutie popped up from behind the couch. "I win!"

"Yes, you do!" Sarah held out her arms and Emmy came running. The little girl climbed right up into Sarah's lap. Sarah hugged her and tickled her and blew a long raspberry against her velvety cheek.

When Emmy finally stopped giggling, she caught Sarah's face between her little hands. "Mommy brought me new books." Piper Bravo, Emmy's mom, was director of the library in town. "Want me to read one to you?"

"Yes, please."

"Okay, Aunt Sarah. You wait right here."

"It's a deal," Sarah replied.

Emmy scrambled down from her lap and headed for her room, Kenzo trailing along behind. She returned a few minutes later with a copy of *The Very Hungry Caterpillar*. Clambering back up into Sarah's chair, she opened the book and started turning the pages, telling the story as she went, seeming to recognize many of the words.

At the end, she tipped her head back to look up at Sarah. "That was good, wasn't it?"

"The best," Sarah agreed. "Thank you for reading it to me."

They both heard the vehicle pull in out front. "Mommy and Daddy are home!" Emmy jumped from Sarah's lap, dropped the book on the coffee table and made for the door.

Jason and Piper were halfway up the steps to the front deck when Emmy yanked the door wide. She raced out to meet them. By the time Sarah reached the threshold, her brother had the little girl perched on his hip and was carrying her back inside as she chattered away, filling him in on everything that had happened while he and Piper were gone.

The couple had been up in Sheridan for an ultrasound. At forty-four, Piper was what they called of advanced maternal age. She would have ultrasounds every four weeks now until the baby came.

Which wouldn't be long. She was thirty-six weeks pregnant as of yesterday. Her baby boy led the way wherever she went.

As Jason hoisted Emmy to his shoulders and headed into the kitchen with Kenzo at his heels, Piper lowered her body carefully into a chair. "How was she?"

"An angel, as always. A very happy, enthusiastic angel. Your daughter can get excited over a snack of sliced apples."

Piper laughed. "It's a gift."

"So?" Sarah asked. "How did it go?"

Piper gently stroked her giant belly. "Just great. Everything's looking good."

"That's what I wanted to hear."

Piper grabbed a throw pillow off the sofa and stuck it behind her to support her back. "I didn't get a chance to ask earlier. How was the interview at the Hale Ranch?"

Sarah thought of Maddox Hale. Tall and fit. Green eyes that seemed to see right through her—eyes with crinkles at the corners because he was around forty. Though he did have a boyish look about him—in his smile, in the way he could seem almost shy now and then. He was charming, really. But then, he would have to be. The Hales had never been rich. Not until after Maddox went off to Harvard, made a bunch of important connections and married an heiress—and yes, Sarah had been Googling the man.

After the interview that morning, she'd come straight home and looked up Maddox Hale online. He was no longer the college boy she'd once asked to hold her snake. Uh-uh. Nowadays Maddox Hale was some kind of huge deal, a high-up executive at a major REIT, which stood for Real Estate Investment Trust. From what she'd read, he really was all that in the world of big-time real estate.

And today, he'd liked her—same as she'd liked him.

But he hadn't *liked* liking her. In fact, she would venture a guess that he'd found it unacceptable that he liked her. And that meant her chances of getting the job at the Hale Ranch were probably slim to none.

And that was too bad. It was just the kind of job she wanted right now, a way to ease back into nursing. A short-term job close to home. Nothing too challenging. And Fergus was a sweetheart. She would have loved working for him. Plus the money would be nice. Her checking account didn't have a whole lot in it at the moment.

"Sarah?" Piper was looking at her funny.

Sarah blinked. "What? Oh! Sorry…"

"You okay?"

"I'm good. Really. It's only… I don't know. The interview went fine. I just have a feeling that job's not for me."

Piper asked, "Did something happen at the interview?"

"No, it went smoothly." And it had. Overall. Talking about the stabbing had been a little rocky, but she'd gotten through it. And it was bound to come up in interviews, so she needed to get used to talking about it simply and clearly without flashing back to the horror of the actual event. "It's just a feeling, that's all." She smiled and played it off. "We'll see. And honestly, it's not a big deal. I only started looking again last week. I'll find something else soon enough. I have an interview scheduled for Wednesday and another for Thursday. The right job is bound to turn up."

"The Hales would be fools not to hire you," said Piper.

"So true," Sarah replied. "I'm the best."

"There you go." Piper shook a finger at her. "You're getting that job."

It turned out Piper was right. Maddox called that night. Sarah was sitting at the built-in table in the trailer she'd been living in on open land about a half mile from her parents' house. It shocked the hell out of her to hear that deep, velvety voice on the phone.

He was so smooth and so polite. "Just calling to let you know you're our choice for the job."

Way to go, Fergus, she thought. Because she had zero doubt that she'd read Maddox right that morning. No way was she *his* choice. Which meant that Fergus must have stuck up for her. She was grinning smugly as she replied, "That's great. I would love to look after Fergus until he's back on both feet again."

"Terrific." He said it like he meant it. But she could hear a hint of irony beneath his charming façade. "I wanted to mention that there will be travel. A week and a half in mid-July. I give an annual party at my house in Southampton. I've convinced my dad to come along and he will need you with him. I realize that you will be working more than five days in a row during the trip so for that ten-day period I will pay you double your rate to compensate you for the long hours."

"That works for me." *Double her rate* sounded excellent to her.

"Good. From Southampton, it's on to New York so that I can catch up on a few things at the office. My plan is to keep the evenings free to spend with my dad—as much as possible, anyway. For you, that means once I get home from the office, your time is your own."

"I understand. The travel is fine."

"All right, then. I've ordered the background check. That will take a couple of days."

She knew they usually took longer. But hers shouldn't. She'd blown through a red light once—no, she was not drunk at the time. And that was her only her run-in with the law. She had great references, what there were of them. True, her bank account was on life support and she had some serious student loans to keep paying back. But everyone had those. Otherwise, she carried very little debt, so the credit check should take no time at all.

"I'm hoping you can start Friday morning," he said. "The way it looks now, they're releasing my dad Friday afternoon. I would want you here to get him settled in, then the weekend nurse will relieve you Saturday and Sunday. And you're back on duty at eight a.m. on Monday."

"Sounds good. So as of now, I start Friday?"

"That's right. At eight in the morning. I'll call you Thursday to confirm."

She made agreeable noises. They said goodbye. She disconnected the call and tossed her phone down on the dinette table.

Take that, Maddox Hale!

She was laughing as she rose from the pleather seat and did a little victory dance on her nine-by-three-foot rectangle of living area floor.

Chapter Two

Sarah arrived at the Hale place right on time Friday morning. Alma greeted her at the door, gave her a key to the house and the code to disable the alarm. Next, Alma showed her to her room on the second floor. The room had its own bathroom and a great view of the stables and the mountains beyond.

"This is beautiful, thank you." Sarah tossed her overnight case on the queen-size bed but kept her work tote on her shoulder.

Alma, who was tall and athletic-looking, with graying blond hair pulled back in a low ponytail, gave Sarah a big smile. "Maddox has had just about every room in the house redone in the past decade or so. Plus, he's added on extensively."

"I noticed." As had anyone who lived within a thirty-mile radius of the Hale Ranch. The ranch house used to be a two-story log home, a comfortable-looking place, but nothing fancy.

Not anymore, though. In the past decade or so, the house had become a sprawling showplace, something straight out of *Architectural Digest*.

"Wait till you see the pool. It's indoors, but with skylights, lots of windows and a comfy, attached pool house that's connected by a wide hallway to the main house. It's beautiful—and usable year-round. It's also Maddox's pride and joy. Do you need some time to settle in?"

Sarah laughed. "I'm only here overnight this time, so no. I've got nothing to unpack, really." She patted her tote. "Except for a few things I brought to make Fergus more comfortable."

"Maddox is up at the hospital. He said that he and Fergus should be here by one or so. How about if I give you a quick tour?"

"I need to see Fergus's room first, get familiar with what I have to work with, see if there's anything missing that I think he'll need. Once I've done that, I would love a tour of everything else."

Downstairs, Alma led the way to the office wing and past the room where Sarah had been interviewed on Monday. At the end of that hallway, a wide door opened onto a spacious one-bedroom apartment. The sitting area was attractively furnished and wheelchair-friendly, with a small kitchenette on one wall. The bedroom included an adjustable bed and a lift reclining chair. As for the bathroom, it had a walk-in shower with a built-in bench seat, a grab bar and a handheld shower head. There was even a sturdy, padded shower stool on which Fergus could rest his injured leg.

Sarah shook her head in wonder at the sight. "This is perfect."

Alma nodded. "Maddox likes to plan for every eventuality. It's a little bit scary, the way his brain works. He added this apartment when he put in the office wing. Told me that a place this size should have an in-law suite. Plus, he wanted his dad to be comfortable if the time ever came when the upstairs primary suite didn't work anymore—though he added an elevator to the second and third floors so Fergus could stay in the primary suite if it was just stairs giving him trouble. But he wanted to have this space ready in case there were more severe problems. Notice that the doors are all wide enough to accommodate a wheelchair." Alma swept out a hand toward the tall windows. "There's a lovely view of the side yard. As for the adjustable bed, lift chair and padded stool, they're new. They arrived yesterday."

"Impressive." Sarah set down her big tote. "Clearly, Maddox Hale thinks of everything…"

"Indeed he does. Now, how about that tour?" Alma wiggled her eyebrows.

Sarah said yes and followed the housekeeper around as she pointed out the features of the house. From the soaring entryway anchored by a giant natural-stone fireplace to the various sprawling living areas with big picture windows and oversize furniture, the house was impressive.

And inviting, too. All those deep sofas and soft leather chairs beckoned a visitor to sit down and relax. The kitchen was on a grand scale, a marvel of chef-quality appliances, dark hardwood cabinetry and stone countertops. But the bedrooms were a little more streamlined, more laid-back.

The indoor pool really was something, a huge space with soaring log ceilings and multiple skylights. There were lush, padded lounge chairs, and also one of those giant roll-up doors of steel and glass, the kind they sometimes used in restaurants, so that in warm weather the pool area could extend out into the yard.

"It's gorgeous," Sarah said.

Alma nodded. "Isn't it? Feel free to use it anytime."

She wasn't so sure about that. "It's okay with Maddox, then?"

"It's okay with Fergus, and he owns the place." Alma chuckled. "Don't look so worried. Maddox won't mind at all if you use the pool. I swim here regularly. Maddox has seen me heading this way in my cover-up, with my beach towel. He always smiles and says I should enjoy my swim."

"Well, all right, then." She would definitely be using the pool.

Twenty minutes later, Sarah and Alma went out the front entrance and down the wide stone steps as Maddox appeared from behind the wheel of a gleaming Mercedes SUV. He was looking very casual today, in old jeans, a pair of Timberlands and a gray T-shirt that clung to his hard, broad chest.

His full lips curved in an easy smile. Ugh. The man was way too good-looking. The frosty way he'd treated her on Monday during her interview aside, he really did come off as thoroughly likable. Probably from years of managing people, learning how to motivate employees and give clients what they wanted while simultaneously accomplishing his own objectives.

"Sarah." He gave her that boyish smile of his. "Did you get settled in all right?"

She beamed right back at him. "Thanks, Maddox. I did."

About then, Fergus leaned out the passenger-side window. "There you are, Sarah! I am so glad to see your smiling face." He pushed open the passenger door. "Hey, Alma!"

The housekeeper gave him a wave. "About time you came on home."

Fergus looked tired, Sarah thought. "It's so good to see you, too," she said. "Let me get your crutches for you." She could see them on the back seat. She grabbed the handle of the back door to get them.

But Maddox stopped her. "Let's use the wheelchair." He lifted the hatchback. "It's kind of a long walk around the side of the house to his rooms."

Fergus's mouth twisted and his eyes got such a mutinous gleam that Sarah was pretty sure he would argue. But then he only sighed. "The wheelchair, it is."

By then, Maddox had lifted the chair out of the hatchback and opened it on the ground. He rolled it around to Fergus's door. And then he slid a glance at Sarah. "I'm guessing you're an expert at getting patients into the chair, but I'm bigger." He said it with a killer grin.

She tried not to giggle. Because that would so ruin her credibility. "Did you transfer him into the car?"

"The aide did that."

"Oh, for Pete's sake," Fergus grumbled. "I can get in that chair on my own."

Sarah shifted her gaze to her patient. "Probably. But if you put any weight on your bad leg, you could make the break worse. We can't have that."

Fergus gave in. "Fine. Have it your way. Transfer me."

Maddox stepped back and let Sarah take charge.

She moved the chair so that Fergus could use his good leg while pivoting into it, locked the wheels, shifted the foot-rests out of the way and slowly helped him from the car and into the chair. He was a strong man and his good leg was sturdy, so the process wasn't as difficult as it might have been, even though she hadn't thought ahead and brought her trusty transfer belt out with her.

Nobody argued with Fergus when he insisted on rolling the chair around to the side door himself. They followed after him carrying his bags and crutches.

A shiny new aluminum ramp had been installed from

the footpath to the side door. Maddox took the lead, striding up the ramp and opening the door. Fergus came next, with Sarah and Alma behind him. Once inside, it was twenty feet along the hallway to Fergus's door at the end.

Alma handed Maddox the bags she'd carried from the car. "I'll get back to work. Buzz me if you need anything," she said, and off she went as Fergus rolled his wheelchair into his new room with Maddox and Sarah right behind him.

"Just set those bags down, son," the older man instructed. "And go on about your business. Sarah and me, we got this thing handled."

Maddox set the bags next to the door. "If you're sure, Dad…"

"I am. Go check on your real estate empire. I will be just fine."

Maddox went to his father and bent close. The two shared an awkward hug and Maddox said gruffly, "It's good to have you home."

"Good to *be* home."

Reluctantly, Maddox left them. Sarah watched him go. The man had a lot flaws, but Sarah couldn't help liking the way he took care of his dad.

In his office down the hall, Maddox caught up with work. Throughout the rest of the day, he resisted the temptation to return to his dad's room, see how things were going.

He kept reminding himself that it annoyed his dad no end when he hovered.

And why should he hover? His father was clearly happy to have Sarah looking after him. As for the woman herself, she seemed both confident and capable.

Better than capable. She liked his dad and she treated

him with respect and fondness. He felt a little guilty for having given the old man pushback over hiring her. She was going to be just what Fergus needed, someone strong, smart and conscientious—and charming as well.

And as for his own bothersome attraction to her, well, he needed to get over himself. Thanks to his obsession with add-ons and improvements, the house was plenty big enough for both of them. They would hardly have to see each other.

Dinner was at six in the big kitchen and included just the four of them—Fergus, Alma, Sarah and Maddox. His dad wheeled his chair right up to the wide plank table. He seemed more relaxed than he had that afternoon, as he kidded around with Alma and Sarah.

Yeah. Things were going well, Maddox thought. Sarah Bravo was a good choice.

After the meal, Maddox went out to check in with Caleb Daws, Fergus's top hand. He found the tall, skinny horse trainer in the stables as usual. Diamond Lady, one of their prize mares, had foaled the night before. Maddox stroked and praised the mare, admired the little one and nodded as Caleb explained that everything was under control, even with the boss out of commission for the next several weeks.

When Maddox got back to the house at half past eight, everything was quiet. He went on up to the media room on the third floor. But the idea of playing online chess or streaming a film didn't have much appeal. He felt restless and considered heading back to his office. There was always more work he could do.

But no. He went on down to his bedroom suite, kicked off his shoes and socks, stretched out on the bed, grabbed the spy thriller on the nightstand, and continued reading where he'd left off the night before. An hour later, bored with the spy story, he glanced out the tall window opposite the bed and saw that the wide, clear sky was thick with stars.

A swim. That was what he needed. He would work off a little excess energy doing laps for half an hour or so. Tossing his book aside, he headed downstairs.

In the pool house, he changed into a pair of board shorts. Then he grabbed a towel, a cap and goggles, and went on out into the pool area itself, which was illuminated at night not only by safety lights but also by the moon and the stars shining in through the windows, the skylights and the big roll-up glass door.

After dropping his towel on a lounge chair, he was putting on his cap and goggles, two steps from diving into the deep end when Sarah Bravo appeared right there in front him. She popped up from under the water like some sort of sea nymph.

Maddox blinked down at her. Her eyes were shut, her face tipped to the skylight above, her hair sleek as a seal's pelt as she brought up her hands and smoothed it back.

For a moment, he wondered if she was really there or if he'd dreamed her up somehow. It was nothing short of otherworldly to enter the deserted pool area only to find her lurking beneath the surface, ready to magically appear and startle the hell out of him.

She opened her eyes. "Oh!" Those eyes went wide. "Uh, Maddox. Hi!"

He couldn't help grinning. She looked as surprised as he felt. Maybe more so. "Sorry," he said. "I didn't realize anyone was here."

"Ah. Right…" She swam to the edge a few feet from where he stood and pulled herself up from the water enough to rest her forearms on the stone tiles. "It's a beautiful pool and the water is just right."

He was staring, and he knew it. Oddly embarrassed, he glanced to the side and noticed what looked like a baby monitor on top of a towel. "Is that—"

"A baby monitor, yes." She was grinning. "I left the transmitter with Fergus. He didn't like the idea of it much. In fact, I suspect he's turned it off. He's been practicing with his crutches today, so he's better at getting around without having to put weight on his bad leg. But just in case he does need something during the night, all he has to do is call out and I'll be there."

"As long as he's got the monitor on."

"Exactly."

"He's a proud man, my dad."

"Tell me about it." She chuckled—and then grew serious. "Listen, I get it if you want the pool to yourself. I was just about to go anyway." She braced her hands on the tiles to climb out.

"No, you weren't."

One dark, wet eyebrow lifted as she sank back into the water. "I wasn't?"

Damn. Those eyes of hers got to him. "Stay." He said it gently. But it was a command, nonetheless. Wondering at himself, at his own intentions, he gave her a shrug and a careful smile. "It's a big pool."

She stared up at him, measuring… What? His honesty? His possible untrustworthy motives?

And then, gripping the edge of the tiles, she stretched out her arms, levered back in the water, lifted her feet to brace on the side of the pool, and pushed off. Her body glided backward through the water. "Okay, then. I'll stay."

He waited for her to reach the other side before lowering the goggles over his eyes. Diving in, he arrowed straight across beneath the surface and popped up next to her.

They stared at each other. He felt energized suddenly, all of the day's pressures and anxieties just dropping away.

Finally, she asked, "Now what?"

"I usually do laps. You?"

"Nothing that structured. I kind of just do whatever comes naturally until I tire myself out. How about you go ahead. I'll stay out of your way."

"Works for me."

For the next twenty minutes or so, he swam at a steady, even crawl up and down the length of the pool, keeping to one side, leaving the other to her. When he was done, he pulled up and stopped at the deep end. He pushed up his goggles and turned to see her floating in the shallows, face up to the skylights.

Her eyes were shut and her hair drifted out around her. Treading water beneath the diving board, he allowed himself to stare at her.

Eventually, she caught on to him. "You're too still." She spoke the words rather loudly as she continued to float in the shallow end with her eyes shut.

He should have answered. But he didn't. He just went on watching her. She was a creature not quite real, adrift at the other end of the pool.

"Are you okay?" she asked at last. "Maddox?" When he still didn't answer, she lowered her legs and stood. The water came to her waist now. All that dark hair clung to her head and down her back. It stuck in snaky tendrils to her slim shoulders, to the red straps of her tank-style suit.

Scowling now, she braced her fists on her hips. "What are you staring at?"

He shut his eyes and drew in a slow breath. His plan to avoid her was not going well. "Sorry. You looked...so peaceful, just floating there." Not to mention, like a mermaid, or some other mythical sea creature. A naiad. A selkie...

She frowned at him down the length of the pool. "Are you all right?"

"I am, yes. I'm also being rude. Again, I apologize."

"It's...okay?"

"No," he said. "It's not." Turning, he hoisted himself out of the pool, rose to his full height and faced her. "You're so good with my dad. He's happy just because you're here. I hope you won't let me scare you away." *Though maybe you should.*

She stood in the water, unmoving, way down there at the shallow end, a water nymph in a red suit. "Of course not."

The strangest thing happened to him right then. He felt relieved that she would stay—and not only for his father's sake. "Good." He crossed the stone tiles and grabbed his towel from the chair where he'd left it. "You are welcome to use the pool at any time. I mean that."

"Thank you." She smiled then. Carefully.

"Good night, Sarah."

"Good night."

What just happened?

Sarah wasn't sure. She watched Maddox Hale walk away. He looked good. Really good, tall and broad-shouldered, filling out his blue board shorts just right. She tried not to think what a great ass he had. And his back muscles...

There ought to be a law against a man being that physically stunning.

But he really had behaved strangely, staring at her that way while she floated, totally oblivious, in the shallow end. What was that all about? She should probably be creeped out by the whole encounter.

But she wasn't.

She was…unacceptably gleeful.

Because Maddox Hale was proving himself to be not only handsome, smooth and way too smart.

He also had an awkward side. He'd seemed a bit embarrassed that he'd stared at her. She got the feeling that he was actually kind of sensitive.

And then there was the way he treated his father. He was a good son. He really did love his dad.

Plus, she was reasonably certain now that he'd changed his mind about her. Maybe he didn't like her, exactly. But now he definitely wanted her to stay.

A little later, upstairs in her room, she put the baby monitor on the nightstand and got ready for bed. When she slid under the covers, she heard a sound.

Not quite a snore, but almost. Fergus had turned on the transmitter unit. Smiling, she switched off the light and settled in for the night.

The next morning, she stayed at the Hale house long enough for a quick breakfast and to meet the weekend nurse, Tansy, who seemed sweet and conscientious.

Back home at the Double-K, there was always plenty that needed doing. Sarah pitched in as usual, looking after the horses, chasing down wandering cattle, helping out in the main house at mealtimes. At the Hale ranch house on

Monday, Fergus greeted her with a giant smile and an enthusiastic, "There you are, Sarah!"

The older man seemed in good spirits overall. He was managing the wheelchair well and practicing on his crutches. The swelling had gone down a bit, which was great as they had an appointment Friday to cast the fractured leg.

That night, she indulged in an hour down at the pool—alone, because Maddox failed to appear. She reminded herself that she didn't care in the least whether he showed up to swim or not.

In fact, it was better if they didn't use the pool together. Because she might as well be honest with herself and admit that when he was near, she was way too... She struggled to choose the exact right word.

Aware.

Yeah. She was much too aware of him.

Boundaries mattered. As Fergus's nurse, she had an ethical responsibility not to get too friendly with her patient or with any member of her patient's family—and okay, she was pretty darn friendly with Fergus and that didn't bother her much at all. That she and her patient got along so well just made her job easier. With Maddox, though, it was a whole other kind of friendly. The dangerous kind. So she swam alone and went to bed early and smiled coolly at Maddox when he showed up at the breakfast table Tuesday morning.

"Sarah," he said with a nod.

"Morning, Maddox." She nodded right back. Strictly professional. No over-fraternizing going on here.

After breakfast, they were back in Fergus's apartment when his cell rang. He pulled it from his shirt pocket and frowned at the screen. "I have to take this, Sarah."

What did that mean? "Er...go right ahead."

He grunted. "Privately, I mean."

"Ah. Gotcha." She held up her own phone. "Just buzz me when you're done."

He made a shooing motion as his phone continued to ring. "Go, go..."

She scurried out, quietly closing the door behind her, wondering what the heck that call was about and then reminding herself that it was none of her business.

But how long would he be? Should she go on outside for a bit or up to her room?

Probably not. Because hopefully, the call would wrap up quickly. They'd been right in the middle of the thirty-minute chair-exercise session prescribed by the physical therapist who had visited the day before, and Fergus would get more benefit out of the session if he didn't take a long break in the middle.

She was leaning against the wall next to Fergus's door, getting caught up on Words With Friends, which she played continuously with Piper and two of her cousins, when a smooth, warm male voice asked, "Everything okay?"

A way-too-delicious shiver slid through her as she looked up from the screen and into those clear green eyes. Maddox stood by the door to his office.

"Fergus had a call," she explained. "He wanted to take it privately."

Maddox's straight brows crunched together. "What kind of call?"

She slipped her phone into her pocket. "I have no idea. It was private, as I said. He asked me to leave the room while he took it."

Maddox seemed to be trying not to grin. "Am I about to get a lecture on patient confidentiality?"

She suppressed a grin of her own. "Do you need one?"

He put up both hands. "Far be it from me to intrude in any way on my father's privacy."

"Well, good, then."

He didn't say anything for a long count of twenty. Oddly, the silence was not the least awkward. Finally, he said, "There's plenty of room for a chair there by Dad's door. I'll ask Alma to get you one."

"A chair isn't necessary."

"Maybe not." He shrugged. "But it can't hurt. You might as well be comfortable while you wait for my father to finish his *private* conversations." His own phone rang then. "I have to get this." With a quick nod, he disappeared back through the office door.

For a moment, she just stood there feeling oddly giddy—and knowing she should not be feeling anything of the kind.

Then her phone rang in her pocket. She put it to her ear. "Hey, Fergus."

"Come on back in."

When she opened the door, he was right there on the other side, close enough that he had to roll his chair back a foot for her to push the door fully open. His weather-roughened cheeks were flushed.

"What's wrong? Did something happen?"

He sat up straighter. "Not a thing. Come on, let's get these damn exercises over with."

For the next twenty minutes, he was a model patient, performing each exercise perfectly. As soon as he finished that last triceps extension, though, he announced, "I'm thinking I could use a walk outside—well, I mean, in my case, a roll outside. It's such a nice day, after all."

He was up to something, she could tell. His smile was forced and his eyes were kind of shifty.

And then he added, "You go ahead and take a break, Sarah. All this fancy landscaping Maddox is so proud of includes a network of nice, smooth paths. I'll have no trouble managing this chair on my own."

She flat-out did not trust that gleam in his eyes. Not to mention that the first time he took his wheelchair out on the grounds, he shouldn't go alone. "If you want go for a *roll*, as you put it, that's fine with me. But I'm going with you."

His craggy face got a pinched look. "You don't need to go. I want you to stay here."

"Fergus, be realistic. I'm here to help you manage your injury effectively. And also to ensure that you are safe while you are healing. Neither one of us knows for sure yet how well the wheelchair will be able to manage those paths. I can't guarantee your safety right now if you take off alone."

Fergus pressed his thin lips together and glared at her mutinously. In response, she folded her arms across her chest and waited.

In the end, he gave it up. "Fine. Have it your way." He started the chair moving. "Let's go."

She fell in beside him and off they went, out the side door and down the ramp.

It really was gorgeous out, the wide Wyoming sky an endless expanse of robin's egg blue. They took the gently winding paths around tall firs, decorative boulders and blue spruce. He seemed to know exactly where he was going and she just followed where he led, mostly at his side but dropping back behind his chair whenever the path narrowed.

It wasn't long before they reached a rail fence that ran along beside the access road leading to and from the highway. Fergus stopped his chair there.

Backing and turning quite skillfully, he faced her. "Okay. This is where I want to be. And I would like to be alone for a bit if you don't mind."

"Fergus, I—"

He stopped her with an upraised hand. "A half hour. I will not budge from this spot and I have my phone if I need you."

His request was perfectly reasonable. If he really wasn't planning on going anywhere, then she had no doubt he would be fine without her. "Sounds fair. I'll just—"

They both heard the vehicle approaching on the road. The car came around a bend and into sight—a silver Escalade. It kicked up dust as it barreled toward them.

The big SUV jerked to a stop just on the other side of the fence from the two of them.

"Too late," muttered Fergus as a blonde woman who might have been any age from fifty to seventy jumped out of the Cadillac.

Chapter Three

The woman wore a broomstick skirt, tooled boots, a soft, snug knit shirt the color of heavy cream and turquoise jewelry.

Firmly shutting the car door behind her, she turned and folded her arms over her generous breasts. "What are you doing out here, Fergus?"

For a tenth of a second, Fergus seemed transfixed, like he'd never seen anything as beautiful as the woman standing on the other side of the fence from him. But then he slanted a glance at Sarah and sat up straighter in the chair. "I thought—"

"That you'd catch me before I got to the house?" The woman gave a husky laugh. "Oops. That didn't work, now, did it?" She turned a big smile on Sarah and held out her hand. Her fingernails were as red as her lips. "Earlene Pugh."

"Sarah Bravo." They shook.

"Nice to meet you, hon. I live out at Sylvan Acres. That's where Fergus and I met. You must be the nurse."

"I am, yes."

"How's he doing?"

"Damn it, Earlene," Fergus interrupted. "Don't go talking about me like I'm not even here."

"I don't see why I shouldn't." Earlene leaned closer to

Sarah and whispered, "He likes to keep me a secret. So the way I see it, talking *about* him instead of *to* him makes us even. You get what I'm saying?"

Sarah sighed. "This is so not my business."

Earlene beamed. "I like you. You're quick. I wonder, could you roll him on back where he came from? I'll just drive the rest of the way up to the house and knock on the door like a civilized person."

"I would, Earlene. But it's really not my call."

Earlene pinned Fergus with a steely stare. "Well?"

"Fine," Fergus said in a growl. "Come on up to the house."

"Why Fergus Hale, I thought you'd never ask."

He scowled. "Just give us fifteen minutes to get back there before you ring the bell."

"Absolutely, honey pie. Whatever you say."

When the intercom buzzed fifteen minutes later, Sarah and Fergus were back in his apartment.

Fergus rolled his chair to the wall and pushed the button to answer. "Alma, that you?"

"Yes, it is. Earlene Pugh is here to see you."

"Fine. Show her in, please."

Three minutes later, Sarah opened the door to Earlene and the housekeeper. Earlene walked right in. "Well, isn't this cozy," she said.

Fergus took charge. "Thanks, Alma. Could you maybe bring us some iced tea and a little snack?"

"Happy to."

Next, Fergus turned to Sarah. "How 'bout a break?"

"I would love one. Give me a call when my break is over."

"Will do."

Earlene wiggled her red-tipped fingers at Sarah. "A delight to have met you, Sarah. And you too, Alma."

Sarah followed Alma up the annex hallway. When they reached the central hallway the housekeeper turned to her. "What a day. I can hardly keep up."

"What's going on?"

Turned out Alma had bread in the oven and chicken on the cooktop. Plus, it was cleaning day, which she explained meant several workers in various rooms engaged in an endless number of cleaning tasks. It was Alma's job to supervise them all.

"Is there any way I can help?"

"Oh, would you? If you could just bring Fergus and his guest their snack, that would be great."

"Happy to."

Sarah followed Alma to the kitchen, waited while she put together a beautiful little charcuterie board to go with the cold drinks, then arranged it all on a serving tray with small plates, crackers, lemon wedges and a bowl of sugar.

"You're a lifesaver." Alma handed Sarah the tray.

"Happy to help," Sarah replied, and off she went to the grandpa suite.

When she got there, the door was wide open. Fergus sat in the doorway, looking glum.

Sarah walked around his chair and set the tray on the coffee table. "Fergus, what happened? Where's Earlene?"

He turned his head away like a small child who thinks you can't see him if he's not looking at you. "She got mad and left." He mumbled the words so quietly that she barely understood them.

"But why?"

"Who knows? *I* don't." His voice got louder with each

word that came out of his mouth. "That woman knows the rules and she breaks them every chance she gets. She does what she wants and then she just gets mad and leaves!"

Sarah didn't have all the facts. She knew she should keep her mouth shut. It was very unprofessional to go spouting her opinions of her patient's acquaintances. But she did it, nonetheless. "Fergus, she's great. Says what she means and puts herself out there. I really like her."

And just like that, he turned on her. "Who asked you?" he shouted.

She almost laughed. Partly from surprise at his sudden vehemence and also because the whole situation struck her as funny. It was obvious Fergus had a thing for Earlene as much as Earlene did for him, but for some unknown reason he wasn't willing to step up and say so.

And on second thought, that *wasn't* funny. That was actually just sad—and none of it had a thing to do with her. She was the nurse and she needed to remember that.

"You're right, Fergus," she said gently. "Nobody asked me. I apologize for sharing my unsolicited opinion."

Fergus just looked at her. His fury had vanished as quickly as it had appeared. Now he looked as though he might break down and cry.

Maddox, on the phone in his office going over his calendar in search of free daytime hours to squeeze in more online meetings, had heard his dad's angry shout. He made a quick excuse to his assistant to wrap up the call and hung up.

When he stuck his head out the door, he saw that the door at the end of the hall was wide open. His father sat in his wheelchair, his gray head hung low. Sarah stood next to him looking...what? Worried? Sad? Deeply concerned?

Maddox went to them. "I heard shouting. What's going on?"

Fergus looked up then and straight at Sarah. As Maddox watched, his dad glared at the nurse and shook his head. Sarah gave him back a miniscule nod.

Maddox had zero trouble figuring out that whatever the problem was, his dad didn't want to discuss it. And Sarah had nodded, which must mean she wasn't going to say anything. He asked, "Come on. What's happening here?"

Sarah lifted her pretty chin and stared at his dad. Her meaning was clear. *You answer, or I will.*

Fergus grumbled, "Just a visitor."

"Who?"

"Someone from Sylvan Acres, checking to see that I'm all right."

"This someone have a name?"

His dad's flinty stare got more so. "Let it go, son. Just leave it alone."

Maddox knew then he wasn't getting any answers from his dad. "You're not going to tell me? Fine." He turned to Sarah. "Has my father upset you?"

She shook her head. "I'm okay."

It didn't escape him that she'd sidestepped his question. "You're sure?"

Her expression relaxed. "I am, thanks."

He turned to his dad again. "If you're going to be a jerk to your nurse, we'll have to find someone bigger and meaner to take care of you."

"Har-har," said Fergus. "Just you try to get rid of Sarah." His expression had softened. "She's the best." He faced

Sarah directly. "Sarah, I am sorry for snapping at you. Please say you'll stay. I promise to be a model patient from here on out."

She actually laughed then. "Don't make promises you can't keep—and yeah. Of course I'll stay."

"Whew. I was kind of worried there for a minute." Fergus swept out an arm toward the tray on the kitchenette counter. "Come on, you two. Alma has whipped up a real nice snack. And I'm going to need some help to do it justice."

Sarah played right along. "I would love some, thanks."

His dad asked, "Maddox?"

"Thanks, but I've got work I should be dealing with."

"Of course, you do. Shut the door behind you, son."

Maddox left the suite and quietly closed the door behind him.

But it wasn't his office he was heading for.

He found Alma in the large hall bathroom on the second floor. It was cleaning day and she always made a point to circulate around the house, checking in with the cleaning crew—and checking *on* them, as well.

"I need a minute," he said.

"Sure." Alma handed a toilet brush to one of the crew and followed him out into the wide upstairs hallway.

"How about your office?" he asked.

"That works," said Alma.

They took the stairs down to the first floor and the small room off the butler's pantry where Alma planned menus and kept track of what needed doing or fixing around the house.

She gestured for him to take the one extra chair and slid into her seat behind the desk. "What can I do?" she asked.

"The doorbell rang a while ago. I was just wondering who it was."

She looked at him sideways. "Let me guess. Fergus wouldn't tell you."

"He said it was someone from Sylvan Acres, checking in to see how he was doing."

"That's right. Earlene Pugh. She asked for Fergus. I buzzed him on the intercom and he said to bring her to his rooms. When I got there, he asked for a snack. I made the snack and Sarah took it down to them. That's all I know."

"Apparently, this Earlene woman left pretty quickly after that."

"Hmm. I didn't hear her leave. But that's not surprising. Things are pretty busy around here today."

"What did she look like?"

The desk chair squeaked as Alma sat back. "Maddox. I think the world of you. And I'm very fond of your father."

He got the message. "That's all you're going to tell me, right?"

"It does seem to me that these are questions for your dad to answer."

What could he say to that? When Alma dug her heels in, no amount of questioning would get him the answers he sought. "Fair point." He pushed back his chair. "All right, then. I know you're busy."

"Thank you. I do need to get back upstairs."

Maddox returned to the office wing, where Fergus's door was shut and all was quiet. Whatever might have happened between his dad and the mysterious Earlene Pugh, if Fergus didn't want to talk about it, that was his right. Fergus might be laid up, but he was still sharp as a tack and more than capable of running his own life without interference from anyone—even his only son.

Damn it.

Sarah really did enjoy being around Fergus Hale. He could be crabby, but he knew when he'd stepped over the line. For the rest of that day and evening, her patient put real effort into making up for shouting at her. He joked with her a lot. When they played chess, she was pretty sure he let her win.

At shower time, same as the other two nights she'd been taking care of him, she waited right outside the bathroom door in case he called for her. But he was managing well on one leg and he never once asked for help. Up till now, he'd been salty when it came time to shower. But tonight, he stayed cheerful right through the process of cleaning up and getting ready for bed.

At eight, when she went off duty for the night, he said, "Thank you, Sarah," then added, "For everything," as she left.

She was grinning as she went upstairs. He was a cagey one, that Fergus. And every bit as charming in his own way as his smooth, New York big-shot son.

In her room, she felt…antsy. Settling in to read, play a game online or watch a show held little appeal.

She thought of the gorgeous pool downstairs. A swim was just what she needed. But given the circumstances, she should probably stay in her room.

Because of Maddox. Because sometimes a woman was better off to steer clear of potential trouble no matter how green his eyes might be, or how charming his smile.

But on the other hand, she would be working here five

days a week for several weeks, anyway. Treating herself to an hour at the pool now and then was just good sense. Swimming was a great form of therapy—good exercise and also stress relieving.

Plus, Maddox lived here, after all. She couldn't turn tail and run every time she caught sight of him. That would be ridiculous. The man had made it clear that she was welcome to use the pool anytime the mood struck. If he happened to be there, too, so be it. She wasn't seeking him out—but she wasn't avoiding him either.

Sarah picked up the remote and turned off the flat-screen on the wall across the room.

Because the mood to use the pool?

It had definitely struck.

She grabbed her suit, cover-up and the monitor, and headed downstairs.

Had she expected him to be there?

Not really. But somewhere in her contrary heart, she might have hoped he would be.

And he was.

In the pool house, she put on her suit. When she came out, he was already doing laps. He was such a good swimmer.

She moved closer to get a better look. And then, for several minutes, she stood on the coping stones right up close to the edge, watching his long, powerful strokes as he glided the length of the pool, turned underwater and headed for the other end, each stroke smooth and measured, perfect in the most mesmerizing way. Even turning underwater in the limited space of the shallow end didn't slow him down. He was fast, slicing through the water like a blade.

She kept expecting him to realize she was standing there

gawking at him. But if he did, he never once let on. He just kept swimming, each stroke as even and sure as the one before it.

Eventually, she started to feel she might be reaching creeper status, so she tossed her cover-up and the monitor on one of the loungers, circled to the far side of the pool and climbed in at the shallow end. The movement of the water must have finally alerted him that he wasn't alone.

At the end of that lap, down at the shallow end with her, he turned under water, came upright and pushed his goggles up onto his cap. "Hey."

"Hey."

They just looked at each other. Like it was some sort of competition—first one to break eye contact loses.

He took the loss. "Exciting day, what with the appearance of the mystery woman from Sylvan Acres."

She saw the questions in his eyes. "Are you going to pump me for information about Earlene Pugh?"

He turned, hoisted himself out of the water and sat on the edge of the pool. "Are you going to tell me to ask my dad?"

She gave him a one-shouldered shrug. "I was there when he essentially told you to mind your own business, so I already know that asking him will get you nowhere. But still. Yes. It's his business, and if you have more questions, you should talk to *him*."

Maddox swiped off the cap and goggles and set them at his side. "That's pretty much what Alma said when I asked her."

"So maybe you should—"

"Leave it alone? Probably. But I'm having trouble doing that. I just want to know…" He frowned.

"You want to know what?"

"Well, I mean, what's up with him? He fell out a second-story window at Sylvan Acres in the morning on a Saturday. I still don't get how that happened. It doesn't add up, not in any way. He said he was there for Bingo. But Bingo was Friday night, downstairs in the Activity Center. And then today, some woman from Sylvan Acres shows up and *something* goes down between her and my dad."

She really wanted to tell him what little she knew. But it was all supposition. She didn't have any real facts. And Fergus had made it painfully clear that he didn't want anyone knowing what was going on between him and Earlene.

"Listen." She said it gently.

He was gripping the edge of the pool, staring into the water as though the answers he sought might have sunk to the bottom. "What?" He looked up at her then, that full mouth twisted with frustration.

"Well, Maddox. Your dad has a right to keep his business to himself."

"I know that."

"Then, respect his wishes. Let it go."

"But I want to help."

She drifted down off the steps and moved through the water, getting a little closer to him. "You *are* helping. You came when he needed you. You hired Tansy and me to look after him. You're doing all you can for him. It's more than enough."

He gave a low laugh. "Nice try. But you don't know what you're talking about. I'm his only child and I'm not here all that much. I fly in a few times a year, but I never stay very long."

"I'll say it again. You're here now. And in case you didn't notice, I've been spending a lot of time with your dad lately.

He thinks the world of you. And he's so proud of you. You're in good with him, believe me."

"And yet, he doesn't trust me enough to tell me what the hell is going on with him." He leaned back and braced his hands on the tiles behind him.

She moved a step closer, the water shifting around her. "Maddox, I honestly don't think he's holding back because he doesn't trust you."

He pinned her with that clear green gaze. "Then, why won't he tell me what's going on with him?"

"I don't know. But you asked what I thought and I think the problem is about *him*, not you."

He laughed then, though there was little humor in the sound. "And if that's true, all it means is he doesn't trust me enough to tell me the truth about himself."

She let out a hard breath. "All right. You can look at it that way, but I wouldn't. Because, as I said, it's really not about you."

Those eyes stayed on her, focusing in. "How old are you, exactly, Sarah?"

Twenty-five at the end of August, she almost said, as though that would make her seem older, more…credible, somehow. "I'm twenty-four."

"I'm forty. That's sixteen years of living between you and me."

More like fifteen and a half, she thought but somehow kept herself from saying. And was he putting her in her place? It sure seemed like it.

But then he went on. "During those years, I've done a lot of things right. And too many things wrong—things that really matter. I haven't spent enough time with my dad— or with my children, for that matter."

She'd never met his kids, but she knew he had a son and a daughter, and Fergus had mentioned they would be coming to stay at the ranch in a couple of weeks.

Maddox continued, "I married the perfect woman and she divorced me because I was—her words—emotionally unavailable and a workaholic."

Omigod. She had so many questions right now.

But did you love her? Did you cheat on her? Did she cheat on you?

Somehow, she managed not to ask. She didn't know him well enough to ask such questions. He'd already told her so much more than she'd ever expected him to reveal.

Plus, there were the ethical issues. His father was her patient. It would be all kinds of wrong for her to get too intimate with her patient's son.

But she wasn't getting intimate with Maddox. They were just having an honest conversation. Weren't they?

He asked, "Was that more than you ever wanted to know?"

"No." She whispered the word. "I…appreciate your honesty."

"You do, huh?"

"Yeah. And now at least you know…" She faltered.

He prompted, "What is it that I know, exactly?" His voice was so cool, clinical, even.

She felt terribly young at that moment and struggled to answer in a calm, level tone. "Well, that the next time you get married, you should do it for love."

"Not going to happen," he said flatly. "Once was enough. I'm never getting married again." The way he looked at her then sucked the breath right out of her body. She knew he meant exactly what he'd said, and that he was warning her off him. Finally, he added, "I should go."

She had to quell the urge to beg him to stay. He was probably right to get out now. He had too much testosterone, along with a willingness to speak honestly and a very big brain. The combination was scary hot, meaning equal parts intimidating—and arousing.

He pulled his feet from the water and stood. "Good night, Sarah." There was finality in the way he said it. She got the message loud and clear. They needed to keep away from each other as much as possible.

Her throat was as dry as a patch of dirt road. She nodded. "Good night."

He left her standing there in the shallow end, wondering what just happened, wishing in spite of everything that she'd asked him to stay.

Maddox set about avoiding his dad's nurse.

He liked her too much. He liked talking to her, staring into those dark eyes, seeing the intelligence shining there. And he definitely liked looking at the rest of her. Too bad looking could so easily lead to touching.

And touching Sarah Bravo would be foolish—foolish and just plain wrong. So he made it a point to swim only when she would be on duty with Fergus. So far, it had worked great. On Wednesday and Thursday, he didn't see her except at meals. That added up to zero opportunities to engage her in overly personal conversation or to enjoy how great she looked in a snug racerback swimsuit.

Friday, he had a deal to close and that meant he needed to be in his office from four in the morning till after end of day on the East Coast, available to massage the transaction and deal with any last-minute holdups. He had Sarah drive his dad up to Sheridan where, if the swelling had gone down enough, they would put Fergus's left leg in a full cast.

She texted him as they left the hospital. All was well. Fergus had his cast.

In the afternoon, Maddox stole a few minutes to check on his dad. Fergus was practicing with his crutches, thumping up and down the hallway in front of the office door.

He seemed in good spirits, and when Maddox stuck his head out his office door, the old man advised, "Get on back to work now, son. I know what I'm doin' here…"

Maddox would have lingered anyway, but the phone rang. He went back to work.

That evening, he'd planned to make it to dinner with his dad, Sarah and Alma, but that didn't happen. Alma brought him a tray and he worked straight through until after eight, at which time he stopped by his dad's room.

When he knocked, Fergus called, "Come on in!"

His dad was in the sitting area alone, looking comfortable in the big recliner, watching an old Clint Eastwood Western. He seemed tired, but okay. Maddox sat with him, watching Clint kill a number of bad guys in interesting ways, until they both heard Maddox's stomach growling.

"Go get some dinner, son," his dad instructed.

"I had dinner at my desk."

"Your stomach is telling you it wasn't enough. Get a snack."

Maddox went out to the kitchen to raid the refrigerator. As he ate, he thought about maybe having a swim. If Sarah just happened to be at the pool, he could check in with her, get her report on how things had gone up at the hospital.

After all, at eight tomorrow morning, she would be off

duty for the weekend and he wouldn't be able to talk to her until…

"Nope." He said the word out loud. "No way."

He'd just spent a half hour with his dad and he knew full well that his dad was fine. There was nothing he needed to discuss with his dad's nurse. If Sarah had concerns about Fergus and his recovery, she would reach out to him.

Yeah, he could use a swim right now, but why kid himself? The real reason he was drawn to the pool tonight was a brunette with a gorgeous smile. In other words, Sarah. He had an itch under the skin to spend a little time with her.

No. Uh-uh. Not going to happen.

They were actively avoiding each other and that was the right thing to do.

Maddox did not use the pool that night. And the next morning, Sarah returned to the Double-K. He spent the weekend hanging out with his dad and also helping in the stables and on the land, making sure the ranch was in good hands while Fergus was out of commission.

Monday, Sarah showed up right on time. He'd left the door to his office open. She stuck her head in and said hi.

In response, he should have given her wave and maybe a friendly "Welcome back."

But no. He had to ask how her weekend went.

She filled him in on the funny things her three-year-old niece, Emmy, had said, and how she and her dad had burned ditches in some pasture out on the Double-K and the fire had almost gotten away from them.

"We got lucky, though," she said. "Got it back under control before things got too wild."

When she headed on down the hallway to Fergus's rooms,

he was left staring at the empty spot where she had stood, wondering what the hell was wrong with him.

He felt like a lovesick kid.

Which was absurd. He'd never been lovesick in his life. Not even over his ex-wife.

He'd met Alexis at a charity event when he was in his mid-twenties. She was beautiful and intelligent, and from a prominent East Coast family. He knew she would be perfect for the man he planned to be, that her name and connections would open doors for him. So he'd swept her off her feet and married her three months after their first meeting.

Had he loved her?

He'd honestly thought so at that time. But now, looking back, he had a chilling awareness that it was his ex-wife's perfection he had loved. She was born and bred in the world to which he aspired.

He'd adored her. He'd admired her. He'd coveted her. He'd honestly liked her.

But love?

No.

As he sat there, staring out the window toward the horse pasture in the distance, pondering the fact that he'd never loved the woman he'd married, his cell rang.

He glanced down as it lit up on his desk.

Alexis calling.

Slightly rattled that she'd called when he happened to be thinking about her, he picked up. "Alexis. Hello."

"Ah. There you are. How's your father?"

"He's doing well, thanks. What's up?"

She drew a breath and then let it out sharply. "I hardly know where to start. Maddox, I need to have a word with you. In person. I thought I would fly out to you Thursday along with the children. I won't stay long—just long enough to talk, and then I'll take the jet back home. Will you please inform the crew that I'll be on the flight with RJ and Stevie and they'll need to fly me back to New York?"

"Alexis. I have no idea what you're talking about."

"Please." She sighed again. "Just make time to speak with me privately as soon as we arrive at the ranch. The jet should remain on hold and I'll need someone on standby to drive me back to that little airport in Sheridan. Because as soon as we talk, I plan to be out of your hair."

"Alexis, I'll ask again. What's this about?"

"And I will tell you—again—that I'm not discussing it now."

"It has to be about the kids, right?"

"Maddox, please."

"I talked to Stevie last week. She was chatting away, happy as ever. I didn't get hold of RJ, but—"

"Next week. I will explain everything then."

"This is not like you." As a rule, Alexis was kind, considerate and clear in her intentions. When she'd asked him for a divorce, she'd done it gently but without any hedging or hesitation. She'd said what he'd been sitting there thinking before she called just now—that he didn't love her and he never had and she wanted a man who did.

"Maddox. Please. I know how you are. If I get into the whole thing now, you will spring into action before I'm even finished laying out the problem."

"What problem?"

"Listen to me, please. I just want to be there, face-to-face with you. I want to have my say before you take over. I promise you that nobody is ill. No one is in harm's way or in danger of dying. And that all you need to know right now is that everything is under control and you shouldn't worry."

Maddox sat very still. He reminded himself that he respected his ex-wife. That she was a fine mother to their children and a good person. That he trusted her judgment.

Unfortunately, right now, he wanted to reach through the phone and shake a little sense into her. She had to know what she was setting him up for.

Now he would be on edge until Thursday when she finally showed up with his children and told him what was going on.

"Maddox."

"What?"

"I will see you Thursday."

"I guess you will."

"Thank you. Goodbye till then." And she ended the call.

Chapter Four

After stewing for a while over his ex-wife's mysterious phone call, Maddox did his best to shake off his frustration. There was always plenty of work he could do, so he focused on the tasks at hand and tried not to obsess over what could possibly be bad enough that Alexis would refuse to share it with him over the phone.

Before dinner, he gave Sarah a break and drove his dad out to the horse pasture where the old man conferred with Caleb and spent some time talking to the horses. It was nice out and Fergus seemed pretty relaxed.

But then, as they drove back to the house, his father asked, "What's the matter, son?"

"Nothing, Dad."

Fergus scoffed. "Don't lie. Just say you're not going to talk about it. I won't like that answer, but at least you won't be lying to me on top of refusing to tell me what's up with you."

He slanted his dad a glance. "If I tell you what's bothering me, will you talk to me about Earlene Pugh?"

His dad squinted out the windshield. Finally, he shrugged. "She lives at Sylvan Acres. I met her playing Bingo."

"A girlfriend, then?"

"A *friend*. Now, tell me what's eating you."

"Nice try. But I'm going to need more information than just that Earlene Pugh is a *friend* you met playing Bingo."

"Well, I can't give you more because that's all I got."

Liar, he thought as he pulled to a stop in front of the house. "Fair enough, Dad." He almost came back with how he'd prefer not to talk about his own problem. But that would just be petty. Plus, his dad was and always had been a good sounding board.

He told Fergus about the call from Alexis.

"Most likely something about one of the kids," his dad said.

"I'm with you. But what?"

"Hmm. She did say it's not urgent, right?"

"Essentially, yes."

"So then, you wait. You'll know on Thursday."

Maddox laughed then. "Good advice, Dad."

"Happy to ease your mind, son." He reached across the console and clapped Maddox on the shoulder.

Right then, Sarah came out of the house and ran down the wide stone steps toward them. She wore turquoise scrubs. The sun glinted off all that dark, thick hair, and Maddox thought of her floating in the pool that first night she'd stayed at the house, a mermaid in a red suit, her hair drifting out around her in a dark, supple halo.

He pushed open his door. "I'll help you—"

"Stay right where you are, son," his dad said. "We got this."

Sarah was already pulling open the back seat door. She grabbed the crutches and held them upright for Fergus to use as support while he carefully exited the vehicle on his own. Once he had a crutch under each arm, they headed around to the side entrance together.

Dinner that evening provided something of a distraction from thoughts of what Alexis might be planning—mostly because Sarah was there. She was really nice to look at while she talked about her intentions to take his dad into town tomorrow. They would go to lunch at Henry's Diner and afterward visit the library. His dad had decided that since he couldn't wrangle horses, he might as well catch up on his reading.

Maddox watched Fergus and Sarah discussing their plans and couldn't help thinking how great it was that his dad had her to keep him company while his leg healed. She was way overqualified for most of the work she was doing right now—but she was exactly what Fergus needed. Essentially, she was his dad's live-in companion and Fergus enjoyed the hell out of having her around.

So yeah, the old man had been right about one thing. He didn't need all the care Maddox had arranged for him. But he sure looked happy sitting there at the table with his broken leg stretched out in front of him, yakking away about his visit to town tomorrow, grinning at Sarah like the two of them were partners in some great adventure.

After dinner, Maddox returned to his office to tie up a few loose ends. By eight, he was up in the sitting room of his bedroom suite, trying to decide what to do with the rest of the evening.

Maybe he ought to drive into town for a drink or something. Too bad he hadn't kept in touch with any of his friends from back in high school. Really, if he was going to drink alone, he might as well do it right here.

Maybe he could watch a show. He grabbed the remote to check out the streaming options and then realized a show wouldn't cut it. He was on edge and he couldn't stop thinking about Alexis and whatever she refused to tell him until they were face-to-face.

Was there something wrong with his ex-wife herself? Was Alexis ill? Dying? What about RJ? Or Stevie. If one of his children was sick...

He cut off that dangerous train of thought. Nobody was sick. Nobody was dying. Alexis had said so before she hung up that afternoon.

Damn it. He was furious at his ex for freaking him out like this—and even angrier at himself for letting the situation get to him.

A swim, he thought. An endless, mindless series of laps might just do the trick. The exercise would relax him and wear him out so he could stop fixating on something over which he had zero control.

And if Sarah was down there, so be it.

Right now, the struggle to resist his attraction to his dad's nurse came in second to his need to stop overthinking whatever news Alexis had to fly all the way to Wyoming to share with him.

Sarah was there when he entered the pool room. She popped up in the deep end as he exited the dressing area. Slicking water back off her hair, she opened her eyes and spotted him. "Oh! Hi."

"Hi."

Without another word, she swam to the edge and hoisted herself smoothly up to the coping tiles. Her suit was bright green tonight, her body every bit as sleek and strong as it had been the last time he saw her here six nights before.

Water beading on her skin, dripping to the tiles as she went, she headed for the nearest lounge chair where she'd left her towel. "I'll get out of your way." She grabbed the towel and the baby monitor and aimed another cool smile at him. "Have a nice swim." She turned for the door to the pool house.

He knew one thing right then—he didn't want her to go. "Wait."

She stopped, turned and tipped her head to the side. "Hmm?"

"Stay a little while."

She gave a quiet laugh, the sound more puzzled than amused. "I don't get it." She touched the smooth, wet skin just below her collarbones and then gestured, open-handed, at him. "I thought we had an understanding, you and me. I thought it was agreed that we shouldn't be hanging out in the pool together anymore."

He considered denying that. After all, no actual words had been said to that effect. But they *had* agreed to avoid each other when no one else was around. They'd just done it without needing to say it out loud.

No. Denial would do him no good at all. It would only make her more wary of him than she already was.

"You're right," he admitted. "We agreed. But I still wish you would stay."

Her eyebrows drew together. She raised the towel and patted her face dry. "You need someone to talk to?"

He couldn't help smiling. Because she was so beautiful. To look at. And in other ways, too. There was beauty in the intelligence that shone in those dark eyes, beauty in her kindness to his father. And beauty in her clear intention to do the right thing.

He shrugged. "I'm that obvious, huh?"

She dropped to the end of the closest lounge chair and quickly ran the towel over her legs and her arms. Then she patted the chair next to her. "Okay. Sit. Talk." She scooted back and brought her long, toned legs up onto the chair. Leaning back, she stared up at the skylight high above. Tonight, the heavens were scattered thickly with bright points of light. "It's a gorgeous night." She slid him a glance. "Are you just going to stand there?"

"Uh. No." He went to the lounge chair beside her, sat down and stretched out. They stared up at the sky together. "Looks so peaceful up there…"

"So, what's going on?"

He turned his head and found her looking at him. It felt good, to have those eyes on him. He started talking, telling her everything that had transpired between him and his ex-wife on the phone that morning.

"It all sounds very mysterious," she said when he was done.

"Exactly. I mean, Alexis is a reasonable woman. I don't get this at all."

"And the not knowing is driving you crazy?"

"Yeah. But she did promise that no one is sick or dying."

Sarah laughed. The sound made him feel a whole lot better about everything. "Hey. That's good to know."

"I guess… Still, it's got me on edge that she wouldn't just tell me what's going on."

"I get it. If I were in your shoes, I would be climbing the walls."

He turned to look at her. "I doubt that. You seem like a woman who accepts the things she can't control. You're just being understanding."

"Maybe. A little."

They grinned at each other. He stared in those brown

eyes and felt better about everything. He said, "The obvious has suddenly come clear to me."

"And that is?"

"If this was some immediate crisis, Alexis would have told me. I really can wait till Thursday to find out what the hell is going on."

"All right, then. See? You just needed to get it out there and talk it through."

He thought of his dad. "I already laid it out for my dad. He said what you just said."

"So then. All will be revealed. You just have to wait till Thursday."

"I'm trying."

"Good. Shall I change the subject, then?"

"Please do."

She pushed the button to lower the back of the chair another couple of inches, then stretched out again. Settling on her side, she tucked her hands under her cheek. "He's doing really well, your dad. Getting around great in the chair and on his crutches…" Right then, she looked impossibly young.

And she was.

Too young for him…

A voice in his head said, *Get up, say good-night*.

He didn't budge. "He's strong, my dad. He and my mom, they were together forever. A love match from high school on. I thought it would kill him when she died. But look at him. Still here, still in good health. As soon as his leg heals, he'll be up every day at four thirty in the morning, running this ranch again." He watched her mouth twist into a grin. "What?" he demanded. "Say it."

"Did he ever tell you what's going on between him and the woman from Sylvan Acres?"

"No."

"He won't tell me, either." She sighed and shut her eyes. "I've asked a few times. No luck. But at least he's gotten nicer about ordering me to mind my own business." Her dark lashes fluttered up.

They stared at each other. He thought about her mouth, those soft, pink lips. About how good she would taste.

And then he was talking again, telling her things she did not need to know. "I haven't been a great father so far. Too…unavailable. Always working."

"You're still working," she reminded him softly. "Long hours every day."

"Yeah, well. I have reasons."

"I believe you." She said it so sweetly. "Reasons like ambition. Wanting to win. Making more money."

"I do not deny it. I like money and I like working. But starting Thursday, when the kids arrive, I'm on vacation. I'm not taking calls from the office. I'm hoping to start showing my kids how much they really do matter to me, hoping to make some headway toward fixing what I've broken when it comes to them."

She reached across the space between their loungers and clasped his arm lightly—just for a moment. He felt that touch like a pulse of electricity, one that vibrated all through him. "I'm glad you're getting this summer with them."

Right then, he realized there were a thousand things he needed to know about her. "Do you get along with your folks?"

She made a thoughtful sound. "My dad's pretty easy. They say he was a tough character when he was younger. But all I've ever known from him is love. He was probably *too* easy on me and my brothers when we were growing up."

"What about your mom?"

"She's tough enough for both of them. Sometimes she's overprotective. If she thinks something's not good for me, she will drive me right up the wall, trying to convince me not to do it. She didn't want me to go to Bolivia. Too far away, a whole different world…"

"But you went anyway." His gaze strayed to her belly and he thought of what she'd revealed the day of her interview. Did she have scars from the knife beneath the sleek fabric of that suit? She seemed completely healed, at least. "Do you regret going to work in South America?"

"Never. I was in the northeastern rainforest. It was wild and beautiful there. And my patients were so grateful for the care I could give them. I'll never forget it. I'm so glad I went."

He watched her lips move and thought again about kissing her.

It was time to go and he knew it. He sat up. "Thanks. For listening."

She swung her legs to the tiles, too. "It was good to talk a little."

He rose. "Good night."

Now she frowned up at him. "Aren't you going to stay for a swim?"

Strangely, he didn't need that now. "No. I'm going on upstairs."

She caught that soft, pink lower lip between her teeth and just stared at him for a moment. Finally, she nodded. "All right, then. See you tomorrow."

He left her sitting there.

Upstairs, he changed into sweats, grabbed the remote and switched on the bedroom flat-screen to CNN. As the

talking heads discussed the news of the world, he wondered if he'd made a fool of himself, spilling his guts to
her like that.

But he didn't feel foolish, not really. He felt...understood.
By his dad's twenty-four-year-old nurse.

Because he really did like her. He was glad that his dad
had made him hire her. She might be too attractive for his
peace of mind, but she was good at her job and she did
keep his dad happy.

And as for his unwelcome fascination with her, it was
manageable. All he had to do was walk away whenever he
found himself thinking unacceptable thoughts about her. He
could do that tactfully. Nobody would ever have to know
that he had a thing for her.

Tuesday and Wednesday, he was careful to swim early
in the morning when there would be little chance of running into Sarah. He saw her at meals, though. He enjoyed
the sound of her laughter and the way she fit right in with
Alma and Fergus. And it was absolutely no hardship looking at her. He just had to take care not to stare.

On Wednesday, he spotted her outside with his dad.
Fergus appeared to be practicing getting around on his
crutches while she pushed the chair along behind him—
apparently in case, at some point, he might want a rest. She
and his dad acted like best friends. They were laughing and
kidding around like a couple of kids, having a whole lot of
fun. And his dad really was getting good on those crutches.

Wednesday at dinner, Fergus announced that he would
start spending a few hours each day with Caleb, keeping
up with his job of running the ranch.

Thursday, RJ and Stevie arrived—Alexis, too. Maddox drove the Mercedes up to Sheridan to meet the jet at the airport.

He was waiting by the back of the car, ready to load the luggage, when his ex and his children came down the airstairs. Alexis led the way. Stevie bounced along behind her, followed by RJ at the rear, nose stuck in his phone.

Once Stevie's feet hit the ground, she darted around her mother and came running, her long, straight blond hair flying, a giant smile on her lightly freckled face. "Daddy!"

Opening his arms wide, he caught her as she threw herself at him. "Hey, baby. Good trip?"

"The best!" She grabbed him around the neck, kissed his cheek and then swung her head the other way to plant another lip-smacker on the other cheek. "I missed you so much!" She levered back with her hands braced on his shoulders and beamed a giant smile at him. "Look. Colors!" She had alternating turquoise and yellow bands on her braces.

"Beautiful," he said. "And I missed you too." He set her down.

Alexis, cool and blonde with cornflower-blue eyes, stepped up. "Maddox."

"Alexis."

She leaned in a bit. He brushed an air kiss in the vicinity of her cheek and she quickly turned for the Mercedes. By then, two men had begun unloading luggage from the rear of the jet.

And RJ. Where had RJ gone?

His son was already at the back seat, pulling open the door.

"RJ," Maddox said. "Good to see you, son."

"Dad," RJ replied flatly. "Hey." And he got in the car.

An hour later, the car had been unloaded, the kids had

been shown their rooms and Stevie was jumping up and down in the living room, begging to visit the horses and swim in the pool—apparently at the same time.

"Please, can we see the horses and swim, Daddy? Can we do that now?"

"Stephanie Angelica, take a slow breath," Alexis advised.

Both of Maddox's children had been named after beloved members of Alexis's family. When the kids were born, Maddox had been so busy making a name for himself at the firm that he'd offered zero resistance when his wife told him the names she was giving their kids. In all honesty, he liked Stevie's full name and she liked it, too. But RJ? He'd demanded to be called RJ from the age of eight and would simply ignore anyone who dared call him anything resembling his given name, which was Reginald Jonty.

Fergus, in his wheelchair, with his crutches in a holder and Sarah at his side, volunteered, "Tell you what, Stevie. We'll take you out to the stables. Won't we, Sarah?"

"Absolutely."

"Where's RJ?" Fergus shot a glance around the foyer.

"He's still in his room. I'll go get him," Stevie volunteered.

Alexis caught her arm. "It's okay, darling. Leave RJ here. Fergus, would you take Stevie, though?"

By now, Maddox had a pretty good idea whom Alexis just *had* to talk to him about. He took his keys from his pocket and handed them to Sarah. "You good to drive the Mercedes?"

"I am." She gave him a brisk smile, strictly professional. Still, just looking at her had him wishing he was going out to see the horses, too. "So, then." She dangled the keys.

"The stables, it is." Her smile grew warmer as she shared it with Fergus and Stevie, who was clapping in delight. "Okay, guys. Let's go out the side door." She turned for the office wing, with Stevie and Fergus right behind her. From the exit there, Fergus could more easily navigate around to the front of the house where Maddox had left the SUV.

A moment later, he was alone with his ex-wife. "A drink?"

Alexis gave him a grateful nod. "I thought you'd never ask."

He led her to what they called the library. It was off the main living room and had a door they could shut. Books lined the walls and there were big leather chairs and Crafts-man tables with Mission-style lamps. Alexis took a chair and he went to the drink cart to mix her a vodka gimlet.

"The house is gorgeous," she said after taking a sip. "So many improvements since the last time I was here. I think it's at least twice the size I remember."

"Yeah. I might have gotten a little carried away."

"Well, it's beautiful." She raised her glass. "And you always did mix a perfect drink. Thank you."

He poured himself a whiskey. "I'm guessing you want to talk about RJ."

She sipped again. "And you're right." Setting her drink down, she opened her giant black handbag and pulled out a tablet. After poking at the device a few times, she handed it to him. "I was called in for a parent conference last Monday, after which I called you…"

Maddox read, *"My Summer Vacation."*

"RJ turned that in last Thursday. It's all about how much he hates being forced to spend his summer in Wyoming, how he…" She hesitated. "Well, I'll just say it. Maddox, RJ writes that he can't stand to be around you because even though everybody likes you and wants to please you, you never cared about anything but making money and bossing people around."

"I see," he said carefully as he skimmed through the thing. It was very well written. His son had a real way with words—even though some of them were the kind of words that shouldn't be found in a prep school essay.

Alexis said softly, "He's been withdrawn lately, as I have mentioned to you before. At school, though, he's been doing fine—at the top of his class as always. To his teachers and counselor, that essay came out of left field. They are very concerned."

"I'm sure they are." It came out sounding condescending. Because he didn't know what to say and because it didn't matter what he said at this moment, not really. He'd screwed up, plain and simple.

Yes, he *had* noticed that RJ had grown distant and disinterested in the past year or so. But he'd written that off as a phase. More recently, he'd told himself he would have July and August to reach out to his son, to get back on a good footing with him.

"Maddox."

He looked up from the screen and into Alexis's worried eyes. "Hmm?"

"You're losing him."

No kidding. "Yes. I realize that."

"I considered asking you to let him stay home, thinking I would get him some counseling, someone to help him deal with all this anger he's obviously having trouble processing."

"But you brought him here to me anyway." Did that sound like an accusation? He really hadn't meant it as one.

And Alexis didn't take offense. "Maddox, the reason I didn't ask to keep him home is that the more I mulled it over, the more I came to see this summer as an opportunity. For him. And for you."

He took a slow breath and said mildly, "Yeah. I see it that way, too."

"Good," she replied, though her expression was not all that hopeful. "I have advice," she added in a rueful tone. Because Alexis always had advice.

"Of course you do."

And he sat there and listened to all of it.

When she finally stopped telling him what he needed to do, he said, "I'm going to fix this, Alexis. I promise you."

"I'm sure this sounds obvious, but please. Try to be patient and understanding with him."

"I will."

"He does need time with you. He needs to be the focus of your attention. He needs a chance to finally understand that you really do care."

"I agree."

She set down her empty glass. "I actually can't think of anything else I wanted to say."

He sent the essay to himself and then handed her the tablet. "Thank you. For coming all the way out here to talk to me about this."

She was suppressing a smile. "Just trying to get your attention." It was something she used to say a lot back when they were married.

"Well, it worked."

"I'm glad." Now she did smile. "This went much better than I expected."

Was that a dig? Maybe. But it if it was, it didn't really

land. Because she was a good mom who loved her children and he was damned grateful for that. No, their marriage hadn't worked out. He knew that was mostly because of him and his ambition at work that drove everything he did. But he was older now, and hopefully, at least a little bit wiser. He'd been a bad husband, but he damn well intended to learn to be a decent dad.

"Are you driving me back to the jet?" she asked.

"I should stay. I'll have one of the hands take you."

"All right, then. Remember that RJ loves you," she said, "no matter how horribly he's behaving at the moment."

"And I love him." Now he just needed to convince RJ of that.

At dinnertime, RJ refused to come out of his room.

Maddox decided to let him have his way for tonight, let him settle in on his own terms. Tomorrow would be soon enough to start tackling the yawning gap between the two of them.

"I'll have Alma send a tray up," he said through the door that RJ had refused to open.

"Thanks," his son answered faintly from the other side. Even with the door between them, Maddox could hear the dismissal in the boy's tone.

He could live with the rejection. For tonight.

Stevie, conversely, was thrilled to be back at the ranch. At dinner, she talked nonstop. She also made a lot of demands. Starting with how she wanted to learn to ride a horse—tomorrow. She wanted to go swimming, too, right away. And to have a picnic by that little creek they went to the last time she was at the ranch. "That was when I was only nine," she said. "And Daddy, I want to go into Medicine Creek and have burgers in that place we like with the long counter and the shiny stools. You remember the one..."

"Henry's Diner."

"That's it. We have to go to Henry's Diner..."

Oddly, Maddox found he didn't mind her constant chatter. With RJ hiding out in his room, only speaking to him grudgingly through the shut door, Stevie's motor mouth made Maddox feel grateful that at least one of his kids was happy to be here.

After dinner, Stevie insisted that they all play a board game together. She ran upstairs to try to coax her brother out to play, too. RJ wasn't going for it. He stayed in his room. But Maddox, Fergus, Sarah and Alma all danced to Stevie's tune.

For the game, they moved from the dinner table to the big living room.

Sarah sat on the sofa. Maddox snagged the big chair directly across from her. He allowed himself to enjoy the view and tried his best not be too obvious about it.

Today, she wore purple scrubs. A few strands of dark hair had come loose from the fat, silky coil pinned high on her head. Those soft little curls brushed along the perfect sweep of her slender neck. He wanted to reach across the big coffee table and give at least one of those wispy curls a tug.

As for the Monopoly game, he won. He tried not to, but he didn't try very hard. Because making money in real estate was second nature to him—even if the money was pretend.

Sarah razzed him about it. "You know, you could be nice and give the rest of us a chance." She beamed him a cheeky smile and he imagined himself slipping a hand around her neck, yanking her close and kissing that smart-ass grin right off her soft lips.

"Yeah, Daddy!" Stevie agreed with Sarah. "You have to be a good sport and let other people win sometimes."

Fergus put in his two cents then. "It doesn't work like that, sweetheart. If you *let* another player win, you're throwing the game and that's even worse than being a bad sport."

Stevie wrinkled her cute little nose. "Some people's dads let them win all the time."

Maddox couldn't let that go. "Those dads are teaching their daughters the wrong lesson."

Stevie scoffed, but in her usual good-natured way. "Yeah, right."

Alma announced, "Losing makes you tough. And it makes you try harder to get better at the game."

"Oh, great," muttered Stevie. "Now losing is *good* for me."

"I know it's awful," said Sarah. "But sadly, what your grandpa, your dad and Alma are telling you is actually true."

Later, after everyone had headed off to their rooms for the night, Maddox fought the urge to visit the pool. He managed to keep a rein on himself, though, and stayed away.

Alone in his bedroom suite, he congratulated himself on resisting the ongoing temptation Sarah Bravo presented. Stretching out on the bed, he focused on tomorrow when he would start finding a way to bridge the wide gap between himself and his only son.

He didn't sleep well. The thing with RJ kept him tossing and turning, staring up at the ceiling, trying to imagine how he might break through to his son.

In the morning, he went to RJ's room first. This time he wouldn't take no for an answer. One way or another, RJ would be coming down to breakfast.

No, Maddox hadn't decided how far he was willing to go to see that his son joined the family for the morning meal. He was thinking he would play that by ear—maybe not the best plan. But at the moment, he just wanted to take a tiny step in the right direction and somehow get RJ to come out of his room.

Unfortunately, when he knocked on the door, he got no answer. After standing there for three or four minutes alternately knocking and calling to RJ to come to the door, he tried the door handle.

It turned and the door swung open. "RJ?"

Nothing.

"RJ, are you okay?"

Silence. No sign of his son.

"I'm coming in."

No answer. Across the sitting area, the bed was unmade, the covers in a tangle.

Maddox went on in, checked the room, the closet and the bathroom. Nothing.

Chapter Five

Maddox gave RJ a call. It went straight to voicemail. Maddox sent a text. No answer.

Maybe the boy wasn't checking his phone, but that seemed unlikely. RJ always had the device in his hand.

However, it was a good thing that RJ had come out of his room. And really, the kid couldn't have gone far.

Downstairs, he found Stevie in the kitchen with Alma. They were making French toast. Neither of them had seen RJ.

Next, he knocked on his father's door, where he found Sarah leading the old man through a series of early-morning chair exercises.

Neither of them had a clue where RJ might be. "I've got his number," Fergus said. "You want me to try calling him?"

Maddox nodded. "Please." Because RJ might just pick up for his grandfather.

Fergus made the call. He got voicemail, too. He left a message. "RJ, give your old grandad a call." When he hung up, he asked, "What now?"

Maddox rubbed at the space between his eyebrows where tension was already gathering. "I'll go looking for him."

"We'll help," said Fergus, and Sarah nodded her agreement.

Maddox called Alma in the kitchen. She and Stevie

dropped the breakfast preparations to search the house. At the same time, Maddox, Fergus and Sarah made a circuit of the landscaped grounds, with Sarah and Fergus going one way, and Maddox the other until they met in the middle—with no success.

Inside, they learned that Alma and Stevie had found no sign of RJ, either. As they all shoveled in breakfast at breakneck speed, both Sarah and Alma tried calling him. They got voicemail, same as everyone else.

At that point, Maddox called Caleb. The foreman hadn't seen RJ, but he mobilized the hands to widen the search.

Leaving Alma in the house just in case RJ miraculously showed up there or someone called the landline with news of his whereabouts, the rest of them headed out to search some more. Fergus and Sarah said they would make another circuit of the grounds. Maddox took Stevie with him. The last thing he needed was for his daughter to wander off, too.

Sarah and Fergus had circled the grounds for more than an hour when Fergus stopped his wheelchair in midroll.

"I'm slowing you down," he said. "We've been over every fancy garden path more than once and shouted ourselves hoarse. It's enough. I'm heading back to the house. You can go faster and farther afield without me, and we both know it."

She agreed with him. Still, she shook her head. "I'm your nurse, remember? My job is to stick with you."

"Not right now, it isn't. I'm going to roll on back to the house easy as you please over these beautiful paving-stone walkways my son spent a fortune on." He held up his phone. "I'll call you if I end up on my ass. You have my solemn word on that. But it's not going to happen, so you don't even need to worry about it."

She hesitated. Because Fergus really was strong and capable. And she could cover some serious ground on her own. "Are you sure?"

"You'd better believe it. Get going. I'll call if I need you."

Maddox was grateful he'd taken his daughter with him. Stevie's presence helped.

For her sake, he stayed calmer. She talked nonstop as they searched on the far side of the fence that surrounded the grounds.

He put in real effort to reassure her that RJ was okay and they would find him soon—even though, as the morning crawled by, he grew less and less certain of that. Maddox kept waiting for his phone to ring with RJ finally returning his calls. And if not his missing son, then Alma, his dad or one of the hands with news of the boy.

So far, his phone was silent. And as each minute dragged by, Maddox grew more and more terrified that something bad might have happened.

After Fergus rolled off toward the side entrance, Sarah decided she needed to go farther afield. She reasoned that everyone else would be scouring the Hale property. Her family's land was right next-door. RJ might have gone that way. So she climbed the decorative rail fence that marked off the landscaped area around the Hale house.

On the other side, she crossed the road onto Double-K land. It wasn't far to yet another fence—this time of barbed wire. Using a post to balance herself, she went over it safely into a pasture full of cattle. Cows and their calves lifted their heads to watch as she passed them.

It was a hot day, already in the eighties. She crossed

the field swiftly, thinking how out of place she felt in her pink scrubs and duty shoes. Most likely, the cattle thought so, too.

But she'd grown up on the Double-K. She could ride a horse by the age of six and there wasn't a pasture, a coulee or draw on her family's land that she didn't know like she knew her own face when she looked in the mirror.

She crossed that first pasture, went over another fence and kept going, calling out for RJ as she went. On the other side of the next fence, she climbed a rise. When she got to the top, she stood under a scrubby-looking willow tree and gazed down on Cottonwood Creek as it burbled along in the shallow ravine below.

"RJ!" she shouted. "RJ!"

When no one answered, she set out to walk that rise above the creek. From up there, she could see across the stream to the open land beyond. And when she turned her head the other way, she saw as far as two pastures over.

As she walked, she cupped her hands to either side of her mouth and called out for RJ. The sound echoed back at her across the rolling prairie. A minute or two later, she would turn her head the other way and call the boy's name some more.

That process went on for a good twenty minutes. Then, pausing, she turned slowly in a circle. The wind blew her hair loose from her topknot. She guided the annoying strands behind her ear and shouted out over the creek below, "RJ! Where are you?"

"Sheesh, I'm right here!" grumbled a young voice from behind her.

Slowly, she turned to look back to the way she'd come. The boy, in baggy sweats and an even baggier T-shirt, his thick dark hair sticking out in all directions, was standing on the rise with her, about ten feet away.

Just when Maddox was about to call the county sheriff and report RJ missing, his phone rang in his pocket. It was Sarah.

He answered. "What?"

"I found him. He's fine."

As he grappled with a thousand conflicting emotions, Stevie took one look at his face and grabbed his arm. "Daddy! What is it? Is it RJ? Is he okay?"

He looked down at her and nodded. "Yeah." It came out in a half-whisper because his throat had clutched tight. "He's fine, honey. He's fine."

"We'll meet you at the house," he said into the phone as his daughter shouted, "RJ's okay! RJ's okay!" and did a happy little victory dance right there on the side of the road.

As soon as he hung up with Sarah, he grabbed Stevie in a hug. She wrapped her arms around his neck and held on tight. She smelled of dust and strawberry-scented shampoo, and he marveled at how quickly she'd gone from a colicky baby who cried every time Alexis made him hold her to this joyful, affectionate creature who seemed to find magic in every little thing.

"Daddy!" she cried. "We found him, we did!" And she threw back her head and let out a loud, "Hooray!"

As soon as he set her back on her feet, he called Caleb to share the good news. Then he and Stevie ran back to the house.

They found Sarah, RJ and Fergus in the kitchen with Alma. Sarah and Fergus sipped coffee as RJ chowed down on French toast.

Maddox took some slow, careful breaths to stifle the powerful desire to grab his son in a grateful hug—and then shout at him that he was never to do anything like that again. But he took his ex-wife's advice and managed to play it calm, hanging back as Stevie ran to her brother.

Tackling him in his chair as he ate, she threw her arms around his neck and hugged him like she'd never let him go. "RJ, you scared us so bad! Where have you *been*?"

"Chillax, li'l sis." RJ gave her arm a quick pat. "I just went for a walk."

"You could at least leave a note," Stevie scolded, letting go of his neck and dropping into the chair beside him.

"Yeah, well…" He frowned, shrugged and then stuck another giant bite of French toast in his mouth.

"Are you all right?" Maddox managed to ask in a level tone.

RJ set down his fork and took his time swallowing. "Oh, come on. How many times do I have to say it? Nothing happened. I'm okay."

Stevie shook a finger at him. "We didn't know that. You're s'posed to tell someone when you go places."

The kid rolled his eyes. "I went early and everybody was still sleeping. I kept walking for a while, and then I sat under a tree by a creek and played Mindustry on my phone. That's all that happened. It's no big deal. Can we just let it go?"

Maddox asked very quietly, "What time did you leave the house?"

"I dunno. Before six."

"So you've been gone more than five hours without telling anyone where you were."

"I had my phone with me. If there was a problem, I would've called."

"We all called you. You didn't answer."

"Yeah, well. I was busy and I knew I would be back soon so…yeah. I let calls go to voicemail—I mean, that's what voicemail's for, right?"

Maddox was not and never had been a shouter. But by then, he wanted to make a little noise. He'd spent several hours trying not to freak the hell out over all of the things that might have happened to a thirteen-year-old boy who'd vanished from his bedroom. Now RJ was back and safe and acting like his taking off without a word to anyone was nothing, like he had every right to hand Maddox serious attitude for caring what might have happened to him.

Well, Maddox could give the little smartass some attitude right back…

He had no idea why he glanced at Sarah right then. But he did. She was already looking at him. His eyes locked with hers. She didn't speak. She only gazed at him steadily. There was something in her eyes…

Encouragement. Support. Understanding—and then she pressed her lips together and gave him a barely perceptible shake of her head. It was a gentle warning not to fly off the handle.

He got her message. All of it.

And he felt the knot of fury and tension in his shoulders relaxing. He recalled the glance RJ had shot at him a few minutes ago—a furtive, angry look, yes. But also an apprehensive one. Maddox had never been one to lose his temper with his kids, so he didn't believe that his son was afraid of him.

No. It wasn't fear that RJ felt right now—at least not fear that his dad might get angry.

However, Maddox could easily imagine his son wondering if Maddox even cared where he'd been or how long he'd been gone.

Okay. Throwing attitude right back at the boy was not the way to go here.

Instead, he said mildly, "The main thing, RJ, is that you're back and you're safe." RJ just looked at him, defiance in his eyes. Maddox went on, "Take your time. Finish your breakfast. And then you and I will talk."

Now RJ wiped his mouth with his napkin. "I think I'll just go up to my room." He took his plate, silverware and napkin, and carried them to the sink.

Maddox had to hide a grin at that. RJ might be trying hard to be bad, but still, he cleared his breakfast dishes like the good boy he really was and always had been.

A half hour later, when Maddox tapped on RJ's door, his son answered at once. "It's open," came the glum voice from within.

He found RJ sitting on the end of his bed. Maddox took a chair. There was a yawning silence while he mentally reviewed and rejected everything he'd planned to say.

Finally, he opened with, "I read your essay about coming here for summer vacation." RJ remained silent. He seemed fascinated with his vintage Nike high-tops. Maddox waited him out.

Finally, RJ glanced up. "Well. It's how I feel."

"I believe you."

"Great," said RJ in a tone that clearly implied *as if I care.*

"I know I haven't been around enough."

"More like *at all.*"

Maddox actively resisted twin urges: (a) to defend himself and (b) to demand that RJ put a lid on the hostility.

But let's get real here. He'd been a mostly absent, uninvolved dad. And his son had a right to be unhappy about that.

He tried again. "Point taken. RJ, I want you to know that I'm sorry I haven't been there when I should have been. I can't promise I'm going to suddenly be the dad you needed all along, but—"

"Good." There was a definite sneer in the curve of RJ's mouth. "Because you're not."

Maddox drew a slow breath before responding. "I work too much, I know that."

That brought a groan from his son. "So, that's it? You're sorry and you know you work too much and that somehow makes everything all of a sudden just fine?"

"I never said that."

"Well, it sure sounded like it."

"How about this? Let's start with right now. What I *can* promise you is that this summer, I'm here. Right here with you and Stevie. We can do stuff together."

RJ shifted his glance just enough that their eyes met— for half a second. Then he was back to looking at his shoes again. "What stuff?"

"Ride horses, go camping, throw rocks in the creek..."

RJ lifted his feet and then dropped them with a thud to the floor again. "What if I don't want to do any of those things?"

"Then we'll find things you do want to do."

RJ let his shoulders slump. "Look. You really have been a crap dad a lot of the time."

Damn. The truth hurt. "Yeah. I get that. I do."

Another sideways glance. "I'm not stupid, Dad."

"No, you're not. Not in any sense of the word."

"It's the truth, what I wrote. I pictured you reading it.

I *wanted* you to read it. They made a big deal about it at school because I'm not the kid who writes stuff like that. But I did write stuff like that. And you know what I thought when everyone was shocked? I thought, great. Maybe somehow you would end up reading it. Maybe you would think about what I wrote. Maybe you would feel bad, you know?"

"I did feel bad when I read it, RJ."

"So, what then? Mission accomplished, is that what you're telling me?"

"If you wanted me to feel bad, you got what you wanted. So yeah, absolutely. Mission accomplished."

RJ grunted and stared at his shoes some more. "Lot of good it will do."

Maddox didn't know what to say. Was this where he was supposed make more promises about being a better dad? He almost wished Alexis was here to tell him what to do next.

RJ grumbled, "It didn't really go the way I wanted."

"How so?"

"I mean, come on." RJ looked up long enough to roll his eyes. "All of a sudden, Mom's all over it, showing up at school for meetings with my teachers. That was embarrassing. And next, she's flying to Wyoming with us to talk to you about it. I don't exactly know what I was after, but all that wasn't it."

"Your teachers were concerned about you."

"No kidding. I had to go see the headmistress. I'm not one of those kids who ends up in the headmistress's office. That's for the kids who pick fights or smoke weed."

"I'm sorry you were embarrassed, RJ. I really am." As he said that, Maddox realized it was true—even though he'd been the subject of all the harsh things RJ had written. "You *are* a good kid. And your teachers know that.

Your essay was so out of character that it raised red flags. It was the school's job to take those red flags seriously."

"Yeah. Right. I get that. *Now*."

"Your mother did what she did because she loves you and she's worried about you."

RJ made a low, unhappy sound in his throat. "I know…"

"As for me, I do get the message. I have to do better by you *and* your sister…" He wasn't quite sure how to go on from there—let alone, how to be a better dad than he'd been up till now. The only silver lining on that front was that apparently, simply paying more attention to his son would be a good start.

RJ groaned. "*What?* Just say it."

"All right. The essay was one thing. I get that you needed to have your say. And it worked. You got my attention. I honestly understand that I've been selfish and oblivious and I need to change. But then this morning, you disappeared and scared us all. We didn't know what had happened to you and we were afraid for you. There's a lot of land on this ranch and on the ranches surrounding us. You could walk miles and miles and not see anyone. Anything could happen to you out there."

"But I just needed to think. I started walking and I kept going. And the longer I was gone, the more I didn't know what I would say when I got back. So I sat down to… I don't know, work it out in my head, I guess. And I started playing my game. I think I went to sleep for a while…" He looked up.

Their eyes met. Maddox felt a jolt of pure hope. This was the first time in too long that his son had looked directly at him.

RJ swallowed. Hard. "When I woke up, I saw I had all

these voicemails and texts on my phone from you guys. And I started to get the feeling that maybe I'd screwed up—again. And then, I couldn't make myself listen to the voice-mails or even look at the texts. And I..." His voice broke.

Maddox coaxed, "You what? Please tell me."

"Okay, Dad. I'm, um, sorry. Sorry I left without telling anybody. I was pissed and I didn't think of..." He shrugged, as though he couldn't decide how to finish.

Maddox took a crack at that for him. "You didn't con-sider all of us freaking out, terrified that you were hurt, or worse?"

"Yeah. That. All that."

"But you do know the rules, that you need to—"

"Stop. Dad, come on. I know I have to tell you or Grandpa or Alma where I'm going when I leave the house. I knew it when I left the house and I left anyway without telling anyone." He was looking down again. He scuffed the heel of his shoe against the floor. "So. Now I'll be grounded, right?"

The idea had not occurred to Maddox. He thought of all the years RJ had always done everything right. He was a smart, quiet kid, an A student who always tried to get along with everyone. Grounding him right now felt all sorts of wrong. "No, I don't think so. Not unless you disappear like that again. And maybe not even then."

RJ's head shot up and his eyes, the same color as the ones Maddox saw when he looked in the mirror, blazed with anger. "So, then, you don't even care where your kid goes?"

"Hey." Maddox put up both hands. "Slow down a minute. I get why you'd think I don't care. I haven't been around enough and I hear you about that. I love you, RJ. And I *am* sorry. I *will* do better."

RJ just stared at him.

Finally, Maddox dared to move closer. He left the chair to sit on the end of the bed next to his son.

For several endless minutes, neither of them spoke. They didn't even move. And then, finally, RJ kind of sagged against him. Maddox wrapped his arm around him.

Was that a start?

God in heaven, he hoped so.

Maddox spent the rest of that day with his children. That night, he went to bed at ten. Sleep evaded him. Around eleven, he gave up and turned on the light. He tried to read. But his mind kept wandering.

To his failures as a husband. As a father.

It made him itchy under the skin, thinking of RJ wandering off that morning without telling a soul where he was going. No, nothing bad had happened to him.

But it could have. He could have stepped on a rattler, cut himself up trying to go over or under a barbed wire fence. He could have ended up in the wrong pasture and come face-to-face with an ornery bull.

The possibilities of bad outcomes were endless and Maddox wasn't going to be falling asleep anytime soon. He pushed back the covers and swung his feet to the floor.

Sarah was floating on her back in the deep end, staring up at the stars through one of the giant skylights, when she saw movement in her side vision.

Righting herself, she shook water off her face and slicked her hair back from her forehead.

Maddox was standing at the edge of the pool, watching her. Really, he was one gorgeous specimen of a man—tall and broad, with those sharply cut abdominals and lean, muscular thighs.

He smiled in greeting. All her lady parts snapped to attention. "One last swim before your weekend off, huh?"

"Yeah. Couldn't resist."

"Good. I'm proud of this pool." He watched her as he spoke, the look in his eye belying the casual nature of his words. "I like to see people enjoying it."

"Well, I am enjoying it. Very much."

He dropped his towel on a lounger and slipped into the water, while she stayed in place, arms and legs gently moving to keep her afloat. He pulled his goggles down over his eyes, surface dived and took off underwater for the shallow end. She watched him go.

And continued watching as he began doing laps. He was mesmerizing—and she was staring. With a groan at her inability to resist the visual temptation he presented, she sank beneath the surface and then popped up and swam for a while in her own completely undisciplined, all-over-the-place style.

He was still going at it like a shark on the hunt when she got out, patted dry and stretched out on a lounge chair. She closed her eyes and listened to the faint sounds of water shifting and splashing as he continued up and down the length of the pool.

She was kind of drifting off when the sounds changed. She heard him climb out of the water. His wet feet made faint slapping sounds on the tiles as he came close and then took the chair beside her. She smiled to herself as he settled in next to her.

"What's that smile about?" he asked.

She did not open her eyes. "I'll never tell—and I'm going

to ask, though I'll completely understand if you don't want to talk about it…"

"Ask." His low voice plucked at her nerve endings, raising goosebumps on her arms and legs. She told herself it was just from the gently circulating air on her still-damp skin.

Had she ever felt such pleasure from just being near a certain man? Doubtful. It was a little like being drunk—this feeling that she might do something dangerous. She might dare to say any old thing that popped into her head.

"How did your talk with RJ go?" she asked.

For several seconds, he said nothing. She turned to look at him, thinking he was about to tell her he really didn't want to talk about that.

He was looking right back at her. "All things considered, it went pretty well, though for the entire time we talked, I felt like I was having one of those nightmares where you're doing something you've never done in your life—downhill skiing at Banff on Delirium Dive, playing first chair violin at the Met. You're faking it for all you're worth and you know it's going to be a complete disaster."

"But it turned out okay, you said?"

"Yeah. I think it did. His running off this morning was completely out of character for him. He's such a good kid—and for that, I can claim zero credit."

Don't ask, the voice of wisdom advised. But then she asked anyway. "Because…?"

"Too busy working to spend time being a dad—or a husband, for that matter."

She dared to ask another question she shouldn't, the one she hadn't asked the other night. "So then…did you cheat on your wife?"

His laugh was deep. Rich. "Sarah. I'm so pleased you feel free to ask me anything."

She knew her cheeks were cherry red. "Sorry. That was completely uncalled-for."

"A little, maybe. But I'll answer it anyway. No, I didn't cheat. Infidelity wasn't our problem. Alexis wanted true love and she never got that from me."

Why not? she thought, but somehow managed not to say.

He must have seen the question in her eyes. He answered it without prompting from her. "I told you before. Alexis was perfect. She knew all the people I wanted to do business with. She was born in the world I wanted to be accepted in. So I married her."

What he said made her heart hurt. "Oh, Maddox. She loved you, didn't she?"

"Yeah."

"She loved you and you wanted her connections."

"I wasn't *that* cold-blooded. I was dazzled by her. You saw for yourself that she's gorgeous and charming. And good—a good person. I liked her from the first, I really did. Still do. And when I asked her to marry me, I believed it was love that I felt for her, that she and I would be like my mom and dad. Together forever. Unbreakable."

"So what went wrong?"

"Over time, I saw the truth. She was the right wife for the life I wanted, but she was not the love of my life."

"That just makes me sad."

"Don't be. We're still on good terms, Alexis and me. We have two amazing children. She's remarried now to a decent guy named Teddy Paulson, a guy she's known all her life, the guy she was with when I met her."

"Does she have true love with Teddy, then?"

"I believe she does, yeah." He seemed pleased about that. Her sadness faded and she smiled. "I'm glad."

His gaze tracked from her eyes to her lips and back to her eyes again. It felt way too good, to have his attention laser-focused on her. "What about you?" he asked.

"Hmm?"

"Are you in love or have you ever been?"

She touched the button on the side of her lounger, raising the chair back so she was sitting up.

He did the same, holding her gaze as he did it. "Tell me," he said.

This conversation was way too personal. Too intimate. And they were not supposed to be intimate in any way. He was her employer and her patient's son...

She answered him though she knew very well that she shouldn't. "I had my first serious boyfriend in high school."

"I'm going to need a name." He looked at her piercingly. A delicious shiver went sliding down the backs of her knees.

"Rudy Blevins," she said. "He played center on the football team and he was a good student, too. Rudy got accepted at the University of Oregon. I went off to Ohio State. That was the end of Rudy and me."

"Who else?"

"Nobody for a while. Not till I moved to Denver for my first nursing job. His name was Aaron Stillwell and he was a software developer."

Maddox was watching her so closely. "That one was serious."

"How did you know?"

"Not sure. The look on your face—kind of tense. Not happy. Disappointed, maybe. From that I get the feeling you really cared for him and it didn't end well."

"You're right. On both counts. With Aaron, it got serious fast. He proposed, I said yes. But then I wanted more from my job. I wanted work that really mattered. I went to Bolivia on a six-month contract. Aaron said he would wait. Five months in, I got an extension to stay on for three months beyond the original six. I also managed to get a week off. I called Aaron. We met up in Buenos Aires to spend those seven days together. On the last day, he said he was through waiting for me. He laid down an ultimatum. 'Come home, or we're done.'"

"You said no?"

She nodded. "I just couldn't walk out on that commitment. I really felt I was needed there and I asked him to please just hold on a few more months. He refused to wait and I refused to go home. Aaron and I were done."

"No one since then?"

She shook her head. "Aaron was it. And three months later, a month before my contract would have run out, I was home again."

"And recovering from the stabbing incident you spoke of in your interview…"

"That's right." She stared into his eyes. He didn't look away. She liked that he didn't.

She liked it far too much.

What was it about her?

Maddox just didn't get it.

Yeah, she was good-looking. But he'd known a lot of good-looking women in his life.

So why did she take up so much space in his head? It made no sense to him.

She was a do-gooder, the kind of woman who would need

to have meaningful work that helped others and made the world a better place. He was a capitalist, plain and simple. He enjoyed making money, closing deals—and living well. Yeah, he donated generously to a large number of good causes, but he was never heading off to Bolivia to provide medical care for those in need.

And then there was the age difference. Given how much he wanted her, the age difference alone should have him leaving every room she walked into.

Instead, he'd started thinking that the age thing didn't matter. She charmed him, she really did. Life felt new and exciting with her around.

And wasn't that exactly what made so many wealthy older men go after younger women? A younger woman made a jaded man feel youthful again. She was watching him. "We shouldn't be doing this," she whispered.

He felt that she'd plucked those words right out of his own head. "I know."

"Nothing can...come of it."

"True."

"And let's just get painfully real here."

He couldn't stop himself from offering hopefully, "Let's not."

She went right on as though he hadn't spoken. "Your dad is doing really well. He's in great shape. He could manage on his own right now, with a little help from you and Alma whenever he needs it. He doesn't actually need a nurse. You realize that, right? Or you could hire a home care aide for less than half what you're paying me."

He didn't want her to go—not if it was up to him.

This thing with them, this magic...

It wouldn't last long. He knew that. But while it did, well, why the hell not make the most of it?

She was like a gift. A gift of all the things he'd always thought he had no need for. Laughter with the right person at the end of the day. Just lying here beside her, just knowing she was there.

Talking to her—about his life. About hers.

Okay, yeah. He wanted more. What red-blooded man wouldn't?

But he knew it wasn't going to happen, that she wouldn't let it happen. And neither would he.

He was honestly okay with that, with knowing he was never going to have her in his bed, as long as she was here. Just for now. For the summer. Something—some*one*—to look forward to at the end of the day.

"Stay," he said. "Take care of my dad who loves having you look after him. Please."

"Maddox. A relationship between us can't happen. It's unethical. You're my patient's son. We can't be—"

"Lovers? I know that. I accept that. Just stay. Just be with my dad because you're good for him. He likes you and trusts you."

"I like him, too. So much."

"I know you do."

"But I meant what I just said. You and me, we are never happening."

He laughed then. "Sarah, we are *already* happening. And there's nothing wrong with that."

"But there is!"

He shook his head. "No. Because I'm not going to make any kind of move on you."

She caught her plump lower lip between her teeth and narrowed her eyes at him. "You're not?"

"No. And you're not going to try to seduce me. Are you? Because actually, I'd be really on board with that—"

A goofy little laugh escaped her. She reached between their chairs and playfully slapped his arm. "Stop."

"Listen. I've never been a man who wants the simple things. I want the big things, the most expensive things that money can buy. I want the life that most people only dream about. And I have that life. It's mine."

She looked at him so steadily now, all trace of humor gone. "Yes, Maddox. You're rich. I get it. Now, what, exactly, are you asking of me?"

"This," he said, staring right back at her. "I just want *this*."

"This? I don't get it."

"This thing, between us, whatever it is. I want more of it. For now, while you're here looking after my dad, I want to spend time with you, just you and me, a little time together at the end of the day. To hang out. Swim. Talk. Laugh."

"And that's all?" Those doe eyes sparked with challenge.

"That's all."

She groaned and covered her face with her hands. "Oh, I don't know…"

"Look at me."

Slowly, she dropped her hands away. "Honestly, what are you doing? This is dangerous."

"Sarah, I promise you. Nothing inappropriate is going to happen." He wanted to touch her so bad—to reach across the space between them, run the pads of his fingers along the perfect line of her jaw, to trace the graceful shell of her ear. He ached to slide his hand under the wet coils of her hair, clasp the back of her neck and pull her in for a long, perfect kiss.

But he did none of those things.

He kept his hands where they belonged. "Nothing inappropriate is going to happen," he repeated. "Because we're not going to let it. And next December, when Christmas comes, we'll be miles and miles apart, living our completely separate lives. I'll be in Manhattan, finalizing the next deal. You'll be off doing good wherever the need is greatest. I'll just be a memory for you—a happy one, I hope."

"Okay. And as for now...?"

"As for now, we're going to keep doing what we've been doing. We'll spend a little time together, enjoy each other's company. And that's all."

She was biting her lower lip again. "I don't know about this."

"Think about it over the weekend."

She gave him a pained look. "Great. Now I won't be able to think about anything else."

Good, he thought, but had the presence of mind not to say. "Meet you here Monday night. For a swim. And conversation."

She grabbed her towel and rose. "Night, Maddox."

"Have a great weekend, Sarah."

"You bet," she said briskly.

And a moment later, she was gone.

Chapter Six

"Miles James," Sarah said tenderly as she stared down at the red, scrunched-up face of her newborn nephew. He weighed seven pounds, two ounces, and felt light as feather in her arms. As she gazed at him adoringly, he yawned hugely and then let out a tiny sigh. "You are so handsome."

In the hospital bed beside her, Piper chuckled. "Oh, come on. He's a newborn. He looks like a little old man."

Sarah slanted her sister-in-law a disapproving frown and then beamed at the little one her arms. "Your mama knows you're perfect. She just doesn't want you to get a fat head about it." She looked up at her sister-in-law again. "You did so good."

Piper groaned. "I have to tell you, at six this morning, I had my doubts he was ever coming out."

Right then, the angel in Sarah's arms let out a fussy little cry. "What do you want, sweetheart?" She rocked him side to side.

Miles James didn't answer. But he did keep fussing.

Sarah passed him to his mama who put him to her breast while Sarah sat in the guest chair and sipped the coffee she'd grabbed in the cafeteria before coming to meet her nephew for the first time.

Piper glanced up from the baby in her arms. "How's work?"

Did her face flush candy-apple red? It sure felt like it. "Fergus is amazing." *And Maddox claims he wants to be my...what? Friend* sounded far too innocent. They were not innocent with each other and he had to know that.

No, he'd never laid a hand on her.

And yet she *felt* him, felt his presence when he entered a room. Heard his voice in her head when he wasn't even near. Thought of him constantly no matter how hard she tried not to.

They were playing with matches and bound to get burned.

"So he's recovering quickly?" Piper asked.

Sarah blinked and ordered her mind to stop thinking of Maddox. "Uh, Fergus you mean?"

Now Piper was giving her a sideways look. "You said that Fergus is amazing...?"

"Right. I kind of feel guilty. He doesn't need me there."

"So taking care of Fergus Hale is nothing like the clinic in the wilds of Bolivia?"

"Understatement of the year."

"You don't feel challenged?"

As a matter of fact, I do. But not by my patient. "I should resign."

"Why? Too boring?"

"No, it's not boring." *Far from it.* "I adore Fergus. I feel right at home at the Hale Ranch. And the money is great." *And I'm considering having a sort-of relationship with Maddox Hale. One with no touching, just...hanging out at the end of the day. Talking. Laughing together...*

And there was nothing at all wrong with that. It sounded perfectly innocent.

But she knew and *he* knew it was anything but.

"So are you keeping the job—or not?" Piper asked.

Sarah laughed then—at herself, at the whole situation. "I have no idea."

"Well, if you like it there and you like the money, it seems like a no-brainer to me."

And it would be if not for the part she wasn't telling Piper. "Yeah. We'll see."

"So how's Maddox?"

Her heart rate spiked—just from the sound of his name. She slid a quick glance at her sister-in-law. Piper wasn't even looking at her. She was making goo-goo eyes at her brand-new baby boy. "Oh, that's right," Sarah said. "You and Maddox went to high school together."

Piper was thirteen years older than Jason and she'd actively resisted falling for him. But they'd had Emmy on the way almost from the first and Jason had been determined that he would be a whole lot more than just a baby daddy to Medicine Creek's hottest librarian.

"Maddox was four years behind me in school," said Piper. "When he got to high school, I was already on my way to college. But as I recall, he was always charming and friendly. And top of his class by a long shot."

"What can I say? Still charming. Still friendly."

"And now filthy rich..." Piper let her voice trail off. "That house. It's really something."

"Yeah."

"It's nice that he's here for the summer. All those add-ons and improvements, all the gorgeous landscaping, and yet he spends so little time here. The man should have a chance to enjoy what he built."

"Yeah…" Sarah stared out the hospital room's one narrow window at the parking lot beyond it.

Piper said, "He's a good son and it's clear he thinks the world of his dad. He even looks a lot like Fergus, though he was adopted. But then that does make sense. His birth mother was Fergus's sister."

"Wait. *What?* Did you just say that Maddox was adopted?"

"Yes. You didn't know?"

"I had no clue."

Piper kissed her baby's nearly-bald head. "Maddox was only two or so when he went to live with the Hales. At least that's what my mother told me." Piper grew up an only child with a single mom, Emmaline Stokely. Emmaline was a local artist and quite a character. "Mary Hale joined one of Mom's art classes years ago. They became friends. It was no secret, the adoption. Mary once told my mom that the day they brought Maddox home was one of the two happiest days of her life. The other was the day she married Fergus."

"Do you know what happened to Maddox's birth parents?"

"I don't have the details, but Mom said they both passed away when he was little and that was why Fergus and Mary adopted him. But you should ask him."

"Wow." The news was a revelation.

Piper was watching her much too closely. "You know, you really should invite him and Fergus and the kids for next Saturday—Alma, too. I know she's like family to the Hales."

Still hung up on the news that Maddox had been adopted, Sarah frowned absently at her sister-in-law. "Next Saturday…?"

Piper laughed, causing the baby in her arms to pop off her breast and let out a squeak of surprise. "Sorry, sweetheart," Piper crooned to the little one. She helped him latch on again before putting on a shocked face for Sarah. "I can't believe you've forgotten your brother's birthday."

Sarah remembered then. On Saturday, her brother Joe would be turning twenty-seven. Her mom was planning a barbecue and inviting the whole Bravo family.

"It's going to be fun," said Piper. "Invite the Hales."

Why not? She pictured Maddox all those years and years ago, blinking down at her in surprise as she held up her snake. "Good idea. I'm inviting the Hales."

Monday evening, after she left Fergus for the night, Sarah returned to her room. She fully intended to stay there. But she lasted exactly twenty-eight minutes before she was grabbing her red suit and heading downstairs.

He was already in the water when she came out of the pool house. Dropping her towel on one of the loungers, she went to the edge and sat down with her feet in the deep end. He swam two more lengths before popping up across from her.

"How was your weekend?" he asked, treading water with one hand as he slid his goggles up onto his cap.

"Piper had a baby boy."

"Piper...?"

"My sister-in-law. She's the director at the library."

"Wait. It's all coming back to me. Piper Stokely, correct?"

"That was her name growing up. She married Walter Wallace, who taught math at the high school. He died eight or nine years ago."

"I remember. And then she married your brother Jason. Don't they already have a daughter…?"

"Yes they do. Emmy is three and a half and the love of my life."

"And the new baby…?"

"His name is Miles James. He's absolutely gorgeous."

Maddox glided to the edge next to her. Rising effortlessly from the water, he turned around and plunked down beside her. "I'm glad you're here."

They stared at each other. It went on for way too long. Fluttery creatures swarmed in her stomach and she forgot how to breathe. It felt amazing, just to sit here with him as he dripped water onto the tiles and looked at her like he wanted to eat her right up.

Though he wouldn't, of course.

They didn't have that kind of thing going on.

"I don't want to talk about it," she said.

"Talk about what?"

"This." She pointed at him and back to herself again. "Whatever this is between you and me…"

He sat there, still dripping wet, smirking at her. Finally, he actually spoke. "Okay, let's not talk about it."

"I'm getting in." She slid off the edge, into the water and under it. When she came up, he was treading the surface a few feet away. They swam for a while, going up and down the length of the pool.

Later, lying on the lounge chair next to his, she invited him to her brother's birthday barbecue Saturday. He said he would be there—and bring the rest of the family, too.

"No gifts," she instructed.

"Aw, come on. What's a birthday without a few presents to open?"

"Joe's turning twenty-seven. He's kind of outgrown presents… I mean, unless you want to buy him a new crew cab."

He laughed at that. "Okay, fine. No presents."

An hour went by, and another. She longed to ask him about being adopted. But to ask felt so…intrusive, somehow. So they talked about his life in New York. And then about her plan to go back to school, earn her master's degree and become a nurse practitioner.

"Why a nurse practitioner?" he asked.

"Because I want to do more for my patients. And to do more, I need to be able to make more decisions when it comes to a patient's care. Different states have different rules. But as an NP, I can prescribe treatments, order tests and diagnose patients. I will be able to write scripts, though in some states I will need to do so under a doctor's supervision. As an RN, I can't do any of those things. I want to work where the need is greatest and the more I can do to help my patients, the better."

"So that's a two-year degree, a master's in nursing?"

"Technically, but it will probably take longer for me. I'll need to be working while I'm going to school."

"What about marriage? Kids?"

"Someday."

He advised, "Take my word for it, the years go by fast."

"I agree. And that's why I want to prepare myself effectively to do meaningful work."

The way he looked at her, his eyes low. Lazy. Like he was considering reaching across the distance between their chairs and touching her in ways that he'd previously made clear he wouldn't.

He'd better not, she thought. At the same time, she tried to suppress a shiver of excitement at the idea that he might.

And she realized she simply could not keep her mouth shut about what Piper had told her. "I...well..."

He watched her so intently. "Whatever's on your mind, you should just say it."

And she did. "This weekend, Piper mentioned to me that you were adopted..." She cringed. "I'm sorry. Did that come out sounding obnoxious and insensitive?"

He didn't even blink. "No. And don't worry. It's not a secret."

"Uh, yeah. Piper said it wasn't. I was just surprised when she told me, that's all. I never knew."

"Why should you?"

"No reason. I just..." *I want to know everything about you. I want to...* She let that yearning thought trail off unfinished. Honestly, what was wrong with her tonight? Did she actually imagine that if she *wanted* him desperately enough he would not be able to refuse her? That everything between them would magically work out and they would end up together forever and ever? *Please.* "Never mind..."

Those green eyes stared right into her, seeing everything. "What do you want to know? Just ask. I'll tell you."

"You're serious?"

"I don't make offers unless I plan to follow through on them."

A few drops of water still clung to his forehead and cheeks. She wanted to touch them, touch *him*. But they had their rules and those rules were very clear—no touching. "Piper said your birth mother was your dad's sister?"

"That's right. Her name was Deirdre. My dad always says she was sweet and shy. And smart. She got a full scholarship to Duke to study economics—and fell in love with one of her professors. Her senior year she dropped out and married the guy. I came along six months later.

"Things didn't go well between Deirdre and the professor. Turned out, he was also a mean drunk. He abused her. I was two the night he went too far. He punched her so hard that when she fell down she never got up."

Sarah gasped. "He killed her?"

"That's right. And then he shot himself."

"Oh, Maddox…"

"Pretty horrible, huh? The shot brought the neighbors. They found the bodies—and me in my crib."

"Were you…okay?"

"Not really. I didn't speak until I was four—or so I've been told. Though when I did finally start talking, I was using full sentences right from the first. I don't remember any of it. My parents did all they could. They got me counseling. I saw a therapist up in Sheridan. I only remember the therapist vaguely, though my mom and dad said I went to see her regularly until I was six. I'm sure she helped."

Sarah's eyes blurred with moisture. She blinked the tears away as she struggled to compose herself. "Sorry. I just…"

"Hey." His voice was gentle. "I only know what my dad and mom told me—and I only know Fergus and Mary as my dad and mom. I don't remember any of my life in North Carolina. I honestly don't."

She nodded. "I've read that people rarely recall anything that happens to them before the age of three."

"I believe that. And if you want to know the truth, I'm glad for it. I had a rough start in life—but then I got very lucky. And I only remember the lucky part." He was smiling now. "Anything else you're just dying to know?"

So much. Everything. But her heart felt raw from what

he'd just shared with her. She wanted to reach across the space between them, wrap her hand around the back of his neck and pull him over onto her chair. She wanted to rock him in her arms like the lost, wounded baby he'd been all those years ago—hold him and rock him, and never let go.

But that was not going to happen.

The large bronze skeleton-style clock mounted on a wall of stone above the sitting area beyond the deep end of the pool showed ten minutes to midnight.

He noticed the direction of her gaze. "It's getting late."

"Yeah." She sat up and swung her feet to the tiles. "I should go." Rising, she draped her towel around her neck and bent to pick up the so-far-completely-unnecessary baby monitor.

"Night," he said, still stretched out on his lounger, as she turned for the pool house.

"Night, Maddox."

A little later, up in her room, she felt edgy and excited, sad and strangely ecstatic, all at the same time. She was sure she would never get to sleep. But she closed her eyes and opened them again what seemed like a moment later—and it was six in the morning on the Fourth of July.

The day went by as usual. She shared breakfast with the family. Maddox took RJ and Stevie into town for the day. Sarah led Fergus through his exercises, after which she drove him out to the stables to meet with the foreman and hang out with the horses.

As she looked after Fergus, the things Maddox had told her the night before weighed on her mind. She felt closer to him after the hard truths he'd shared. Closer and full of yearning—and foolish, too.

Because getting closer wasn't going to go anywhere for them. She knew that. They'd agreed on that.

So getting her heart in deeper, falling harder...

Well, that was just plain reckless of her. She ought to know better. But her heart didn't seem to be listening to the warnings going off in her mind.

That evening, Sarah and Alma joined Maddox, Fergus, RJ and Stevie for the Independence Day celebration put on by the merchant's association in Patriot Park. They all rode into town together in Maddox's SUV.

It was a great time. They bought food from the various booths, visited with friends and with Sarah's large extended family. When night fell, they watched the fireworks explode in the wide Wyoming sky.

After the fireworks, there was dancing under the stars. Sarah watched Maddox dance with Stevie, who couldn't stop yawning.

Sitting under a hackberry tree strung with party lights, with Fergus on one side and RJ on the other, Sarah thought how much more relaxed RJ seemed in the past few days. Apparently, he and his dad had come to something of an understanding.

On the dance floor, Maddox bent to whisper in his daughter's ear. Stevie nodded up at him, beaming. And Sarah let herself wish that Maddox might ask her for a dance, too. She really would enjoy that, especially a slow one so that she would have his arms around her.

Because that was the great thing about slow dancing. It didn't have to mean anything. People slow-danced with strangers. It could simply be a friendly social activity.

But then, slow dancing with Maddox was bound to feel

a lot more than merely friendly. And that meant she probably wouldn't be doing it.

Scratch *probably*. She wouldn't. Absolutely not.

"What the...?" muttered Fergus, who sat a few feet to
her left. All evening, he'd seemed perfectly happy hanging
out with his son and grandchildren, celebrating the Fourth.

Right now, though, he craned forward in his chair and
scowled at the couples out there on the portable dance floor
as they swayed to a cover of an old Willie Nelson song. It
took Sarah a minute, but then she spotted the problem—
Earlene Pugh.

Earlene was dancing in the arms of a very attentive older
man. She looked every bit as captivating as she had that
morning two weeks ago, this time in a denim skirt with a
different pair of fancy boots. Her hair was swept up in a
pile of curls. As Sarah—and Fergus—watched, she went
on tiptoe and whispered something in the ear of her partner.
The man threw back his head and let out a laugh.

"That about does it," announced Fergus. "Sarah, I'm
going to go wait by the car." He spun his chair around and
off he rolled toward the parking lot.

Sarah rose to follow after him.

RJ looked up at her. "What's with Grandpa? Where are
you going?"

"Just to check in with him. I'll be right back."

"I'm going too." He was already on his feet, falling into
step beside her.

They caught up with Fergus on the edge of the parking lot.

When they got close, he stopped and turned the chair.
"What?" He glared at Sarah and then at his grandson. "A
man's not allowed to go for stroll on his own these days?"

"Grandpa," coaxed RJ. "Don't be grouchy."

"Humph. You two go on back where the action is. I'm doing fine on my own." Sarah opened her mouth to remind him that it was her job to stick close to him, but he beat her to it. "I know, I know. I'm your job. But right now, Sarah, I want to be—"

"Dad!" Maddox came jogging toward them, Stevie close on his heels, with Alma taking up the rear. "What happened? What's going on?"

"Not a thing," grumbled Fergus. "And even if there was, it is not your concern."

Maddox turned to Sarah. "What's this about?"

Alma spoke up then. "If you ask me, it's that woman from Sylvan Acres." She moved in close to Fergus and patted him on the shoulder. "I saw her back there on the dance floor with some smooth operator. They were laughing and having a grand time."

"Nobody asked you, Alma," Fergus practically shouted. "Just leave it alone!"

Alma dropped her hand from his shoulder and stepped back. "You got it." She pressed her lips together and her cheeks flushed deep red.

To his credit, Fergus realized right away that he was out of line. "Sorry, Alma," he muttered. "I know you're on my side…"

Now they all just stood there, surrounding Fergus, on the outer rim of the parking area.

Finally, Maddox said, "It's getting late. Why don't we head on home?"

Nobody objected. Sarah helped Fergus get comfortable in the car and the kids climbed in, too. Alma and Maddox went back to collect the big blanket and the folding chairs they'd left near the dance floor.

The ride back to the ranch was uneventful. RJ and Stevie nodded off. Everyone else kept their thoughts to themselves.

Sarah tried not to regret the dance she might have had with Maddox. It helped to remind herself that there wouldn't have been a dance. Because if he'd asked her, she would have turned him down.

Back at the ranch, she got Fergus settled in and went on up to her room. It was a little after midnight by then. Too late to head downstairs.

And yet she ached to go for a swim.

But she made herself remain in her room. Because she really did need to get a grip on this situation with her employer—either that or get honest and quit her job. Quitting would be the wisest move. If she quit, she could pursue an honest, upfront relationship with him. And if an honest relationship wasn't happening, then at least she could start getting over him.

Getting over him...

Talk about irony. She'd never even kissed the man and already she was trying to figure out how to get over him.

Maddox did go swimming that night. Long after he'd finished his usual forty laps, he stayed at the pool hoping Sarah would show.

At one thirty in the morning when he finally went upstairs, he was both disappointed that she hadn't appeared—and frustrated at himself that he cared so much.

He had a problem and he knew it. But that wasn't going to stop him from showing up again the next night.

And the one after that. Both of those nights, she was already in the water when he got there. They swam and then they talked and laughed together. It was exactly what he needed. He wanted every moment he could steal with her.

And there was nothing wrong with that, he reassured himself for about the fiftieth time. Nothing wrong at all. As long as he kept the whole thing in perspective, enjoyed being with her and didn't make any move to take it to the next level, what was the harm?

Saturday was her brother's birthday. Maddox took the family to the Double-K for the party. It went great. There was plenty of beef and a giant array of sides. He caught up with a large number of Bravo family members, and his dad and the kids seemed to have fun. There were horse-shoes, darts and ping-pong. The kids—there were a lot of them—played twister and Jenga Giant with blocks made of two-by-fours cut to foot-long lengths.

After Joe blew out his candles and everyone had cake, Maddox gathered up his family to go. Together, the Hales said goodbye to Joe and their hosts.

Sarah said, "Thank you for coming." She gave him that beautiful smile.

"See you Monday..."

She nodded.

That was the extent of their interaction that day. It was so far from enough. He couldn't wait for the damn weekend to be over. To have her to himself in the evenings again.

Was he an embarrassment to himself?

Probably.

Not that he even cared.

Monday, as usual, she showed up at breakfast. He wished he was sick so that she could be *his* nurse. He wanted her taking care of him in her plum-colored scrubs, bending close to tuck in his covers, taking his temperature, soothing his fevered brow with the light press of her cool hand.

It was a simple fact that just the sight of her made the day brighter.

After the meal, she went off with Fergus while Maddox took the kids out on horseback. They swam in Cottonwood Creek and then shared a picnic Alma had packed for them. Stevie was a joy to be around and Maddox was getting along with RJ pretty well now most of the time. However, his son still looked at him with wariness now and then, like he was waiting for Maddox to disappoint him again. Maddox was determined that wasn't going to happen.

RJ didn't appreciate being told how to do things, so Maddox was learning to step back and let his son try to figure things out on his own. The boy had a surprising understanding of the way things worked. RJ could discuss the pros and cons of electric vehicles based on solid facts. And when he and Maddox played chess, RJ won a third of the time.

Maddox was proud of both kids. He was finding he really did get a lot of satisfaction in having time with his children. He reminded himself that these were the moments that mattered—him and RJ and Stevie making memories to last them the rest of their lives.

After dinner that evening, he and the kids watched *Spider-Man: No Way Home*. Both RJ and Stevie had already seen it, but they had no objections to watching it again on the giant flat-screen in the media room on the top floor.

Later, after he'd kissed them both goodnight, he headed for the pool. Feeling suddenly on edge, he wondered, *Will she be there?*

"She'd better be…" he muttered under his breath and then shook his head at himself.

If she'd had enough of him and the swimming and the talking and the carefully-not-touching, well, how could he blame her?

He couldn't. And he wouldn't.

But then, he entered the pool house—and miracle of miracles, she was there!

Her slim bare feet were visible beneath the drawn curtain in one of the four changing cubicles. Pure happiness radiated through him and suddenly he was grinning like a fool.

Her toes were painted the same plum color as the scrubs she'd worn that morning. And he was just standing there staring at her purple toes when she pushed the curtain back.

Blinking, he brought his gaze up over her smooth, strong legs to the perfect outward curves of her hips in that sleek purple suit—and on up past the tempting dip of her waist to the soft fullness of her breasts.

Eventually, he met her eyes. "I..." He swallowed. Hard. "Hi." Why was it he so often felt like an awkward boy around her? He was supposed to be the mature one, after all.

"How long have you been standing there?" she asked with a lift of one dark eyebrow.

"Longer than I should have."

Her gaze met his so steadily. She didn't look away. The gleam in those big eyes said he was in for it. "It's not nice to lurk in the pool house."

"No. It's not. Not nice at all."

She took a step toward him and then another, stopping when she'd closed the small distance between them. Now her bare toes were an inch from the toes of his shoes. "Did you have a good day?"

His brain was a fog of need. His body, too.

"It was a great day."

"You spent it with the kids?"

"That's right."

"How's RJ?"

"I don't want to get ahead of myself, but I think RJ and I are doing pretty well."

"Good." She searched his eyes. "What about you and me?"

He sensed a trap—but what kind? "What about us?"

"Do you think we're…doing well?"

Damn. She was so beautiful. And he had it so bad for her.

How had he let this happen?

And now that it had, shouldn't he want it to stop? He had his rules, after all. He wasn't cut out for true love or marriage. He didn't want another relationship. He wanted an occasional night out with a pretty woman who expected good company in and out of bed. No one too young—and certainly not his father's nurse.

So many rules he had. And Sarah Bravo tempted him to break every damn one.

"Maddox?" She lifted her hand and laid it, light as a breath, over his heart, which instantly went wild in there, throwing itself at the walls of his chest like it would break right through to get to her.

The problem was, it felt so good to have her hand on him. He wanted more. Reaching out, he eased an arm around her waist.

"This is wrong," she said.

He really didn't want to hear that. So he pulled her close and claimed her mouth with his.

Chapter Seven

Wrong...

The word echoed inside Sarah's head as his lips touched hers, so hot and hungry and perfect.

Wrong...

His big hands roamed her bare back, learning her skin, mapping the shape of her. He kept one arm wrapped around her waist as the other moved upward over her back. His warm fingers eased under the heavy mass of her unpinned hair to clasp her nape. Her heart pounded in her ears, demanding *more, more, more*, as faintly, far in the distance, her rational mind screamed, *stop!*

Wrong...

So wrong and yet somehow so absolutely right.

His tongue slid across the seam of her lips, seeking entry. With an eager sigh, she let him in. He bit her lower lip—not hard. Just enough that she moaned in excited response. And then both of his hands were at her waist, lifting her. Her feet left the floor as his mouth continued to plunder hers.

Eagerly, she raised her legs and wrapped them around him nice and tight.

And now...

Oh yes! She could feel him, so hard and big and ready, pressing against her core.

More, her heart cried and her body agreed. *More. Yes. Never stop*...

But some small shred of self-respect remained to her. With a moan of sheer frustration, she brought her hands up between them and pushed him away.

His eyes blazed green fire. "Come back here."

She pushed harder. "Stop."

That single word did the trick. His arms loosened. Her feet touched solid ground. He stepped back. They stared at each other.

And then, with a low, tortured sound, he reached for her again. She put up a hand to stop him.

It worked. His arms dropped to his sides. "Sorry," he said roughly. "I won't do that again."

Did she believe him? Not a chance. "Maddox, this is no good."

He hung his head. "You're right. I know."

"You know...*what*?"

"That we can't be doing this."

"Exactly. And yet, here we are."

He straightened his broad shoulders. "As I said, it won't happen again."

"Now you're just deluding yourself."

"Sarah, I swear to you..."

It was too much. She did what she had to do. "Maddox, I quit. And this time, I mean it."

"Whoa!" He put up both hands and patted the air between them. "No. Come on. Don't do that."

"There's no other option here."

"Yes, there is." He forked his fingers back through his hair. "Please, Sarah. Don't overreact."

"Oh, but I'm not. If I stick around, you know where this is going to go. And it's just flat-out unethical. We've already agreed we're not doing this. And yet look what just happened. If I worked for an agency, I would rightfully be fired for kissing my patient's son."

"But you don't work for an agency."

She scoffed. "Please. Yes, I am an independent hire and there's no one to fire me if you don't. But that doesn't make my kissing you any less wrong. Nurses have no place getting emotionally involved with a patient or with anyone who has influence over the patient. Situations like this one can potentially cause all kinds of damage."

"My dad is not that kind of patient. He knows his own mind and he makes his own decisions. There's no way I'm going to use you to subvert his best interests. Plus, we both know that you're not going to hurt him or anyone else."

"Rules are rules. How many times do I have to say it? If we keep doing this, I could—or at least I *should*—end up before the licensing board and lose my nursing license."

"That will never happen. Who's going to report you? No one."

"Oh, Maddox." She took a step back from him. "Listen to yourself. *Okay, it's wrong but don't worry because no one will ever know.* That is not reassuring. Not in the least. I don't see how we can—"

"Slow down. Just hear me out…"

She shut her eyes and shook her head. "Maddox, you are a very smart man. You have to know that this argument just goes around in circles. We can't talk ourselves out of the truth. It's painfully clear now that neither of us has what it takes to keep our hands off each other. I have to go."

Maddox knew she was right.

And yet the hopeless fool inside him just wouldn't give

up. Even though he knew he would lose her anyway—that he would never really *have* her, not even if she agreed to stay. It wasn't as though they had a future together. They wanted completely different things from life. Not to mention he had no interest in creating a future with anyone. He liked being single. He wasn't going to change.

And yet, he'd developed something of an obsession with the woman glaring up at him now, and he couldn't bear the thought of her leaving. If he couldn't be alone with her, at least he could see her, share a word or a smile with her, during the day.

"It's only here, alone together at night, that we get into trouble. I'll leave the pool to you in the evenings. You won't see me here again. Will that work?"

Her mouth was drawn down at the corners. "We've been through this. The best way to solve this problem is to make absolutely certain we have no opportunity to break the rules. My leaving this house is the only way to guarantee that."

"How many ways can I say it? There's no need for you to quit."

"Sorry, but it's my career and self-respect on the line and I say that there is."

"Now that we're fully aware of the fact that we can't be alone together, there's an obvious solution to the problem. I'll stop coming for a swim in the evenings. You'll have the pool to yourself."

"It's not that simple. I think you know that."

"Look, you said yourself that you need the money. And my dad is crazy about you. He's going to be hurt if you leave and he's also going to demand an honest explanation of why the hell you had to go."

"So tell him the truth."

"Oh, great. Tell my dad that we can't keep our hands off each other and that's wrong, so you quit."

She winced. "Okay. It's not the kind of thing you want to explain to your dad. I get that..." She looked up at him so earnestly.

Damn. He was pitiful when it came to her. He did have a serious problem here. He needed to let her go every bit as much as she needed to leave.

And yet...

Really, they could fix this. She could keep her job taking care of his dad and he could have the rest of the summer with her in all the harmless, innocent ways that meant so much to him.

Why couldn't they have that much, at least?

A smile across the breakfast table. A glance as they passed in the hallway. Board games with his dad and Alma and the kids. They could even use the pool together, in the daytime, when there were others around.

"It's an easy fix," he reassured her. "We won't be alone together. Problem solved."

"Maddox, it's not a good idea..." She whispered the words.

"Stay. You take such good care of my dad and he loves hanging out with you. He's not used to being cooped up inside, unable to ride or to work with the horses. You keep his spirits up. And the trip to New York is right around the corner." They were leaving Thursday. "Come with us to the beach house in Southampton. Spend a few days in Manhattan. In Southampton, there will be a weekend of parties. I'll be busy with my guests. No chance I'll behave badly, I promise you. And then, in the city, RJ and Stevie will go to their mother for the week while I catch up at the office. It will be you and Dad at my place. You'll rarely see me. And I will never again put you in a situation like this one tonight."

"Stop blaming yourself. I'm just as much at fault as you are."

"All right. It's your fault, too." He tried a smile, but knew it wasn't very convincing. "Feel better?"

She folded her arms and sighed. "Not really."

"Just stay. Please."

Silent now, she gazed up at him. Somehow, he kept his mouth shut as well, though it took superhuman effort not to keep right on begging her. He didn't understand himself at all—not when it came to her. He should just let her do it, let her go, end this thing between them that he never should have allowed himself to start.

But then she nodded.

And he realized he'd done it. Somehow, he'd convinced her not to do what she *should* do. He dared to breathe again.

"All right," she said. "I'll stay, on the condition that we have no more time alone together."

"Agreed."

"We'll give your plan a try." She turned, ducked back into the dressing cubicle, grabbed her clothes and faced him again. "Good night, Maddox."

"You don't have to…"

She cut him off with a finger to her lips. "Good night." And then she turned and headed for the door that led into the house.

For the next two days, Sarah rarely saw Maddox. She avoided the pool completely. If she saw Maddox coming, she turned and went the other way.

Fergus asked her twice if she was okay. He said she seemed far away and maybe a little sad.

She assured him that she was just fine. "Sometimes I get like that."

"Like what?" Fergus demanded.

"I don't know. Thoughtful, maybe. You know, there's so much to do in life and if we're not careful time kind of slips away."

"Okay," grumbled her patient. "Now you're making *me* sad."

She laughed at that. "Sorry. I'll cheer up. Just you watch me."

"I'm holding you to that. You see if I don't."

Thursday morning, they—Fergus, Sarah, the kids and Maddox—drove up to the airport where Maddox's jet was waiting for them. That was cool, sitting in what amounted to a sleek, modern living room that just happened to be flying through the sky.

They played card games—rummy, hearts and crazy eights. Lunch was served in the air. It was fun. The only hard part for Sarah was avoiding eye contact with her patient's son.

A big car was waiting at Teterboro to take them to Southampton. They arrived at Maddox's beach house late in the afternoon.

Sarah tried not to gape in awe at the splendor of the place. Inside, it was all open and airy. Walls of glass faced north and south to take advantage of the panoramic views.

Outside there was a large sundeck, a forty-foot swimming pool, a big, beautiful pool house. A boardwalk led down from the pool deck, over dunes thick with beach grass, to the white-sand beach and the Atlantic Ocean beyond.

Such splendor required serious staff—including a cook, a housekeeper and a burly guy who took care of the pool and grounds. Fergus told Sarah that only the housekeeper lived on the property full time. The others came and went.

Thursday night was family night. Sarah made her excuses, went to bed early and spent a mostly sleepless night considering her options. The way she saw it now, the less time she spent acting like one of the family, the better for everyone. Professional boundaries mattered—especially in a situation like this.

She couldn't let herself get too relaxed or too comfortable. The more she let down her guard, the more likely she would be to let Maddox get too close again—or to throw her professional ethics out the window and beg that man for things that would be so, so wrong.

Friday, she stood on the sundeck beside her patient, who sat in his wheelchair. They watched Maddox and the kids run down the boardwalk to the beach.

"The grandkids love it here." Fergus swiped off his faded Cowboys cap and let the wind ruffle his white hair. "They've been coming here in the summers since Maddox bought the place eight years ago and they have friends here that they meet up with every time they come."

"They do seem excited to be here," she said.

"They are. Stevie always has a great time. RJ, too." Fergus squinted up at her. "RJ seems better lately, don't you think?"

"He does, yeah."

Fergus settled the cap back on his head. "Maddox says that he and RJ have gotten into it more than once, but when that happens, they take a break and then they get together and talk it out. That seems to work. They're getting along pretty well now."

Sarah smiled down at him and then gazed off toward the beach, which was invisible between the higher dunes and the Atlantic beyond. "Everybody's out of sight."

"Yep—hand me my crutches. I need to get out of this chair."

Fergus spent the rest of the morning and early afternoon using his crutches instead of the chair. Sarah hung around with him, careful not to crowd him. He was growing more and more independent, rarely needing her help to get around or to manage his physical needs.

She could hand in her resignation today and rest easy in the knowledge that her patient wouldn't struggle without her. She liked to think that Fergus might miss her. She would definitely miss him. But he didn't need round-the-clock care, not anymore—if he ever really had.

And *she* didn't need any more opportunities to behave inappropriately with her boss. Over the long, restless night before, she'd made her decision. When they returned to Wyoming, she would hand in her notice and move on. Even if Maddox tried again to convince her to stay, she would remain firm. She was leaving. There was nothing more to talk about.

Friday evening, Maddox hosted Stevie and RJ's local friends and their families. Down on the beach, they shared a Hamptons-style bonfire-in-a-tin and cookout. Fergus rolled his wheelchair down the boardwalk and then, one arm wrapped around Maddox and the other around the groundskeeper, he hopped on one leg across the sand and settled in a cushioned folding chair to join the fun. Sarah stuck close to him, doing her job. The kids had a ball. Maddox seemed relaxed and happy. Sarah's gaze kept straying his way, her heart heavy with longing she shouldn't allow herself to feel.

Saturday morning, Maddox's business colleagues and their families began to arrive. The giant schmooze-fest went on all day and late into the night. Fergus knew a few of the guests from previous visits, apparently. He hung out with them and with the kids. Sarah felt increasingly unnecessary. She went through the motions anyway, keeping an eye on her patient, who'd become a dynamo on crutches.

Most of the people there that day seemed to look right through her, which felt a little insulting but also made total sense. She clearly was not on hand to network. After all, she wore scrubs and she stuck close to the guy on crutches.

But she did overhear a tall, balding man asking Maddox, "Who's the nurse?"

Maddox said nothing. Apparently, he was pretending he hadn't heard the question.

But that guy was not deterred. "She's gorgeous," he said, loud enough that Sarah could hear him clearly. She made the mistake of glancing his way. He looked her up and down as though she wasn't really human, just an object to be acquired, like a fancy car or a high-dollar speedboat. And then he added, staring right at her as he did it, "The young ones are so much fun, aren't they? All that energy and enthusiasm. There's nothing that gets me going like a pretty young thing…"

Well, that settled it. The jerk did see her as a *thing*—and Maddox took him by the arm.

"Whoa, Hale," muttered the jerk. "Back off."

Maddox pretended not to hear him. "I need a minute,"

he said, all friendly and smooth. And he pulled the guy over to a deserted corner of the pool deck.

Sarah couldn't hear what was said, but that guy didn't get near her again that evening—which was good. Really good. Because his attitude pissed her off and if he'd actually approached her she might have said just about anything. And she might have said it good and loud, too, which could have put a damper on Maddox's fancy party.

Sunday, the staff packed up one of the big luxury SUVs from down in the beach house's five-car garage and Maddox drove the kids, Fergus and Sarah to his penthouse in an area of Manhattan known as Turtle Bay.

The apartment was every bit as gorgeous as the Southampton beach house, full of light, with views of the city all around. Fergus told her that Maddox had bought it a year after RJ was born when he'd closed his first major real estate deal. It was a half-hour commute from there to the financial district. Maddox could have found something just as nice closer to work, but RJ and Stevie had started out in Turtle Bay and both of them considered it their home. Alexis, Fergus said, loved the area, too. She and her second husband, Teddy, had bought a townhouse nearby.

The car was barely unloaded when Alexis appeared to collect the children for a weeklong trip to Portugal. Once the kids were gone, it was just Maddox, Fergus, Sarah and the housekeeper/cook, Evan, at the penthouse. Fergus had RJ's room. Sarah got the guest room directly across the central hallway from him.

Maddox's suite was down at the end of that same hallway. He disappeared into it right after dinner. Which was perfect, truly. For as long as she remained Fergus's nurse, the less she saw of Maddox Hale, the better for both of them.

Monday, she barely saw the man. He left the penthouse early in the morning. Evan told her at breakfast that Maddox would be eating dinner out—and that was great, she kept telling herself. Perfect, even. Maybe he would be gone all day, every day and into the night for the rest of the week. Maybe she wouldn't have to deal with him at all till they got on the plane for the return trip.

She should be glad for that. Too bad her foolish heart ached for him. She wanted to be near him. She yearned for those nights by the pool.

It was a real problem. But at least it reminded her that she'd made the right choice about handing in her notice as soon as they got back home.

And her own dilemma aside, what about Fergus— dragged all the way to Manhattan and then abandoned? What was Maddox thinking?

She asked Fergus if he'd like to go out and explore New York City a bit.

"I would," he replied. "Just get me back here by nine tonight. Maddox said he'd be home by then."

When she heard that, for no logical reason at all, she felt hurt—because Maddox hadn't said a word to her about when he'd be home.

And seriously. *Hurt?* Please. She had no business letting herself feel hurt over anything Maddox Hale did or didn't do. He did not have to communicate his schedule to her. Clearly, she reminded herself for the umpteenth time, the less contact she had with him, the better for her heart, her career and her self-respect.

On a happier note, she enjoyed her day with Fergus immensely. The New York streets were hot and muggy, crowded with people from all walks of life. She loved it—

all of it—the crowds, the noise, the muggy heat. There was an energy to the city, a pulse that she could feel rising up through the concrete, a kind of call to action that made her want to get out and get things done.

They got a wheelchair-accessible taxi van to take them to Central Park, where there were trails Fergus could manage in his chair. For more than an hour he rolled along beside her in the shade of the spectacular elm trees. It was gorgeous. Too soon, they headed back to the spot where the taxi van would meet them.

The driver let them out near Maddox's apartment, where they had lunch at a bistro—well, okay, it was a food truck with three café-style tables huddled close on either side, each with an umbrella to keep diners shaded at least a little.

Fergus joked, "You know we'd be more comfortable back in the penthouse. And Evan would cook us whatever we asked for."

"We're having an adventure," she informed him with a grin as she went to work on her excellent coq au vin.

But he was watching her too closely. "You're smiling. But your eyes are sad. You've been sad for days now. What's the matter, Sarah? Homesick already?"

"No. How could I be? New York is fascinating. I love it here."

"Then, what is it?"

She sipped from her can of sparkling water as she came to the conclusion that her patient should know of her plans. But they weren't easy to explain, not when there was so much she had to hold back. "Oh, Fergus…" Where to begin? Stalling as she searched for the right words, she ate some more of the delicious chicken.

Fergus leaned closer. "Talk to me. Come on, now."

She set down her plastic fork. "I don't know how to say this. But let me just start with how much I have loved working with you. You're the best."

"What in the holy hell?" Fergus sat back in his chair. "You're quitting."

She was no crier. Never had been. But all of a sudden, her eyes blurred with moisture and her throat clutched.

"Aww, now..." Fergus sighed heavily and held out his extra napkin. "Dry those pretty eyes."

She took the napkin and blotted up the tears. "It's time, that's all. You don't really need me. You are taking care of yourself and doing a great job of it. We both know that."

His forehead was all crinkled up. He reached across and squeezed her shoulder. "Tell me the rest."

She drew a shaky breath and sat up straighter. "That's all. It's time for me to find another—"

"Bull crap." His eyes had narrowed. "This is about you and Maddox, isn't it?"

Her mouth fell open. "Uh..."

"Isn't it?"

She just couldn't lie to him. He wouldn't believe her anyway, and he'd be hurt that she'd refused to trust him. "Yeah. It's about Maddox."

He grunted. "I knew it."

She groaned. "You don't get it."

"I think I do. It ain't rocket science. You two are a pair. You like him and he's wild for you."

"Wild?" she asked hopefully, before slapping her hand over her mouth. "Forget I said that." Fergus cocked a brow and chuckled. She went on sternly, "It's not right for me to get involved with Maddox."

"Seems pretty damn right to me. You got a problem

because he's older? What do they call that when you have something against older people—an ageist? Sarah, are you an ageist?"

"No—his age is not a factor. Not for me, anyway. The big problem for me is that you're my patient. This is my job. My falling for your son is not acceptable."

"But you *have* fallen for him." He must have taken her unwillingness to argue the point as confirmation—which it was. "I knew it," he muttered. And then he went further. "And in case you didn't notice, Maddox feels the same about you."

Her pulse sped up. "Please. How can you possibly know all this?"

He waved a big, rough hand. "I know my son. And Sarah, I'm not blind. I knew it that first day, when we interviewed you for this job."

"What are you saying?"

"I'm saying that Maddox was a goner the minute you walked into his office at the ranch."

"You're exaggerating."

"No, I am not. I was still in the hospital then, remember?"

"Of course. You interviewed me remotely."

"That's right. The laptop in Maddox's office was turned toward him when you walked in the door. I saw his face. Bam! Like in *The Godfather*, hit by the thunderbolt."

She probably shouldn't be this happy to learn that Maddox had been strongly attracted to her from the beginning. But she was. Still, she tried to play it off. "You have no idea what you're talking about."

"Wrong."

"I mean, honestly. I just thought he disapproved of me for some reason."

"You got it right. He did disapprove—but not of you. Uh-uh. He disapproved of his own reaction to you."

"I don't know about that…"

Fergus grunted. "Well, I do."

"Fine. Have it your way."

He actually winked at her. "I will, don't you worry."

"I'm just saying that I walked out of that interview feeling absolutely certain that he wouldn't hire me."

Fergus wore a smug little grin. "But he did hire you, now, didn't he?"

"Right. Because of you."

He reached across their little table and gave her arm a squeeze. "Please don't quit. You need the job and my son needs you."

She shook her head. "Oh, Fergus. It's not that simple."

"Sure it is."

"No. It's not. As in all professions, there are rules of behavior. If you break them, there can be serious consequences. Not to mention that to break them is just plain wrong."

"What rules of behavior?"

"As a nurse, I need to be objective. I can't be distracted, can't be tangled up in a relationship with anyone in my patient's family, can't be subject to the potential for undue influence. When I'm working, my mind has to be focused on the person I'm caring for. There can't be any question that I might have made a decision that's not in the patient's best interest."

"Whoa, that's a mouthful, what you just said. And I'm sure you're right about the dangers in some situations—if, for instance, I was at death's door and Maddox wanted to get rid of me and started cozying up to my nurse to help him do it. But this is no murder mystery. Nothing like that is going on here. Your rules don't apply."

"Sorry, Fergus. Rules are rules and they always apply."

He was silent for several seconds as he studied her face. "I'm not having any luck changing your mind, am I?"

She shook her head again, slowly this time.

Fergus heaved a heavy sigh. "They got beer in that food truck? 'Cause I think I need one."

When Maddox entered the apartment early that evening, he found Sarah and his dad in the living area watching one of those *Jesse Stone* mysteries that Fergus loved.

"Good news!" he announced. "My dinner meeting had to be rescheduled."

"Great." Fergus grabbed the remote and paused the show. "Evan made chicken potpie—and this is almost over."

From Sarah, he got a guarded smile. Since that night in the pool house a week ago now, all her smiles were guarded—at least the ones she aimed at him. "Hey," she said with a nod.

"Hey," he replied. "So then, you two already ate?"

"Not yet," his dad said. "Evan left the food warming in the oven. We were planning to eat as soon as this show is over."

"Sounds good." Maddox took a corner chair well away from the beautiful brunette in the sunny yellow scrubs. "Have I seen this one?"

"I think we watched it last summer," said his dad. "It's the one about the pregnant teenager who drowned in the lake."

He vaguely recalled that one—and he could smell that chicken potpie. His stomach grumbled. "Okay, then. Let's get to the end. Dinner's waiting."

When the credits rolled, Sarah stood first. "I had a big lunch, so I think I'll skip dinner and say good-night to you two." She cut a glance at Maddox. "If that's all right."

It wasn't. Though they were careful and distant with each other now, he couldn't stop himself from wanting her near whenever the opportunity presented itself. The summer was racing by. He would never have another night by the pool, just the two of them talking about things he would only share with someone he knew he could trust absolutely. But even if he couldn't have that, he *could* have time with her like this, with someone else around to keep them honest, and he didn't want to give it up.

"Of course it's all right," he lied. "Good night, Sarah."

"Night," said his dad.

She rose and left them. He didn't realize he was staring after her until his dad coughed. By then, she'd disappeared down the hall.

"Ready to eat?" Maddox asked.

"You bet—and son?"

"What, Dad?"

"We need to talk."

Rap-tap-tap.

Sarah woke from a fitful sleep to the sound of someone quietly knocking on the door of her room. She felt around on the nightstand for her phone. When the screen lit up, she saw it was just past midnight.

Rap-tap-tap.

With a groan, she sat up and swung her bare feet to the floor. Pulling down the hem of her faded Buckeye Nation T-shirt so it covered her to midthigh, she padded barefoot to the door. When she pulled it open a crack, she saw Maddox glaring at her from the other side, his hair sticking out every which way, like he'd been raking his fingers through it.

"What is it?" she whispered.

"Let me in," he muttered ferociously.

Alarm skittered through her. What was the matter? She opened the door a fraction wider, enough to see that he was barefoot in joggers and a gray T-shirt. "What? Is it Fergus? Is he—"

"He's fine. He's in bed. Let me in."

"Maddox, I don't see what—"

"*Please.*"

With a heavy sign, she stepped back. He crossed the threshold. She still had hold of the door and stood slightly behind it, keeping it as an admittedly ineffective barrier between them. "Now what?" she demanded—quietly, for the sake of her patient sleeping right across the hallway.

"Shut the door."

"Whatever you say," she whispered, heavy on the irony. As she pushed the door closed, he began to pace the room. She let him stalk back and forth a couple of times before inquiring, "What's this about?"

"I couldn't sleep." He paced to the chair in the corner, turned and came toward her again.

"And this is my problem, how?"

He stopped right in front of her. "My dad says you're quitting as soon as we get back to Wyoming."

She shut her eyes and drew in a slow breath. When she opened them again, he was still right there, inches away from her, six-foot two or so of hot, disheveled, pissed-off manliness. She could smell his cologne, a scent of cedar and mint.

"Well?" he prompted.

"Yes. I'm quitting."

"Don't you think you should have spoken to me about this first?"

Once again, her pulse had set up a racket. It pounded in her ears. "Fergus is my patient. I thought he should know." She fell back a step, claiming a bit of much-needed space.

He simply stepped forward and closed the distance she'd created. "Why?"

"Why?" She almost threw back her head and laughed out loud. "You know why. It's no good, my working for you. There's too much…tension. I need to go."

"What about my father? He depends on you."

She gave a snort-laugh at that one. "Please. Fergus is doing great. Hire him a caregiver if you must, but he's not going to roll over and die without me."

He said nothing to that. And his silence? It had weight and urgency. Plus, there was the way he looked at her, like he needed to get his arms around her, and he needed to do that now. That look sent hot shivers skittering down the backs of her knees. She glared at him and mentally dared him to reach for her.

But that would be wrong and his clenched jaw told her he knew it. He held himself in check.

Barely.

The solution to her dilemma came to her then. She knew what to do.

"Maddox."

"What?" he demanded, low and silky, through gritted teeth.

"I changed my mind about quitting."

He blinked at her—both suspicious and hopeful. "Yeah?"

"Yeah. I'm not waiting till we get home to give notice.

I'm quitting right now, tonight. As of this very moment, I am no longer your father's nurse."

He looked crushed. "You can't—"

"But I am." And then she closed those six inches that separated them, slid her hands up his hard, hot chest, surged to her toes and crushed her mouth to his.

Chapter Eight

Maddox couldn't stop himself. He wrapped his arms tightly around her and returned her kiss.

Damn. It was heaven, holding her close, kissing her like his life depended on it. He didn't like that she'd quit—in fact, he hated it—but at least now she seemed more than okay with having his arms around her.

He should be glad that at last, she was letting him hold her—and he *was* glad. But at the same time, guilt ate at him.

After all, he had so many years on her and they looked at the world so differently. He didn't want to hurt her, but if they let this go further, he most likely would.

He should call a halt.

But he didn't. He wanted her too much to push her away.

And she wanted him. At last, he had her in his arms again, so strong and soft and perfect, her hair smelling of lemons and flowers, her mouth tasting of toothpaste and heat.

There was no damn way he could make himself call a halt to this.

Never. Not in a million years. Instead, he stood there in the middle of the room with her wrapped around him like a climbing vine, knowing he should peel her off him…

And doing no such thing.

On the contrary, he grabbed her closer, kissed her harder,

held on tighter as he staggered backward toward the waiting bed.

When the backs of his knees met the mattress, he sat down. She climbed right onto the bed with him and wound her arms and legs around him, pulling him even closer to her than before.

He could feel her, the feminine core of her, hot and soft and welcoming, pressing against his suddenly painful erection. It all seemed unreal, that she was offering him everything he wanted—everything that he had absolutely no business letting himself have.

She grabbed his face between her hands. His eyes popped open. She was glaring at him, brown eyes blazing gold as she pulled her mouth away from his just far enough to whisper desperately, "Don't you dare stop now."

"Sarah…" It came out as a groan.

"Don't you dare," she warned a second time. And then her mouth met his again, opening, inviting. He slipped his tongue inside and all his scruples went winging off somewhere far away and out of sight.

She pushed him back onto the bed and followed him down, kissing him wildly. Her loose hair fell all around them, her hands were on him, her fingers gliding along his arms and up again across his shoulders. They dipped down the front of him, skating so sweetly over his chest and around to either side of his waist.

She tugged on his shirt. "Come on. Let's get this off you."

That did it. He caught her hands. "Wait."

She glared down at him with an annoyed little sigh. "What is it now?"

He felt like a kid again—out with the hottest girl he'd

ever known, totally unprepared for how lucky he was about to get. "I don't have a condom."

Her kiss-swollen lips quirked in a tiny smile. And then she was lifting that sweet body off him.

"Hey..." He tried to catch her hand.

But she was already off the bed and turning away. Still flat on his back, he lifted his head to watch her walk to the closet, pull open the door, flip on the light and kneel by her suitcase.

Unzipping one of the front flaps, she took something out.

A moment later, she'd shut the closet door and leaned back on it. "It's not a problem," she said. "I always have condoms. Even if I never use them, being prepared is the safe thing to do." She flicked on the floor lamp a foot away and stuck her hand under the light. "See? I bought these when I left for Bolivia." She peered at them more closely. "Still good." And then those big eyes were focused on him again. "I also take a contraceptive shot. I mean, just in case you have concerns that condoms alone aren't enough." She looked at him so earnestly, a responsible young woman ticking off all the sexual health-and-safety boxes.

He sat up. This was the moment—his last chance to walk away. Realistically, he knew he should get the hell out.

Sarah must have read his thoughts from his expression. She crossed her arms, lounged against the door and asked, "Are we saying good-night after all, then?"

Damn. She was something, with those big eyes and all that wild, dark hair, slouching there in her too-big T-shirt, one bare foot crossed over the other.

He really needed to stop lying to himself. He was going nowhere.

"Well?" she asked.

He held out his hand.

With a happy little laugh, she darted back to the bed. Taking the hand he offered, she turned it over, set the condoms in his palm and folded his fingers to cover them. He dropped them on the nightstand.

"Come here," he coaxed, taking her other hand, too, pulling her back onto the bed with him.

She didn't hesitate. Bracing one knee to either side of his thighs, she straddled him, pushed him back onto the pillows and bent close. Her hair fell around them again, a curtain of dark silk. The scent of her, sweet and tart, thrilled him.

With an eager little sigh, she lowered her mouth to his for a quick, hard kiss. And then, going up to her knees again, she took hold of her big shirt and whipped it off and away. The breath fled his body at the sight of her, naked except for a pair of little pink bikini panties.

It was then that he saw the two lines of rough, still-red scar tissue a few inches to the left of her navel. "Sarah..." He took her by the hips.

She rested her hands on his arms and gazed down at him, her expression so sweet and tender. "I'm okay. Honestly. They're healing up fine."

Gently, he brushed his thumb along one scar and then the other. "You could have been—"

"But I wasn't." She grinned.

He grunted. "You're proud of these."

She gave a low laugh. "I am. They make me feel tough, you know? It's like, whatever life throws at me, I'm going to do what I have to do. One way or another, I'm going to help where I can, and you'd better believe I will make it through alive."

"Come down here." He caught her hand and pulled her close again.

They kissed for the longest time, until finally she urged him to sit up. They stared at each other as they tore off the rest of their clothes.

"At last," she said softly when there was nothing between them. No smallest scrap of clothing—and no reluctance, not for either of them. There was only Sarah and Maddox. Naked. Together.

Not too long ago, he'd promised them both that they wouldn't do this. Never in his life had he been so happy to call himself a liar.

He took her in his arms. They stretched out on the bed. Staring down into her shadowed eyes, he saw that little girl he'd met all those years ago, the one who held out a skinny garter snake that had wrapped itself around her small, grubby wrist.

A tear escaped the corner of her eye.

"What's wrong?" he asked as he kissed that tear away.

"Nothing, honestly. Everything is very, very right." She lifted her arms and twined them around his neck. Her fingers brushed up into the hair at his nape. "I just never thought that you and I would ever be here, like this, together..."

"And yet, here we are." He took her lips again, kissed her slow and deep. He ran his hands over her body, touching every inch of her skin, needing to memorize the shape and feel of her so that when she was gone he would still have the ghost of her to haunt all his dreams.

She was bold and fearless, claiming the top position, tracing patterns on his chest with her naughty tongue. Moving down his body, she wrapped her fingers around his erection and lowered her mouth to take him in.

He almost lost it then. He could so easily have let her lure him right over the edge.

But no. Not yet. Not this time...

This time?

As though tonight was only the beginning.

It wasn't. It was the end. She was leaving. Probably tomorrow—or was tomorrow already today now?

There wouldn't be another time.

This was it. Their one night together. Right now was all that mattered. Right now he held her, so smooth and fine and eager, close in his arms.

She licked a slow path along the aching length of him.

Taking her by the shoulders, he rolled her under him, regaining control. He groaned. "You'll kill me..."

"As a medical professional, I can confirm that you're still breathing," she said playfully as she laughed up at him, a low, throaty, intimate sound.

He kissed the end of her pretty nose and marveled that such dark eyes could be so full of light.

And then he was taking those soft lips again in a long, deep kiss. Her mouth was so fine. But her mouth wasn't enough. He went lower, mapping the satiny skin of her throat, dropping a quick line of kisses across the elegant sweep of her collar bones.

He caressed his way lower still, lingering on those soft, tempting breasts before moving on to discover the satiny curves and hollows of her belly, the tender indentations beneath her hip bones—and the ragged beauty of those twin scars.

Carefully, he eased his shoulders between her open thighs. Settled there at the core of her, he kissed her for a long, sweet time. She was eager, clutching his hair in both her fists, spreading those strong thighs even wider, moaning his name like a plea.

Until, at last, she broke wide open. He kept kissing her, touching her, stroking her as she came so sweetly on his tongue.

When her climax faded down, he slid back up her limp body and reached for the nightstand. Taking one of the foil pouches, he tore it open, removed the condom and rolled it into place. She stared up at him, her eyes soft. Dazed.

And then, very slowly, she smiled. "Maddox."

"Sarah."

She reached up and brushed a slow finger down the side of his face as though to prove to herself that he was actually here with her, naked in this bed, all the barriers between them broken down—for this one night, anyway.

"Didn't we agree that this would never happen?" Her tone was teasing.

"We did." He hated to ask, but he knew that he had to. "Do you want to stop?"

She let out a sound of pure disbelief. "Are you kidding me? No way."

"You're sure?"

Her eyes turned so soft then. "Absolutely. I'm just a little bit amazed, that's all—that we're here, together, you and me."

"So, then. No stopping...?"

"That's right. No stopping. No way..."

He lowered his mouth to hers and brushed his lips, lightly, slowly, across hers.

She sighed. "Oh, Maddox. I'm glad for this night with you. I truly am."

"That's what I needed to hear." He kissed her more deeply then, sharing her breath as he settled between her open thighs. She wrapped her legs around him, spread her hands at the small of his back and pulled him into her. They groaned together as he filled her.

It was so good, her body soft and welcoming, cradling him as he moved within her. He felt so close to her right then, in a way that went far beyond the physical. It was sex the way he'd heard it could be but never for a moment believed—intimate. Open. The most natural thing in the world. Thrilling and comforting, both at once.

Maybe he'd lost it. Gone over the edge. Or beamed himself up to some other universe.

Whatever this was, he never wanted it to stop. He imagined them here, in this bed, forever. The world going by outside this room, spinning on without them. Leaving them to spend the rest of forever in each other's arms.

Too soon, she cried out, a soft sound, but urgent, too. He felt her body pulsing around him.

With a low moan, he joined her, surging hard into her as his release rolled through him. Swept away on a wave of pure pleasure, he closed his eyes and let sensation have him.

"Maddox…" She said his name on a long, happy sigh. "So good…"

He gave a low growl of agreement and pulled her closer.

Sarah woke wrapped in Maddox's arms.

When she stirred, she felt his lips in her hair. "You're awake," he said.

"Um-hmm." No light bled in around the curtains. "What time is it?"

"A little past two in the morning." He tipped her chin up. They smiled at each other.

She wasn't sure what she felt. Relaxed. Satisfied. And

also a little bit sad. Was this the end, then? Would he pull on his joggers and T-shirt and leave her alone in the middle of the night?

His eyes were steady, holding hers. "Did you mean it?"

"About quitting?" At his nod, she answered, "Yes. Maddox Hale, I no longer work for you."

A muscle flexed in his jaw. He didn't seem very happy with her answer. And then he suggested, "You could change your mind, you know."

"But I won't." She held his gaze steadily. "Face it. I quit."

He stroked a hand down her hair and then leaned in to brush a kiss on her lips. "What will you do?"

She eased away from him a little, plumped her pillow, and came to rest on her side, facing him. "I'll find a flight home and when I get there, I'll start looking for another job."

He watched her from the other pillow, those green eyes stormy. "Stay."

"Maddox, we've already been through this. I can't keep working for you—especially not now, after what we just did."

"I know."

"Then, why are you asking me to stay?"

"Because I don't want this to end yet."

Yet. She got that message loud and clear. There was no hope for them long-term. She already knew that, but it still hurt to hear him remind her. Even if it could never work, couldn't he at least leave the future open to possibility for this one night? Couldn't he leave off the word *yet*?

"Just listen," he said. "Just hear what I have to say. You could spend a few days here in New York, see the city, alone or with my dad—but only if you want to, as my guest instead of my employee. If you feel you have to leave now, Evan will keep an eye on him when I'm not here. You don't have to worry that he'll be alone."

A few days in New York...

That sounded wonderful. And she *had* felt kind of guilty about deserting Fergus. "I love hanging out with Fergus. You know that."

Now he was smiling again. "It's only a few days. And then you can fly back with us on Sunday."

She wanted to.

So much.

However, she needed a paycheck. For the past month, she'd been socking her earnings away. But that was over now. She should head home and get to work finding another temporary job. If all went according to plan, she would be accepted into a top-rated graduate program by the fall and starting school again in January. In the meantime, the more she could save, the better.

But come on. Five more days in New York and a free flight home on Sunday? Was she honestly thinking of passing that up?

"Your guest," she repeated. "That's what I'd be?"

"Yes, you would. A very welcome guest. And I swear to you, it will be strictly hands off, if that's how you want it."

It wasn't. After last night, she wanted all she could get of him for as long as it lasted—which couldn't possibly be long enough as far as she was concerned. She asked him, "What do *you* want?"

His eyes changed. Her stomach hollowed out at that look on his face. "I'll take whatever you're willing to give me."

Her breath got stuck in her chest. Because he wanted more, too. Just...not as much as she wanted.

And how was she going to feel when they went home? Wouldn't five more nights only make it all the more painful when it was over? She drew a careful breath. "There's Fergus to consider, too. I mean, he's always struck me as pretty traditional. He might be a little put off by his son and his used-to-be nurse heading for bed together every night. He also might get the wrong idea, assume it must be serious between us, that we could have a future together..."

"Sarah, we both know there's no future for you and me."

To hear him say it right out loud like that—it hurt. Disappointment, like a dead weight, pressed on her chest. She willed it away. Because he was right and she needed to face the truth. Their lives were on separate tracks. Forever was never going to happen for them.

She drew a slow breath and nodded. "I get it. This thing with us is going nowhere—but as for your invitation, yes. If you're sure it won't make problems with your dad, I would love to stay and come home with you and the family on Sunday."

"Excellent." His voice was low, full of delicious promises. He reached out, caressed her shoulder, let his finger trail down along her arm, his touch slow and sweet as poured-out honey.

Those eyes of his made promises. But only for the next five nights. If she were to spend those nights in his bed, how much more would it hurt when she had to say goodbye?

"About my dad," Maddox said. "He's a big boy. He understands that we're going to make our own choices."

"Yeah. I get that. Still, this, what just happened between us, it's private."

He was smirking now. "So you *are* seriously considering spending a few nights with me?"

"I don't know, Maddox. I'm really not sure that's such a good idea."

"Damn." Those fine lips turned down in a disappointed frown.

"You should go," she whispered. "It's getting pretty late…"

They stared at each other. Her heart was banging around like a wrecking ball inside her chest. He pushed back the covers and swung his feet to the floor.

"Wait…" She caught his arm.

He turned to look at her. "What is it?"

"One more time?" she whispered.

"Hell, yes." He pulled close as she lifted her mouth to his.

"You know, I didn't think you'd go straight to Maddox with the news that I was quitting," Sarah said gently late the next morning.

It was just her and Fergus, sitting near the fountain in Greenacre Park, which was only a couple of blocks from Maddox's penthouse. The small park was absolutely beautiful, with exotic flowers blooming everywhere in giant stone pots. Sarah wore jeans and a tank top instead of her usual scrubs. Because today, she was no longer Fergus's nurse.

"I was hoping he would talk you out of it," said Fergus. "Didn't work, though, huh?" When she shook her head, he added grumpily, "I still can't believe you're leaving me."

She tried to look stern. "It's time and you know it. You do everything for yourself now. The truth is, you didn't need a full-time nurse, even at first."

Fergus waved her words away. "Oh yes, I did. Because my full-time nurse was you. You make everything easier. Plus, we get along, you and me. I like having you around."

"Thank you. You're my favorite patient. Ever."

"Yeah, right."

"It's the unvarnished truth. And stop sulking. I do live next door to you and I'll be over to check on you often."

"You better. And about you and Maddox, I—"

"Fergus," she warned.

"Don't give me that look. It won't shut me up. I'll say what I mean to say. I'm not blind. I know damn well that you two have something going on together."

"Fergus, it's not—"

"La-la-la." Like some overgrown kid, he plugged his fingers in his ears. "I can't hear you."

She reached over and tugged on his left arm. "Stop."

He let his arms drop. "Then be quiet and let me talk." When she scowled at him, he demanded, "You quiet?" At her grudging nod, he said, "I just want you to know that I'm glad, that's all. I am giving you and my son the Fergus Hale Stamp of Approval. You two were made for each other."

Tell that to your son, she thought. She said, "Is that all? Because there's nothing for you to approve of."

"Liar."

She felt so sad suddenly. "Listen, I…care for Maddox."

"I know that." His voice was gentle now. "And he cares for you."

"But we're at different places in our lives. We don't match up in the ways that matter."

"Why, because he's fifteen years older?"

"Fifteen and a half, technically speaking," she corrected him.

"Whatever. Fifteen and a half years is nothing. Men marry younger women all the time and it works out just as often with them as it does with any other couple."

"It's not only the age thing."

"What? He's too rich for you?"

"In a sense, yes. We want different things."

"Well, get over yourself. Having money is nice. Take it from someone who knows. You would get used to it."

"Fergus, I think we just need to agree to disagree."

He looked at her so fondly. She wanted to grab him and hug him. "Well, now, Sarah, I *can't* agree with you. Because you're wrong."

"Can we just let it go, please?"

"Fine, fine," he grumbled. "Whatever you say."

"Let's talk about the next five days instead."

"What about 'em?"

"We have five days to hang out in Manhattan, you and me. It's going to be fun. We can do all the touristy stuff. We can visit the Empire State Building—which is fully ADA compliant, by the way. And I would love it if we could get in to see a Broadway show. Unfortunately, from what I've been reading online, wheelchair-access-wise, the theater situation isn't quite so ideal. Those are some really old buildings, which means they're hard to retrofit to make them accessible. But a few of them offer decent wheelchair access. I'm hoping Maddox can pull some strings, get us tickets to a show in a theater where you can get around easily."

"You want to take me to a Broadway musical?"

"You bet. You're going to love it."

Fergus gazed off toward a giant blue hydrangea in an enormous concrete pot. "Yeah," he said glumly.

Now what? "Are you trying to tell me you have no interest in going to a Broadway show?"

"A Broadway show sounds great." He was still focused on that hydrangea and he sounded downright sad.

She waited for him to say more. When he didn't, she gave him a nudge. "What is going on?" He bounced his good foot and kept looking glum. "Whatever it is, you might as well just tell me."

He threw up both hands and then dropped them in his lap. "Okay." Still refusing to meet her eyes, he said, "All this talk about you and Maddox has got me thinking about Earlene. And if you just have to know, Earlene likes to go to shows. Truth is, she was always after me to take her down to Cheyenne to some little theater she's heard about there..."

"Earlene... She's the woman from Sylvan Acres, right?"

He finally looked at her then. It was a very cranky look. "How many Earlenes do you think I know?"

Her heart turned to mush. Fergus Hale was inching up on confiding in her. Softly, she suggested, "What I think is that you miss Earlene."

"Humph. And what if I do?"

"Then, I don't see what's stopping you from doing something about that."

He scoffed. "What's stopping me? I will tell you what's stopping me. I loved my Mary. She was my everything. I thought I would die when I lost her. Earlene is...special to me, but Mary was my whole heart. And my only wife. I am never getting married again."

"Are you telling me that Earlene wants to marry you?"

His forehead crinkled up. "How would I know if she wants to get married or not?"

"So you're saying that you haven't talked to her about marriage, then?"

"Why would I do that? I won't be getting married again, so there's no point in talking about it."

"Well, Fergus. Sometimes you need to talk things over, kind of get everything you're feeling out in the open."

"Humph," said Fergus. Again. "I'm not one of those men who's inclined to blather on about *feelings*."

"I'm only saying that you could tell her that you don't intend to get married again. It's very possible that she doesn't want to get married, either."

"Humph."

"No, really. Maybe she's looking for marriage and maybe she's not, but I'm sure she wants to know where things stand. It seems to me that you really do care about her. What can it hurt if you spend a little time thinking about ways that you might work it out with her?"

"Well, now you went and put it in my head, I'll probably be thinking about her a damn sight more than I have been—which is already a lot—and I don't even know why I'm talking to you about this. What's the point? You saw her dancing with that fool in the park on the Fourth of July. Looks like she's not that interested in working things out with me, anyway."

Sarah felt a distinct niggle of annoyance at him. "Okay. You know Earlene better than I do, so you may be right. But at the risk of pissing you off, I feel it's only fair to point out that she came to see you at the ranch back in June."

"You think I don't remember? I'm old, but my memory still works just fine."

"Good to know. And I was there, too, that day Earlene came to the ranch. I was there and I saw how you behaved toward her. You were rude to her. You rejected her. You acted almost ashamed of her, trying to keep anyone from realizing that she'd come to visit you. I see no reason why she wouldn't want to dance with some other guy who seemed proud to be seen with her."

Fergus was silent. He sat very still in his chair, his head tipped down.

Sarah dared to ask, "Fergus, when you broke your leg, was it Earlene's window you fell out of?"

He finally looked up. "So what if it was? Earlene and me, we had an agreement. And that agreement was that nobody else would know that we were spending time together."

She prompted, "Spending time...?"

"Damn it, Sarah. If you just have to know, I stayed over at her place after Bingo that Friday night before the incident with the window."

"I see," Sarah replied, and then waited for Fergus to continue.

"I don't know why I'm telling you this," he grumbled.

"If you don't want to talk about it—"

"Oh, what the hell? I could maybe use a little feedback, if you know what I mean."

"Okay." She said it softly. "I'm listening."

"Ahem. So I stayed at Earlene's place after Bingo Friday night. Then, in the morning on Saturday, I was getting ready to go when she starts in about how she doesn't want to be my dirty little secret anymore."

"Wait. Who used the word *dirty*?"

"She did."

"Not you?"

He sat straighter in his chair. "Of course not. I never said any such thing."

"Good."

He eyed her sideways. "You mind if go on?"

"Please. Continue."

"Okay, so when she said she didn't want to be my dirty little secret, I said that keeping what we had private was what we'd agreed on. She said that wasn't working for her anymore. I said, *What do you want me to do, Earlene?* She said that we should change the agreement. I said no. By then, there might have been shouting."

"Who was shouting?"

"Both of us. And then Laverne Dixon, the woman who has the unit next door to Earlene's, started pounding on Earlene's door, shouting, *Earlene, is everything okay in there?* Earlene went to answer the door and I knew she was going to let the Dixon woman in."

"So you…?"

"I jumped out the window and broke my damn leg."

Chapter Nine

"Wow." Sarah longed to leap up and hug him—and then to call him a fool. But she had a feeling a hug might not go over so well right now. As for calling him a fool, why rub it in? She could see from the guilty look on his face that he already knew he had not behaved well when it came to Earlene Pugh.

She settled for, "You *really* didn't want anyone to know that you were seeing Earlene."

"Figured that out, did you?"

"Because of Mary?"

Fergus sat in silence, visibly lost in thought, for a minute or two. Finally, he confessed, "I never in my life thought I would ever be with any woman but my wife. And then, all these years after losing Mary, Earlene comes along. And she's beautiful and smart and a whole lot of fun—and she doesn't take guff off of anyone. I liked her the minute I saw her. And I hated myself for betraying Mary in my heart."

"You are not betraying Mary."

"Maybe not. But it sure has felt like it. Especially at first. That's why I didn't want anyone to know."

"So really, whether or not to *marry* Earlene isn't the question."

Fergus shot her a sideways glance. "What are you getting at now?"

"That the real question at this point is are you willing to go public in your relationship with Earlene."

"Doesn't matter. It's over. You just said so yourself."

"I said no such thing. I said you were rude to her and that I wouldn't blame her for dancing with someone else."

"Same difference."

"Fergus. If you want to be with Earlene, you really do need to make an effort. You're going to have to apologize to her for your thoughtless behavior that day she came to the ranch to see you, and you're going to have to agree to give up all the secrecy and make it clear that you're proud to be with her."

He was quiet again. Finally, he muttered, "Yeah. You're right on both counts. I know it." He looked her square in the eye. "I miss Earlene, Sarah. I truly do."

"I can see that—and that's why, in addition to your apology and your agreeing to go out with her openly, you need to tell her directly that you don't want to get married again. Because if she does want marriage, you need to know that. And she'll need to know that marriage isn't in the cards if she's with you."

"Yeah. I suppose so."

"And don't forget to tell her what you think of her, that she's smart and beautiful and you can't get her out of your mind."

"That all?" he muttered.

She took the hint. "Okay, okay. I guess that's enough advice for one day."

He stared at the waterfall. "I'm going to need to talk to Maddox about this thing with Earlene, too. Kind of get him up to speed."

"Great idea."

"I'm not exactly looking forward to admitting why I went out that window."

"You'll figure it out."

Fergus shot her a glance then. "And about you and Maddox, you'll think about what I said?"

"I will, thanks." Not that thinking about it would do much good. "Now, how about that Empire State Building?"

"I'm ready. Let's do it."

She took out her phone and checked ticket prices. They weren't cheap. But she could get them tickets for that afternoon, the ones that included going all the way to the top deck. She bought them. "Okay. We have the tickets. Now I'll arrange for the taxi van…"

Maddox had meetings lined up for all of that day—but no dinner plans. When he got back to the penthouse at five thirty, he found Sarah and his dad out on the terrace, sipping margaritas and enjoying the city views spread out around them. Evan appeared with a drink for him.

It was still hot and sticky out. Maddox took off his light jacket, draped it over a chair and sat down to enjoy his scotch, the view—and especially the company. His dad seemed almost lighthearted as he described their visit to the Empire State Building.

"It was a good day," said Fergus and held up his glass to Sarah.

She tapped hers lightly against it. "Yes, it was."

Maddox watched them. They were such great friends, kidding around together, squabbling over little things. He wished he could figure out a way to convince Sarah to stay on as his dad's nurse for the rest of the summer.

But it wouldn't work and he knew it. If she stayed, they

would end up in bed together again. He was sure of it. And that would be just fine with him.

Not with her, though. And he couldn't ask her to cross that line. Not when he knew how important it was to her.

No. He'd already convinced her to stick around for the rest of the week and hang out with his dad. Better to let her start looking for the right job as soon as they got back to Wyoming.

He was staring off blindly toward the East River, thinking about the woman sitting to his left when his dad said, "Tomorrow, we're going to the Museum of Natural History. Any chance you can come with us?"

Maddox thought of tomorrow's calendar. Booked. He would be lucky to get home by six.

Fergus said, "I know that look. Never mind, son. Just thought I'd ask."

Maddox felt pretty damn guilty. If Sarah hadn't agreed to stay on, he would have had to come up with something better than letting his dad hang around with Evan in the apartment all day. He offered ruefully, "I'll try to get home before dinner."

"That'll do," his dad said with a nod and a smile. And why shouldn't Fergus be smiling? After all, he was spending the day with his best buddy, Sarah.

And that reminded him. Had Sarah paid for the visit to the Empire State Building? And what about meals out, and the special cabs they had to use to accommodate the wheelchair?

At the very least, he needed to reimburse her for whatever was coming out of her pocket.

Yeah, they would have to talk.

Tonight. After Fergus was in bed.

* * *

Sarah was propped up against the pillows, watching *Say Anything* on the flat-screen across the room, and wondering what had happened to grand gestures in romantic comedies, when the tap came on the bedroom door.

She knew it was Maddox. Who else would it be? Evan had left the apartment at a little after six and Fergus would be in bed by now.

The tap came again.

She turned off the movie, padded barefoot to the door and pulled it wide. "What?"

He was still dressed in chinos and a white shirt. She, on the other hand, was all ready for bed.

"I just want to talk," he said. "It won't take long. Ten minutes, no more."

"Sure." She swept out a hand toward the corner of the room where two chairs and a small square table formed a sitting area. "Have a seat."

He came in and she shut the door. They each took a butter-yellow club chair and faced off across the low table.

He said, "Tonight, my dad mentioned that the two of you are seeing the sights—and I know that means buying tickets, paying for cabs, eating in restaurants and whatever else you decide to do. That can get expensive. I'm guessing you're picking up the tab and my dad is assuming that I'll reimburse you."

"You're here to reimburse me?" She didn't believe for a minute that he'd come to her room at nine thirty at night solely to settle up the miscellaneous expenses.

"That's right." His voice was firm. "I was thinking five hundred a day and then if it goes over that amount, you'll let me know and I'll cover the balance as well."

She hadn't spent five hundred—not yesterday or the day before. But why quibble about this? He was willing to foot the bill for the fun she and Fergus were having and why shouldn't he? He could certainly afford it. "Okay. Five hundred a day is great. Thank you. I use Venmo. Just send the money to my phone number."

"Sounds good. And my dad also said that you two want to see a Broadway show in a theater where he can get around in his wheelchair. My assistant will find the tickets. How about for a matinee on Saturday? I'm done working Friday and I'd planned to spend Saturday with Dad, anyway. So it would be the three of us, if that's all right?"

She really should not allow herself to be so pleased about this. "Great. Your dad will love having the day with you."

He leaned in. "Could we…talk a little more?"

Her heart lifted. "Of course."

"My dad finally told me about what went on with him and Earlene Pugh, how he ended up going out her window at Sylvan Acres. He said you know all about it." At her nod, he continued, "He also said that he cares for Earlene. That he wants another chance with her."

"Yeah, he and I talked about his feelings for Earlene. I think it's great he's ready to try to work things out with her. He also shared a little about your mom."

Maddox looked away. Her heart sank. She was suddenly certain that he would get up, say he had to go and walk out the door.

But he didn't. His eyes were full of shadows as he faced her again. "It almost killed him when she died. He wouldn't come out of his room for days."

"I'm not surprised. They always seemed so much in love." She couldn't stop herself from adding, "It must have been really hard for you, too—to lose her like that, with no warning at all."

He shifted in the chair. Again, she just knew he would jump up and announce that he had to go.

But no. He was still right there, still leaning in close. "It was bad, yeah." His voice was a low, rough whisper. "She was there and then she was gone. In an instant. And I was two thousand miles away, here in Manhattan, when it happened."

"Maddox. You can't blame yourself."

"I don't. I just wish that I'd been there." He made a low, thoughtful sound. "She was kind, my mom. And fun, too. Always up for anything. She was a skilled horsewoman. She spent a lot of days and long, cold nights working out on the land alongside my dad and the hands—and me, when I was young."

"I remember. She and Fergus were always a great team…"

He nodded. "She loved being a rancher. She loved me, loved being a mom. She loved my dad so much, with all her heart. She always seemed so strong…"

"Seemed?"

"Was," he corrected himself. "She *was* strong. But then, one morning in late September fifteen years ago, she sat up in bed and said, 'Fergus, something's wrong.' And then she fell over sideways, already dead of a massive heart attack."

Sarah blinked away the sudden tears. "I remember the story. It's so sad and I'm so sorry."

Maddox stared into the middle distance. "I didn't know that she was gone until hours later when my dad called me from the funeral home to tell me what had happened. I couldn't believe it. My mom was a rock. She and my dad were everything to each other. For a while after she died, I

didn't think he'd make it. He wanted to be with her so bad,
I thought he might…" He let that sentence go unfinished.

Sarah gulped down more tears. She longed to say something reassuring. But no words came to her.

"Why am I telling you all this?" Maddox's face had gone
blank. "First the awful story of my birth parents. And now
I give you the total rundown on my mom's sudden death.
You must think I'm one of those guys who has to *share*
every difficult moment he ever went through."

"No." She wanted to reach for him, to put her hand over
his. But she feared that her touch would only send him running for the door. "Maddox, I appreciate your telling me.
I honestly do."

He did get up then. She rose as well. They faced each
other across the small, low table. "I should go." He was already turning for the door.

She sidestepped and put herself in his path. "Wait."

"Sarah, I really think—"

"Just listen."

His eyes were bleak. "I don't know what's wrong with
me, to be laying all that on you."

"Nothing," she replied. "Nothing is wrong with you. I
wanted to hear about your mom. Thank you for talking to
me about her."

He stared down at her for the longest time. "I, uh, yeah.
Well, now you know. And I should…"

She caught his arm. "Stay…"

He shook his head. "Sarah. You don't want that."

She stepped even closer. "I do, Maddox. Yes. I do."

His eyes burned into hers. "Tell me to go."

"No way. Stay."

For a moment, neither of them spoke. Again, she was

certain that he would shake off her hand, step around her and head for the door.

Instead, with a low, rough sound, he reached for her. His mouth touched hers. She opened for him as she slid her hands up over his chest, feeling the heat of him, the muscled contours beneath the crisp white cotton of his shirt.

"Sarah…" He whispered her name like a secret prayer. And then he scooped her up and carried her to the bed. Laying her down, still kissing her, he started pulling off her shorty pajamas. In seconds she was naked.

He stroked a slow hand down the center of her, from the notch between her collarbones to the space between her breasts, over the hollow beneath her ribcage and lower still to the secret place where her thighs met.

"You're so beautiful," he said. It was one of those things men always tell women, but she believed him anyway. Because he meant it. She could see the truth right there in his green eyes.

He dipped a finger inside her. "So wet," he whispered and added another.

She moaned. It felt so good, to have him here with her, to have him touching her, to have him holding her close. "You have too many clothes on," she chided, and got to work fixing that problem. First, she shoved at his chinos and boxer briefs.

He kicked them off along with his sneakers.

But he still wore the white button-down.

By then, she had no patience for buttons. Straddling him, she took the sides of his shirt in either hand—and yanked. A few buttons slipped from their holes. The rest went flying.

"That shirt will never be the same," he remarked as she tossed it away. Now they were both completely naked.

"I'll pay to replace it."

He smirked up at her. "Such a big spender."

"Take it out of my sightseeing allowance," she suggested.

He reached up, wrapped his fingers around the nape of her neck and pulled her down to him. She splayed her hands against his chest as she kissed him. It was glorious—the two of them, pressed together, with no clothes in the way.

He rolled her under him.

She twined her legs and arms around him. They were still kissing. It was a perfect kiss, the kind of kiss that becomes the next kiss and the kiss after that. She could go on like this, kissing Maddox, held tight in his powerful arms for the rest of the night and just possibly on into tomorrow.

He felt for the nightstand drawer, found a condom, got it out of the pouch and lifted up to his spread knees to roll it down onto himself. When he came back to her, she pulled him close and gasped in pleasure as he filled her.

Taking his face between her hands, she kissed him again. She moaned against his mouth as he rocked within her.

No, they didn't have a hope for forever. On Sunday, they would fly home to Wyoming and go their separate ways.

But for right now, for tonight, he belonged to her. So what if it was no more than a sweet, thrilling lie she was telling herself? She didn't care. She let her heart have its way. For now. For tonight.

He rocked into her and she met him, held him, cradled him close.

She rolled and he took her cue, going over on his back so that she was on top. She sat up, braced her hands on his chest, and moved slow and easy, hoping to make this perfect moment last.

But the tension built swiftly and her finish came at her—sweet, hard and fast. She threw back her head and cried out his name.

And then he rolled her beneath him again. He surged into her so deep. They stilled. She pressed her lips to the side of his throat and then sank her teeth in lightly. He groaned. She felt him pulsing as he came.

A few minutes later, he was pulling the covers up over them and gathering her into his arms.

"What time is it?" she asked drowsily, her eyes drifting shut.

"Shh. Sarah. Sleep…" His lips brushed her forehead, so softly.

So tenderly…

When she woke it was daylight. She was lying on her back, alone in the bed.

A shaft of sunlight sliced across the ceiling. She stared up at it, grinning, remembering something Maddox had said on one of those nights by the pool.

Nothing is going to happen between us because we're not going to let it…

Wrong. She grinned at the thought, feeling smug. Something had definitely happened between them.

But there was another, much sadder prediction he'd made that night by the pool…

Something about how by December, when Christmas came, they would be miles and miles apart living completely separate lives.

Her smug grin faded. She and Maddox were not meant to last and both of them knew that.

But hey. Why not enjoy themselves during the next four nights in Manhattan? Four more nights…

She needed those nights. And then, when they got home on Sunday, they would end it for real.

Chapter Ten

That day, she and Fergus spent hours in the Museum of Natural History. After the museum, they bought a late lunch at a taco truck on Columbus Avenue.

They got back to the penthouse at four. Maddox came home at a little after five. The three of them had dinner outside, beneath a wide red umbrella at a steakhouse half a mile from the apartment.

That night, Sarah went to Maddox's room. He opened the door just wide enough to grab her hand and pull her inside. She stayed with him all night. Early in the morning, she kissed him and slipped away.

They met up in the kitchen for breakfast. Fergus was already there. They made plans to go out again that night, the three of them.

After Maddox headed for work, Sarah and Fergus decided on a morning stroll. They ended up at Greenacre Park again. Fergus liked the waterfall and the showy profusion of flowers. When lunchtime came around, they got sandwiches from Carol's Cafe right there in the park.

Around one, they started back to the apartment, but then kept going to Rockefeller Center instead.

It was beautiful, with the gold statue of Prometheus out in front, the fountain behind it and the gorgeous sixty-seven-story skyscraper soaring up into the clouds. She couldn't help feeling wistful, thinking of Christmas again like a sentimental fool. The giant Rockefeller Center tree would be up then, framed by the skyscraper, and the ice rink would be open, full of skaters all bundled up in winter gear.

Maddox might bring RJ and Stevie here to skate…

"You okay, Sarah?" Fergus was staring up at her, a worried look on his craggy face.

She promised she was just fine.

They headed back to the penthouse a few minutes later. That night, Maddox took them out for Italian.

And later, Sarah joined him in his bed. Like their three nights before that, Thursday night was a great night. In the morning, she slept a little later than she meant to. At eight Friday morning, she woke to find Maddox was already gone.

When she stuck her head out his bedroom door, Fergus was sitting in his wheelchair a few feet away. "Mornin', sleepyhead," he said with a grin—and then, without another word, he turned his chair and rolled off toward the kitchen.

She zipped into her own room to shower and get dressed.

Once she was ready to face the day, she found Fergus in the kitchen finishing off his breakfast and visiting with Evan.

"Scrambled eggs with ham?" Evan offered.

She realized she was starving. "Perfect. Thank you."

Fergus stayed to keep her company while she ate. He said nothing about that moment in the hallway and she was grateful that he didn't bring it up.

Honestly, what was there to say?

When she asked him what he had in mind for today, he

shrugged. "How 'bout we take it easy, just hang around the penthouse?"

She agreed. But then, by eleven, she was feeling antsy. "Let's go out, take a walk…"

Fergus shook his head. "You go on. I'll be right here when you get back."

Outside, she wandered freely, enjoying the bustle and variety of the city. She found a coffee place and got a latte to go. Several blocks from the penthouse, she passed a family clinic. For a moment, she paused on the street, staring through the glass door into a granite-walled entry hallway with wide stairs going up and an elevator on the left. The clinic in question was in there somewhere.

She really did want to get a look at it. It was an old game for her, picturing herself in different medical settings.

She pulled open the glass door and went in. At that moment, nobody was manning the sign-in desk. She scribbled her name on the open book there. The sign on the wall between the stairs and the elevator said the clinic was on the second floor. She took the stairs up.

The clinic was down a hallway, the third office on the left. When she stuck her head in the door, she saw a woman in a lab coat speaking softly to another, younger woman with a baby in her arms. The woman with the baby said, "Thank you so much, Dr. Belo."

The woman in the lab coat nodded. "She should be fine now. We'll see you in two weeks…"

Sarah knew she was pushing it—lurking in the doorway, eyeing the reception area, listening in on a private conversation between a patient and her doctor. With a final sheepish wave for the receptionist who was watching her from behind the counter, Sarah backed out and shut the door. She was down the steps and out on the street a minute later, feeling a bit guilty for poking her head in just to gawk.

But not that guilty, really. More…wistful.

She needed to get focused on her career goals again. Taking care of Fergus had been a good transitional job for her, and the money sure was nice, but she had never planned to be a private duty nurse. It was time to get a job at a family clinic or maybe up at the hospital in Sheridan. And she really had to get her applications in if she wanted to be back in school this coming January.

Back at the apartment, Fergus was having a nap. Sarah went to her room, got out her laptop and started looking at job boards, seeing what was available.

Maddox returned at a little after five. They had dinner on the terrace and capped off the evening with one of those Jesse Stone mysteries Fergus loved so much.

In bed, she and Maddox made slow, tender love and then fell asleep in each other's arms. When she woke, the sun was already up on their last full day in New York City.

That day went by at the speed of light. Maddox took them to breakfast at a nearby café. They were seated in the orchestra when the curtain went up on *Chicago* that afternoon. It was a great show and a really lovely day—and it was over much too soon.

That night was the same. She spent a good portion of it in Maddox's bed. But at two in the morning, after three intense bouts of lovemaking, she was wide awake.

Carefully, so as not to disturb the sleeping man beside her, she eased back the covers to slip from the bed.

She got one foot on the rug before his hand snaked out and closed over her wrist. "What's going on?"

"I'm going to go on back to my room." She eased free of his grip.

He blinked, grabbed the bedside clock, scowled at it and set it back down. "It's not *that* late…"

She swung her other foot to the floor and reached for her sleep shorts and cropped top. He watched her as she pulled them on.

"Damn it," he said low. "I miss you already."

She tugged her top into place and then combed her fingers back through her hair. "I miss you, too." And she did. "Oh, Maddox…" She went back to the bed and into his arms. Their kiss was sweet and hot.

But then she pulled back. If she stayed, she might say things she shouldn't. "Really. Gotta go…" Once again, she slipped from his hold.

He caught her just as she reached the door. Taking her gently by the shoulders, he turned her to face him. She looked up into his eyes and longed to fall into his arms, to beg him to take her back to bed, to never, ever let her go.

But in the end, he *would* let her go. He'd already made that perfectly clear.

Easing a curl of hair behind her ear, he said, "The kids and I are in Wyoming through Labor Day."

She answered reluctantly. "I am aware."

His finger strayed down her cheek, over her jaw and along the side of her neck, rousing sparks under her skin, making her belly hollow out and her pulse roar in her ears. "I don't want to say goodbye yet, Sarah. I know that's probably the wiser way to go, but I want every minute I can get with you."

She wanted that, too. So much.

But every moment she spent with him only made her

want him more. Simple logic seemed to indicate that the longer she let this thing between them go on, the harder it would be to say goodbye.

His warm fingers trailed down her arm. He caught her hand, smoothed it open and pressed a kiss into her palm. "Will you think about it?" His breath whispered across her skin. "Sarah…" His arms went around her.

She didn't even try to resist. His mouth came down on hers and it was heaven. She kissed him back with all her yearning heart.

When he finally lifted his beautiful, dangerous mouth from hers, she said, "Okay, I'll think about it."

He framed her face between his hands. "You'll let me know, then?"

She drew a slow, careful breath and nodded.

For a minute that seemed to stretch into a lifetime, they stared at each other.

Finally, she shook herself. "I'm going to go back to my room now."

He seemed about to argue, but then he nodded. "Of course. Good night."

She pulled open the door and slipped out before she could throw her arms around him and promise to give him anything, everything, whatever he wanted—for as long as he wanted her.

Back in his bed a minute later, there was no way Maddox could sleep. He stared up at the shadows near the ceiling and couldn't figure out how he'd managed to let himself get so attached to Sarah. It wasn't like him at all.

He was totally gone on her in a way he'd never been before. He was also an idiot for allowing this to happen. The least he could have done was let tonight be the end of it.

But no. He'd begged her for more.

He just couldn't bear to lose her. Not yet. It was so good with her. And if she said yes, they could have the rest of the summer. By September, they might even be over each other. Right now, that seemed about as likely as the sun suddenly rising in the west.

But it could happen.

And even if it didn't, at least he would get what he'd literally just begged her for—more time.

Was that so much to ask?

He knew that it was. But that didn't stop him from hoping she would end up saying yes.

Sunday morning went by in a flash. Alexis brought the kids over at seven and they were on their way to Teterboro by eight.

During the flight, Sarah was friendly with the kids and Fergus. She seemed relaxed. She explained to his children that she was leaving her job with Fergus because their grandpa didn't need a full-time nurse anymore. "But don't worry," she added. "I'm right next door and I'll be stopping by to check on you guys."

He didn't know how she managed to say goodbye so warmly. So gracefully.

Because he didn't feel graceful in the least. On the contrary, he was kind of a wreck.

But he focused on Stevie and RJ, and that helped. He heard all about the trip to Portugal—the beautiful beaches, the aquarium in Lisbon, the fabulous marine waterpark in Guia.

Stevie talked nonstop about the wonderfulness of everything. As for RJ, he seemed relaxed. He'd even let Maddox hug him when Alexis dropped the two kids off. Maddox hoped that if he did his part, made sure to keep the connection going between him and his son, he and RJ might eventually have the kind of closeness Maddox had with Fergus.

It was late afternoon when they arrived at the ranch. Sarah went inside with them. She spent a few minutes chatting with Alma and then headed upstairs to her room. He was busy with the kids, getting them settled in again, hearing more details of their trip, so he wasn't sure when Sarah put her things in her little Jeep and drove away. But when they all sat down at the table for dinner, she wasn't with them.

The next day, Earlene Pugh appeared at the front door. Maddox just happened to be the one to answer when she rang the bell.

Earlene smoothed a fat blond curl back over her shoulder and gave him a giant smile. "Hello, Maddox. I'm Earlene Pugh, here to see Fergus."

"Earlene." He took her hand. "Hello. I've…heard so much about you."

She laughed. "Of that I have no doubt—and don't look so worried. Fergus asked me to come." A small grin tipped up the corners of her red mouth. "Well, *begged* me to come is more like it. And I'm just a sucker for a man who begs." Her gaze shifted. Now her grin was aimed over his shoulder. "Fergus. Tell your son that it's okay for me to come in."

"There you are." Fergus was beaming ear-to-ear. "Son, where are your manners? Let the lady in."

Maddox stepped back. "Come on in."

"Why, thank you."

A minute later, Earlene and Fergus headed toward the office annex and the grandpa suite.

Earlene stayed for dinner that night. Later, they all played Monopoly. Maddox won, as usual. But Earlene came in a close second. By then, Maddox not only liked her, but he also respected her. She had determination, the will to win and a talent for thinking strategically.

And she fit right in with the family. The kids liked her from the first. She treated them with warmth and respect. And when she asked either of them a question, she took the answer they gave seriously.

When the game was over, she went off to the grandpa suite with Fergus. In the morning, she was gone. But she showed up again on Wednesday, and she stayed all day and into the night. Already, Maddox wouldn't have minded if she just moved in. He hadn't seen his dad this happy in fifteen years.

Truthfully, Maddox was a little jealous—okay, more than a little.

Seeing how happy his dad was to have Earlene back in his life made it even harder for him not to think about Sarah. He hadn't seen or heard a word from her since she ducked out on Sunday without saying goodbye.

He did get a call from the hospital up in Sheridan, though. She'd applied for a job there and listed him as a reference. He'd given her a glowing recommendation.

Damn. Why didn't she call him?

She'd agreed she would reach out to him, let him know if she was willing to spend some more time with him over the rest of the summer—hadn't she?

Or had he just assumed she would be knocking on his door, ready to fall into his arms, prepared to take whatever he was willing to give her? And then to meekly accept his departure when September came along and he called for the jet, packed up his children and headed back to Manhattan without her.

Looked at from that perspective, he was a giant ass, one who had no reason to be surprised if she refused to get near him ever again.

Early on Thursday evening, Sarah sat alone in her trailer on the Double-K. She was nursing a beer and thinking of how she ought to go on over to the main house and have dinner with the family.

Also, she should visit the Hales. If she didn't get over there and say hi as she'd promised, the kids and Fergus would start thinking she didn't care about them, that she'd just walked away and never looked back.

But then she reasoned that it had only been a few days since she left. She could wait another week and not be considered the kind of person who didn't keep in touch when she said she would.

She put the beer bottle to her lips and drank. The cold brew tasted great going down. Maybe she'd have a second one. And then a third. Maybe she'd skip dinner with the family and get falling-down drunk.

After all, in the trailer, there was never far to fall.

Even in her morbid mood, that struck her as funny. She was chuckling to herself when someone tapped on the door.

At that light, sharp sound, her heart did something alarming inside her chest. She couldn't help hoping that her visitor might be Maddox—that he'd realized he didn't want to live without her. That he was here to beg her to give him another chance to…

What, exactly?

Spend every night in his bed until September?

Yeah. That.

The truth was, Sarah wanted more nights with him, too.

But she had a problem. More nights would not be enough for her. She wanted everything from Maddox Hale. Everything until death did them part.

Too bad the man had issues. Issues he showed zero interest in dealing with, let alone resolving. And his issues meant that she needed to keep her distance and start getting over him. She had stuff do in her life. She couldn't waste her time pining over some guy who was never going to be ready to commit.

"Sarah?" It was her mom's voice.

She knocked back another big gulp of beer. "It's open."

The door swung wide and Meggie Bravo came up the retractable steps and into the confined space. Sarah's mom had thick dark hair with streaks of silver at the temples. Her eyes were dark, too. Looking at her mom, Sarah thought, was like looking at an older version of herself.

"Want a beer?" Sarah asked.

"Good idea." Meggie helped herself, taking a bottle from the fridge under the counter, knocking the cap off with the opener mounted on the cabinet next to the door. Sarah scooted over a bit and Meggie sat down next to her at the table. "Any news?"

She nodded. "I got lucky. They need a temporary staff RN in the ER up at the hospital in Sheridan. Long story, but it's a twelve-week job. I'm stepping in for a nurse taking family leave to have her baby. Bobby Dahl interviewed me." Bobby was a friend of the family. He and her brother Jason had been buddies in high school.

"You got the job?"

"It's not a done deal, but it looks good. Bobby got me in

for the interview Tuesday, and right away, he was asking what day I could start. They'd already hired someone, an RN from Buffalo, but he backed out when he got offered something permanent."

"Congratulations!" Her mom raised her beer in a toast.

Sarah tapped the bottle with hers. "It will take them a week or two to tick all the boxes, but that's like the speed of light for getting hired at a hospital. And I have to tell you, I'm feeling pretty good about it. I don't want to sign on for anything long-term right now, anyway." She needed her MSN degree. That was the top priority. And that meant she wouldn't be staying in Wyoming for all that long.

Her mom nodded and sipped. "So I've been thinking…"

Sarah groaned. "What is that look? What's going on, Mom?"

Meggie picked at the label on her beer bottle. "Your grandma Sharilyn has told me more than once that I need to—her words—'Butt out of other people's lives…'"

Grandma Sharilyn, who was Sarah's dad's mom, lived in Los Angeles with her second husband, Hector. Meggie wanted Sharilyn and Hector to move to Medicine Creek where she could look out for them. But Grandma Sharilyn had a mind of her own. She and Hector had a dinky apartment in East Hollywood. It was their home. They loved living there. Result: Meggie kept pushing Grandma Sharilyn to move and Grandma Sharilyn dug in her heels and constantly reminded her daughter-in-law to back off.

Meggie added, "Maybe your grandmother has a point…"

"Mom. Just go ahead and say it. I can take it. What's on your mind?"

"The Hales came to Joe's birthday cookout."

"I was there, too. I remember."

Her mother sipped more beer. "I saw you and Maddox Hale together."

She shouldn't ask. But she did. "And that matters, why?"

As always, Meggie laid it right out there. "It's obvious. You care for him. He feels the same about you."

Sarah laughed. There might have been a trace of bitterness in the sound. "Let me put it this way. Maddox Hale has told me to my face that he's never—that's *n-e-v-e-r*—getting married again."

"So? You in a hurry to get married all of a sudden?"

"Well, someday. It's what I want for my future, so there doesn't seem to be much point in getting invested in a guy who doesn't want the same thing. Even though you're right—I care for him. But I can't let myself get too attached. Because he's always going to keep a certain amount of emotional distance from me. That's who he is."

"Because he said so?"

"Yeah. More than once."

Meggie waved a hand. "That man is completely gone on you. He'll change his tune—or he will if you give him half a chance."

"Mom. I love you so much. But you've got no idea what you're talking about."

"Hmm. I think I do. If you really want someone to be with you, you need to be flexible."

"You think I'm not flexible?"

"I'm not talking about you. I'm talking about me."

"Okay, I'm not following. *You're* not flexible…?"

"That's right. I've never wanted to live anywhere but here on the Double-K. And yet I chased your father all the way to Los Angeles and lived with him there."

"Mom. I do know the story."

Meggie smiled way too sweetly. "For your father, I was flexible."

"Right..."

"Even though he'd already flat-out rejected me, I didn't give up. I tracked him down in LA."

"Mom. We both know it wasn't that simple. According to the terms of Grandpa Kane's will, you had to—"

"Who's telling this story?" Her mom gave her the evil eye.

"Okay. Sorry. Go on."

"Thank you. So anyway. When I caught up with your father in LA, he turned me down again. And still, I refused to give up. And look at us now. Deeply in love. Married forever with three terrific kids and two adorable grand-children."

"Mom. Dad and Maddox Hale are nothing alike."

"You'd be surprised. Some men require a whole bunch of patience from the right woman."

"There is no *right woman* for Maddox Hale. And be honest. Are you trying to tell me that you aren't at least a *little* concerned that Maddox and I are so different, that he's a decade and a half older than I am and divorced, with two half-grown children, that he's very unlikely ever to come live in Medicine Creek again?"

"You're not going to be staying here at home, either. You'll always be off doing good work, sometimes under conditions that your mother, frankly, does not want to know about. I've accepted all that. As for the age difference, look at Jason and Piper. She's more than a decade older than he is and yet they are just right for each other."

From what Sarah had heard, her mom hadn't exactly been Team Piper at first. But whatever. "I don't know how many ways to say it, Mom. There is no future for me with Maddox Hale."

"Now you're just being obstinate."

Sarah laughed again. "I do love you, Mom."

"And I love you." Meggie chided, "Don't let your chosen one get away."

"Get away? If he's trying to escape, are we so sure he's the one for me?"

"Ha-ha." Her mom looked at her, deadpan. "May I finish?"

"Go right ahead."

"Thank you. Sarah Ellen, you need to do whatever you have to do. Kick every obstacle right to the curb. Think about what you *really* want. Don't settle for anything—or anyone—less."

"Tell me the truth, Mom. How many beers have you had?"

Meggie picked up her half-finished bottle. "This one, that's all." She raised the bottle high. "Be bold, baby girl. Go after what you love and don't give up. If you want that man, you'll need to be flexible. And you'll need to get to work helping him to understand that he can't live without you."

"It's open!" Maddox called when the tap came on his office door.

It was early afternoon on Monday and he expected the door to swing open on Alma or one of the kids.

But no.

It was Sarah, her dark hair pulled back in a low ponytail, wearing jeans, boots and a dusty shirt. She had her hat in her hand. "I was just riding by," she said with that smile that could drive a man to distraction.

"Hey," he said. Because *hey* was the sum total of his vocabulary at that moment.

"I spent a few minutes with Fergus, Stevie and RJ already. Alma, too. I've missed them and I didn't want them to think I'd deserted them."

And what about me? he longed to demand, like some whiny child. *Did you miss me?*

"I'm glad," he said, his tone cool and even, despite the emo boy carrying on inside him. "And they've missed you."

She leaned against the door frame. "I notice Earlene is here, too."

He nodded. "Dad finally got his head out of his ass and reached out to her."

"Good for Fergus. The two of them were looking real cozy together when I stopped in at the grandpa suite just now."

"Yeah. She's here all time."

"That's great news." She glanced down at her boots. "I'm happy for them."

He couldn't help wondering if she still needed a job.

Not that Fergus even needed a nurse. His dad was getting along fine without a full-time caregiver. In fact, the weekend nurse had moved on, too. But Maddox would hire Sarah anyway. She just had to say the word. Even if he never got to touch her again, he would love to have her here, in the house, for the rest of the summer.

Because he missed her. He missed her a lot. "How's the job hunt going?"

She gave him a big, proud smile. "I start next week up at the hospital in Sheridan."

So, then. They'd hired her. "Congratulations."

"Thank you."

"I can't say I'm surprised. They called me for a reference. I gave you a big thumbs-up."

"I appreciate that."

Damn. This was awful—the ten feet of distance between them that felt like ten miles, all this meaningless chitchat. And in a minute, she would go.

Which was for the best. Unfortunately, the fact that her leaving was the right thing didn't make it any easier to bear.

"My birthday is Thursday," she said. "I'm hitting the big two-five."

"Impressive," he replied dryly.

"I know, right? Twenty-five is practically ancient. And not only am I getting old, but there will also be the usual Bravo family barbecue on Saturday at the Double-K to celebrate. You're invited—and the kids and Alma. Fergus and Earlene, too."

Tell her you can't make it. "We'll be there."

"Great. Two in the afternoon. No gifts, no food. No need to bring anything, just yourselves. The party will go late if you want to stay. There will be a local band and a dance floor."

"Sounds fun—but you know Alma. She won't show up empty-handed."

"If she insists on bringing a dish, that's great. Her choice."

Those nights in New York. And the nights by the pool... Do you think of them, too? Lately, I can't think of anything else. "All right, I'll tell her."

"Great. See you then."

"Can't wait." He realized that he sounded like he meant it. Probably because he did.

With a last sweet smile, she was gone.

He sat there staring at the empty spot where she'd been, wondering what was wrong with him.

Total avoidance. That was the best thing for both of them. He should have wished her a happy twenty-fifth and expressed his regret that he couldn't make it Saturday.

But apparently, he was now incapable of doing the right thing. Worse, he didn't even care. Saturday, he would see her again. Nothing else mattered.

Chapter Eleven

On Saturday when Maddox and his family arrived at the Double-K, the birthday barbecue was in full swing.

Meggie Bravo greeted them. She was all smiles, chatting away, looking so much like an older version of her daughter that Maddox kept having to remind himself not to stare at her.

RJ went off to play ping-pong and horseshoes and Stevie ran to catch up with a couple of girls she'd met last month at Joe's party. Fergus, on his crutches, quickly found a chair to settle into. Earlene sat down beside him. As for Alma, she headed for the table with all the casserole dishes on it to add her special Hot German Potato Salad to the mix.

Meggie took his arm then. "Come on and say hi to Nate." She led him over beneath the shade of a couple of big oaks where her husband and their sons had two smokers and three grills going. For a few minutes, Maddox made small talk with the Bravo men.

It wasn't long before he moved on—just enjoying the party, he told himself, stopping now and then to greet people he'd known since he was younger than Stevie. No ulterior motive at all.

Except there damn well was. He was on the hunt—for Sarah.

On the far side of the field from the grills and smokers, a six-piece band played country favorites. A few guests were already up and dancing on the temporary dance floor. Party lights were strung from tree to tree. After dark, they would give off a nice glow.

He passed three long tables covered with bright cloths and set with stacks of paper goods and plasticware. There were pitchers of cold tea, lemonade and margaritas along with coolers full of soft drinks and beer.

On one table, a three-layer birthday cake had Sarah's name written on it in green and pink icing.

But where was the birthday girl herself?

"Hello, Maddox." Her voice, from directly behind him, sent a hot charge of pure awareness zipping up and down his spine.

He faced her. Damn. She was beautiful in a snug lace top, a long skirt and boots tooled with flowers.

Today, all that shining dark hair curled loose past her shoulders. The Wyoming wind teased at it, lifting the soft strands so they shifted and danced against her smooth throat.

"Sarah." His voice came out scratchy, out of practice, like he'd somehow managed to forget how to talk. "Happy birthday." At least that came out sounding close to normal.

"Thank you."

He pretended to glance around them, though in truth, the only thing he could see right now was the woman standing in front of him. "Looks like a great party," he heard himself mutter, and then had to gulp down the sudden urge to laugh out loud at his fumbling behavior.

As a rule, he could work a room—or an open field, in this case—like nobody's business. He knew how to make small talk, to come off as warm and friendly without giving away so much as a hint of his true feelings or motives.

Today, though, he'd stared like a fool at Meggie Bravo because she looked so much like her daughter. And right now he was tongue-tied with Sarah herself.

She moved a step closer. A whiff of citrus and flowers seduced him. "I'm so glad you came." She said it sweetly.

But that look in her eyes was not sweet. Those eyes said dangerous things, made promises he couldn't wait to insist that she keep.

"What are you doing?" he asked in a ragged whisper.

"Want to see my trailer?"

He blinked. Because she could not be serious. "Now?"

"Yeah."

All around them, people were laughing, dancing, drinking, playing lawn darts and bocce ball. "But it's *your* party."

"Exactly." She let out a big fake sigh. "And that means we won't be able to stay long."

"In your trailer, you mean?"

She nodded and then she gave him a one-shouldered shrug. "But that's okay because there's not a lot to see in there. A dinky kitchen that doubles as the living area. A tiny square of bathroom. And the bedroom. I mean, the biggest thing in there is the three-quarter bed." Her eyes were so soft, almost innocent. But not quite. "So that's what I'll do. I'll show you my three-quarter bed."

This was the most ridiculous conversation he'd ever participated in. Not that he cared. He got the message loud and clear. So clear that he was already hard.

And the plain truth? He could not wait to see that trailer. "Now?"

"Didn't I already say that?"

"Sorry. I seem to be a little bit…out of my depth."

She smiled again. That smile was powerful. It caused his knees to feel shaky, made his pulse race and his blood burn.

"Tell you what." She pointed toward a row of maple trees beyond the band and the dance floor. "It's not far past those trees. I'll head on over there. Count to thirty slowly and then follow me."

And just like that, she was gone. He watched her walk away from him and was so completely mesmerized by the swaying of her hips in that pretty skirt that he forgot he was supposed to be counting.

When she disappeared from sight beyond the stand of maple trees, he blinked like a man slowly waking from a trance.

That was when he remembered that he should have been counting. Had enough time passed that he could just go find her?

Oh, to hell with it.

He headed for the stand of trees, certain that any second someone would step into his path and try to engage him in conversation or ask where he was going.

But nobody stopped him. He wanted to run, but that would draw undue attention. Instead, he maintained a slow, steady pace past the dance floor and the band, between the maple trees.

A rail fence blocked the way ahead. But there was a gate. He went through to another dirt road, stood in the middle of it and looked left.

Nothing.

But when he looked to the right, on a grassy spot about fifty feet from the road, he saw the trailer. It was the kind a lot of cowhands owned. Not fancy, just a very small, not very comfortable home away from home.

He went right to it and tapped on the door, backing up a step when that door swung outward.

"Come on in." Her eyes sparked with challenge and she wore a bad-girl grin.

He went up the metal steps. She moved to the side for him to enter, then stepped close again and pulled the door shut.

They faced off between the door and the sink. He could smell her perfume and he wanted nothing so desperately as to reach out and haul her close.

He tried to play it light and easy. "What do you know? Bathroom, living area with kitchen…" He glanced over his shoulder. "Bedroom nook. This is very cozy."

"Too cozy," she replied with an eye roll. "And we don't have much time."

"We don't?"

"Maddox. Keep up. It's my birthday and I should be out there with my guests. As for you, your children might already be wondering where you disappeared to."

"Ah," he said, his brain a hot fog of need. "Right."

"So we'll have to skip the quickie I fantasized about in favor of getting everything out on the table."

No quickie? He didn't know whether to be wrecked with disappointment—or ecstatic that she seemed to imply…

What?

He had no clue what she might be trying to tell him. "Just give me a hint. What's going on?"

She took his hand in both of hers and pressed it between those beautiful soft breasts. Maybe he would get lucky and she would hold it there forever. "It's like this," she said.

"I'm going to be working twelve-hour days, three days a week for the rest of the summer. And you're here until…?"

"We're staying through Labor Day," he finished for her. "Why?"

She gave him a wistful smile. "Well, Maddox. I can't stop thinking that there's really nothing standing between us now." He liked where she was going with this—liked it a whole lot—so he kept his mouth shut and waited for her to continue. "Your dad is no longer my patient," she said. "I no longer have an ethical obligation to keep my distance from you."

Did they really need to go over that again? He was already completely up to speed on her *ethical obligations*.

She went on, "And so, well, I've been thinking. What's keeping you and me from spending some time together this summer?"

"Not a damn thing." It was exactly what he wanted. He should give her a resounding yes and do it now. But when he opened his mouth, he just had to ask, "You're serious about this?"

"I am, yes—for the rest of the summer. Then you go back to New York. And I—"

"Sarah. I know what happens at the end of the summer."

She studied his face for a long, uncomfortable moment. "You go your way, I go mine…"

What was she getting at? "You have an issue with that?"

"Not an issue, no. I was just wondering if there was any chance you might have started to see things differently."

"No. Nothing's changed."

She made a throaty little sound and let go of his hand. He let it drop to his side. "I see," she said.

Damn. Was this the deal-breaker, then? It seemed like

she wanted at least the possibility of more. For him, that wasn't happening—did that mean they were done without getting started? He wasn't a liar, but why couldn't he come up with some diplomatic way to imply that they might have a future together?

Because it wouldn't be right, that was why. He owed her the truth at the very least.

So instead of convincing her to forget about the future and live in the moment, he just stood there and waited for her to back out.

She shocked the hell out of him when she shrugged. "So, okay, then. What do you say? You and me till the end of the summer?"

Relief poured through him. He eased his hand from her grip, but only so that he could slide his fingers up over her shoulder and wrap them around the nape of her neck.

He should have sense enough not to ask. But he did it anyway. "You're sure?"

"I am." She stared up at him so steadily. "You?"

He stroked his hand down her hair, caught the ends of it and wrapped the silky strands slowly around his palm. Gently, he tugged, tipping her head back until her lips were positioned directly beneath his. "I'm sure."

And then, at last, for the first time in fourteen grim, endless days, he kissed her.

Sweetness exploded through him as she surged up. Her hands glided over his chest to clasp the back of his neck. He hauled her even closer and kissed her more deeply as he dared a step backward toward the bed.

She stopped him by pushing him away. "No, really, Maddox. Not now. I need to get back."

He stared down into those huge dark eyes and asked gruffly, "When, then?"

She gave him that slow, perfect smile. "I could stop by tomorrow evening. Maybe for a swim?"

The rest of the summer. His mind was spinning. Another month with her...

Yeah, he knew it would only make it harder to say good-bye when the end finally came. But some things, not even the strongest man can resist. This woman was one of them. They would have the rest of the summer and then they would cut it clean. He would put two thousand miles of distance between them. The distance would force them to get on with their real lives.

"Maddox?" She gazed up at him, waiting for him to speak. Too bad he'd forgotten the question. "Tomorrow night?" she asked again.

"Yes! Come on over whenever you can. Early is good. Dinner around six as usual. You can visit with the family. They're always glad to see you."

She looked at him doubtfully. "How about this? Let's not bring the whole family into it. Let's make it just you and me—for this first time, at least?"

As if he would argue. However she wanted it, that was how it would be. "Sure. Just you and me."

"Text me when you're free for the night. I'll come right over."

"All right. When do you start the new job?"

"Tuesday. It's classic nurse's hours. Seven a.m. to seven p.m. Tuesday, Wednesday and Friday."

"So then, tomorrow night you can stay late?"

Her answer was a slow nod and a very wicked smile.

* * *

Sunday night, Sarah got the text at nine forty-five. The coast is clear.

Laughing for sheer joy at the very idea that she would see him in a few minutes, she tapped out a quick, I'm on my way.

And then she stuffed her blue swimsuit in a beach bag, climbed in her Jeep and headed for the Hale place.

He was waiting on the front steps when she drove up. She jumped out and ran to him. He grabbed her close and kissed her—the perfect kiss, hard and deep and full of heat.

When he lifted his head she asked, "Where should I park?"

"Leave it where it is." And he kissed her again.

They stood there in the glow of the porch lights on the wide front step, kissing endlessly, like they had all the time in the world. To touch. To laugh. To be together…

When he finally pulled her inside, they went straight up to his room, which was big and manly—with an enormous platform bed, everything in tan, white, brown and gray. Functional and luxurious at the same time.

She dropped her tote on the nearest flat surface and reached for him. They kissed for the longest time.

She was trying to peel his shirt off him when he grabbed her hands. "What?" she frowned up at him. "You want to keep your clothes on?"

He chuckled. "Absolutely not."

"Whew." She started pulling on his shirt again.

"I just need a minute," he whispered against her parted lips.

"For what?"

He lifted his hand and she saw that he held up a beautiful pendant necklace—a teardrop-shaped peridot on a delicate gold chain. "I meant to give this to you yesterday, but once we got into your trailer, I was so busy fantasizing about getting my hands on you, I forgot all about giving you your gift." He unhooked the clasp. The green stone glittered. "Happy birthday."

Her throat clutched at his thoughtfulness. She had to try really hard to look stern. "I said no presents."

"Rules." His shrug dismissed such things. "Made to be broken. Turn around."

"Oh, Maddox…" She was already turning and lifting her hair.

"A peridot. The stone of compassion. Perfect for you." His warm fingers brushed her skin as he worked the tiny clasp. "There." He caught her hand and pulled her into the en suite bathroom, where he took her by her shoulders and turned her to face the mirror.

"I love it," she said. It really was perfect. Not only her birthstone, but also exactly the kind of piece she would have chosen for herself—spare and elegant, with a short chain. "Thank you. I love it."

"I'm glad." He turned her around.

She looked up and met his eyes as his mouth came down to claim hers. He tasted so good and she'd missed him so much. In no time at all, she was standing there naked, her clothing strewn across the floor.

Before she could even get his shirt off, he was scooping her up and setting her on the soapstone countertop. "It's been two weeks and a day," he murmured. "Far too long." His lips started on a journey.

She moaned as his teeth scraped lightly along the length of her throat. And she gasped as he caught her nipple in his hot mouth and sucked.

She might have cried his name out loud as his fingers danced down the center of her, over the curve of her belly, pausing briefly to caress her scars before gliding on into the secret place between her open legs. He stroked her there, slowly at first and then more rapidly.

Letting her head fall back against the mirror, she made way too much noise as he coaxed her body to rise, and she cried out within minutes as a sweet, shivery climax rolled through her.

She'd barely started to come down from that experience when he sank to his knees. Suddenly, his mouth was right where his fingers had been, his tongue sliding along her eager flesh, delving in.

Time—it just flew away. She braced her feet wide on the bathroom counter and let him have his way with her.

Later, in his big bed, they moved together, eyes open, lost in each other. She pretended that tonight and the summer nights to come would last forever. Because why shouldn't she indulge in a beautiful fantasy?

What good was a fantasy anyway, if a woman couldn't let herself dream that it might someday come true? Right now, they were pressed close together, holding on tight. Right now, they were everything her yearning heart could ever desire.

Right now, tonight, she pretended to believe that somehow it would all work out for them.

"Morning, Sunshine." Maddox's soft lips brushed her cheek.

Sarah opened her eyes. The room was still dark. But morning light peeked around the edges of the curtains. "What time is it?"

"A little after seven."

Her eyes popped open wide then. "I stayed all night?"

"Yes, you did."

"I really wasn't planning to sleep over. I should get…"

He silenced her with a finger to her lips. "It happened. Roll with it."

For some reason that struck her as funny. She snickered. "Now what?"

"We get up. We have breakfast." He whispered the words in her ear and then bit her earlobe.

"Ouch—won't that make a bad impression?"

"On whom? My dad and Earlene, who have probably spent last night together in his apartment?"

"I was thinking more of Stevie and RJ—and wait, Earlene spends the night here?"

"She does—and more often than not this past week."

"Go Fergus! I'm so happy for him."

Maddox gave her a slow grin. "So, then. Breakfast?"

She wanted to, but… "I don't know, Maddox. I guess I kind of pictured us keeping things low-key."

"Hmm. You mean, I'll text you after the kids are in bed, sneak you up here to my room, then sneak you back out when you're ready to leave?"

"When you say it that way it sounds a bit sleazy."

"Because sneaking around is a bad idea. Here's what I think. We get up, get dressed and have some breakfast, you and me and the family. They'll be glad to see you. I guarantee it."

"But PDA-free, right?"

"Not that it'll be easy keeping my hands off you, but yes. It's a family thing, after all. G-rated is the way to go."

"I have to ask. Are Stevie and RJ accustomed to seeing your girlfriends at the breakfast table the morning after?"

His big shoulder lifted in a lazy shrug. "No. But that's a completely different situation."

"How so?" she asked, instantly jealous of said girlfriends, whoever they were.

"The kids already know you," he explained. "They love you. You're part of their life here now. You're not some strange woman appearing out of nowhere at the family table." So his girlfriends were strangers to his kids? This was getting more depressing by the moment. He went on, "You're the one who took care of their grandfather. You're their next-door neighbor."

She wasn't sure what to say to that. He did confuse her. He seemed to want every minute he could get with her, yet he wouldn't even consider the idea that they might try to find ways to keep seeing each other after Labor Day. "I don't know, Maddox."

"But *I* do—So how about we pull it together and join the family for breakfast" He tried to flip back the covers.

She held on to them. "Wait."

Now he was frowning at her, the skin between his eyebrows all crunched up. "What's the matter?"

"Well, now that we're talking about your girlfriends, is there a woman waiting for you in New York?"

"What? No!"

"But you do have *girlfriends*, plural?"

He gave her a classic Maddox Hale look—both aloof and endlessly patient. "*Girlfriends* was your word."

"And you didn't call me on it. In fact, you immediately started listing the differences between your girlfriends and me."

He fell back against his pillow and glared at the ceiling. "Okay, Sarah. Where are we going with this?"

"I just want some...context."

He scowled harder at the ceiling. "Context. You want context."

"Who are your girlfriends?"

"Just to clarify, they are not really my girlfriends. They are mature, intelligent women I usually meet socially, women I'm introduced to by mutual friends or acquaintances. Women I enjoy spending time with. We might have a drink together. We might have dinner. And sometimes we might spend the night together."

Okay, now. That just made her sad. "So what you're saying is you might spend a night with one woman on Friday and then another woman a few nights later, right? You have no commitment to any of them?"

"You make it sound like it's a revolving door."

"Just answer the question. Do you have any kind of commitment to any of the women you go out with?"

"Sarah, it's a date. The only commitment is to behave like a decent human being and to try to have a good time together."

"What about safe sex?"

"Absolutely. Safe sex is a given."

"Hmm."

He narrowed his eyes at her. "What does that mean, *hmm*?"

"It means I'm thinking. And what I'm thinking is that what you describe doesn't work for me."

He braced up on an elbow then and raked a hand back through his sleep-scrambled hair. "I don't get it. We weren't talking about you."

"No, we were talking about the women you date. Which

does not include me as we have never once been on a date together. But date or no date, I just want to make it very clear to you that I'm not okay with your taking a night off from me to go visit one of your other girlfriends."

He looked like she'd poked him with a hot stick. "What the hell are you talking about?"

"I'm saying, for the rest of the summer, as long as you're spending nights with me, there will be no other women in the picture."

He blinked. "That's all you're getting at here?"

"Yes. I need your agreement. No other women as long as you're with me."

His eyes changed, went from ice green to something much warmer. "Agreed." He leaned in closer, until their noses almost touched. "Nobody but you, Sarah." He kissed the tip of her chin. "Say it back."

"Nobody but you, Maddox."

He ran a finger down the side of her throat and out along the slope of her shoulder. His touch felt so good. It always did. "Excellent." He bent close. They shared a light kiss. "Now, come on. Let's get breakfast."

She still wasn't sure if breakfast was such a good idea. "I don't know..."

"What now?"

She lifted up enough to kiss him again, then made herself pull back. "Not today, all right? I've got stuff to do at home."

"Tonight, then?"

"Sorry, can't."

He actually pooched out his lip in a pouty face. "You're pissed at me."

"No." It was halfway a lie. She was still smarting a bit

about those other girlfriends. About the fact that he insisted everything between them would stop dead on the day after Labor Day. But she wasn't vetoing tonight because of either of those issues. "Tomorrow, I start a new job. I need to get to bed early to be fresh for my first day."

"Damn." He kissed the end of her nose. "Guess I can't argue with that."

Ten minutes later, she went out the front door and climbed into her waiting Jeep without encountering Alma, Earlene or any of the Hales. That morning, she groomed horses and baled hay, then spent the afternoon getting ready for her first day in the emergency room. She ate with the family and went to bed early.

Still, Tuesday morning came much too soon. She was on her feet all day, dealing with everything from an accidental encounter with the business end of a pocketknife to GI bleeds to cardiac arrest. Her twelve-hour shift felt like it lasted for an eternity. She didn't actually leave the hospital until eight thirty. When she got home at nine, she had a quick shower in her trailer, ate microwaved stew and fell into bed.

Her eyes were just drifting closed when her phone buzzed with a text from Maddox. She squinted at his name on the screen and couldn't help smiling.

Hope it was a good first day, he'd written.

She called him.

He answered on the first ring. "So, how's the new job?"

"Grisly. Altogether, too much bleeding occurs in the ER."

"Are you going to quit?"

"No way. And I have a question."

"Go for it."

"How long is it going to take people to stop putting flour on burns? Because they're still doing it, even though a simple internet search will yield nothing but reasons why *not* to do that."

"Old wives' tales die hard. When can I see you?"

"Maybe tomorrow night?"

"You sound far too doubtful."

"It all depends on whether or not I'm dead on my feet when I get home."

"But don't you have Thursday off?"

"So?"

"Just get yourself over here. You can sleep late."

She rolled to her back and grinned at the funky ceiling panels overhead. "Aren't you the eager one."

"You have no idea."

The truth was, she missed him, too. She wanted to spend every moment she could in his arms. That didn't bode well for the possibility of her getting over him after Labor Day. However, a girl can hope.

She wrapped her hand around the green stone on the necklace he'd given her. Slowly, she slid it back and forth along the chain. "I'll text you when I get home tomorrow night."

"Thank you. Sleep well, gorgeous."

She hung up smiling—and was sound asleep a few minutes later.

Wednesday was every bit as grueling as the day before had been. As soon as she got back to the trailer, she texted Maddox. I'm home.

He texted back, Playing Grand Theft Auto with RJ—don't judge.

Have fun, she replied and headed for the shower.

Once she was clean, she brushed her teeth and went to bed. Maddox roused her from sleep at a little before ten.

She answered with a groggy, "Huh?"

"The kids are in their rooms for the night. How about if I come to you?"

It was tempting. But it bothered her that Stevie or RJ might need him in the night and discover he'd somehow vanished from the house. "I'll be there in fifteen minutes."

"I feel guilty making you come to me. You sound beat…"

"So I'll just stay here, then…?"

"No! Come on over. Please."

When she drove up, he was waiting on the front steps, same as the other night. This time, she'd brought an overnight bag. She grabbed it from the passenger seat and rushed to his arms. In his room, they stripped in record time and crawled under the covers.

But then she yawned. "Sorry. New job, extra exhausting. But don't worry. In a week, I'll be an old hand at it, ready to party till all hours when I get home."

He kissed the end of her nose. "You need sleep."

She yawned again. "You noticed…"

He pulled her closer. She turned in his arms so they were spooning.

"Rest," he whispered. His breath stirred her hair and his lips brushed her temple so lightly…

It was the last thing she remembered until after seven the next morning when she woke to his hand slowly sliding down her thigh. *"Mmff,"* she said, and almost dropped off to sleep again.

But that hand of his kept moving. It felt really good—good enough that she rolled to her back in his arms and blinked up at him. "Please continue," she advised groggily.

And he did.

In no time, he had her calling out his name. Groaning, he covered her mouth with his hand. "Shh…"

"Right," she whisper-moaned. "Mustn't frighten the children…"

That special wakeup call ended in a heap of twining limbs, with both of them breathing hard—and a sudden tap on the door. "Daddy?"

"Stevie," Sarah whispered. She winced. "Is the door locked?"

"It is. Don't worry."

"How much do you think she heard?"

"Relax." He nuzzled her cheek. "She didn't hear a thing."

"Daddy!" the sweet voice called from the other side of the door. "Alma says breakfast is ready! Are you coming down?"

"Be right there, sweetheart!" he called back.

"Okay, don't take too long. Your frittata will get cold!"

"I'm on my way…"

There was silence on the other side of the door. They waited for a long count of ten.

Then Maddox said, "Come on. Let's get breakfast."

"I should go…"

"You should get breakfast first."

"It's not good for me to be wandering into the kitchen from your bedroom in the morning. That will only confuse your children."

"No, it won't. We'll fake it. It will be fine."

"Fake it, how?"

"Simple. We go down together. I say, *Look who dropped by.*"

She waited for the punchline. It failed to materialize. "And then what?"

"And then everybody's happy to see you. We have breakfast and enjoy each other's company."

"You think they won't ask questions?"

"I'm reasonably certain they won't. They know you. They like you. You said you'd be stopping by and here you are. What's to ask questions about?"

Why did that make perfect sense to her?

Probably because he was right. Stevie and RJ saw her as their grandpa's former nurse, not as their dad's new girlfriend—which she wasn't—not in any permanent way.

In September, this man beside her and his children would fly back to New York. She would move on, putting her focus on getting her MSN and going forward with her career. For her, Maddox Hale would become a sweet, sexy memory—just as she would for him...

"Sarah?"

She blinked. For some reason, her throat felt tight. Because this, with him?

She loved it. It wasn't only the sex—which was absolutely amazing. It was the closeness. The way they could sometimes finish each other's sentences. It was the laughter they shared, the sheer joy and contentment she felt when they were together.

She was having more and more trouble imagining her life without him in it—which was a real problem. Because he'd made it very clear that to get serious about him would be a giant mistake, that this thing between them was just for now and going nowhere.

She'd thought that she'd accepted the situation. She'd told herself she'd come to grips with the fact that her future would not include him.

But she hadn't. Not in the least. And as each day went by,

she inched closer to facing the scary truth that she wanted more from him—and *with* him.

After the disappointing way it had ended with Aaron, she'd come to the conclusion that she was perfectly fine on her own. She'd accepted that her life was about her career first, that love was secondary for her. She'd believed that the right man would somehow come along when she was ready for him, that he would be everything Aaron had not been. He would understand her need to put her work first and love her enough to accept her as she was.

Maddox did seem to understand how much her work mattered. Too bad he had no intention of making a life with her.

She kept telling herself that she needed to remain realistic. This thing with him, it was an interlude. A sweet summer fling with a definite end date. Because in no way was Maddox Hale the right man for her. She knew it. He knew it.

And yet, at this moment she could not help thinking that walking away from him was all wrong somehow.

"Sarah?" Maddox asked again. He definitely sounded apprehensive now.

And the concern for her in his voice? It tripped a lever inside her.

He cared more than he wanted to. And she loved that he did. Because she cared, too.

Everything was starting to become painfully clear. This, the two of them, just for the summer...

It had seemed like enough for her when she'd decided to go ahead with it. She'd thought she could be with him, enjoy him for a few perfect, romantic weeks.

And then just move on.

But now, finally, she saw the flaw in her plan. Moving on from Maddox Hale would not be that simple.

Her mother was right.

Giving up without a real fight just wasn't in her nature.

And that meant she was going to have to closely examine her plans for the future. Because those plans...

They would have to change.

"Sarah, are you okay?" He looked so worried.

She smiled at him tenderly. "Yes. I'm just fine."

"You sure?"

"I am, yes."

"Okay, then." He seemed at a loss. Probably because she was behaving strangely. "So...what now?"

"Let's do what you suggested—go on down and get breakfast."

He smiled then. "You mean that?"

"Absolutely."

Downstairs, it went just as Maddox had said it would. Stevie was delighted to see her. RJ played it cool but seemed perfectly okay with her presence. Fergus slanted her a knowing look. Alma bustled off to get her a plate.

As for Earlene, she greeted Sarah with a big smile and a "Howdy, Sarah. Great to see you again."

Nothing had changed.

And yet somehow, Sarah's whole world had tipped on its axis.

Chapter Twelve

The way Maddox saw it, his powerful infatuation with Sarah Bravo presented no problem for him because their time together was self-limiting. He and Sarah would have these few weeks together and then cut it clean.

And that made it okay for him to steal every last moment he could get with her. Time was ticking away. They only had so much of it to share. Better not to waste a minute.

That day, he talked her into hanging out with him and the kids. Alma packed up a picnic and he, Stevie, RJ and Sarah took one of the crew cabs out to a swimming hole he remembered on Crystal Creek. When Sarah tried to back out because she didn't have a swimsuit with her, he said they'd drive over to her place and pick one up on the way.

When she hesitated, Stevie piled on. "Yeah, Sarah! Come with us. It's going to be fun."

Stevie's enthusiasm did the trick. Sarah gave in. They stopped at her trailer, and she ran in and came out wearing shorts and an unbuttoned shirt over her green swimsuit. He smiled at the sight of that suit. It brought back memories of the two of them, alone by the pool during those first nights when they'd just started getting to know each other. He kind of wished it was the red one—it was his favorite. If the kids hadn't been there, he might have asked her to change.

It was a great day—hot, but with some cloud cover and a nice breeze. The spot on the creek was very much as he remembered it, with willows on the shallow side to provide shade and a nice-sized swimming hole rimmed with rock formations on the deep side, the kind of rocks just right for diving.

The kids did a lot of cannonballing. They also played air ball—a variation on volleyball with no net and a beach ball.

Maddox loved every minute of that day. His kids were happy. Sarah was there. It was all pretty much perfect until Sarah insisted that they drop her off at her place on the way back. He missed her the minute she disappeared inside that tiny trailer.

Friday evening, he called her to invite her to join him, RJ and Stevie on a weekend camping trip. They would leave the next morning and return Sunday afternoon. It should have been perfect for her because she had weekends off.

Sarah said she couldn't go. "Thanks for thinking of me, but tomorrow and Sunday, I need to help out around the Double-K a little."

"But you just worked three twelve-hour shifts at the hospital. What you need is a break."

"Sorry, Maddox. I've got work to do here."

He and the kids went camping alone. It was great. But it would have been exponentially better with Sarah along, even if they had to sleep in separate tents so that his children wouldn't realize that he and Sarah had something more intimate than friendship going on

Things got worse.

All the next week, she put him off. She said her new job was demanding and that she also really did have to do her share on the family ranch. She couldn't be sneaking out in the middle of the night just to roll around in bed with him.

Why not? he thought but somehow managed to keep from saying.

He really liked rolling around in bed with her and he knew damn well that she liked it, too. Plus, they had a limited amount of time to roll around in bed together and they ought to be doing that every chance they got. The summer was flying by and he hadn't so much as set eyes on her in the past seven days.

Saturday, he tried again. He called at seven and was more than a little surprised when she actually picked up.

"Hello, Maddox." She sounded resigned. Why? She didn't want him calling now? He just didn't get it.

"What's the matter? Are you all right?"

"Yeah. I'm okay."

He made himself speak gently. "Sarah. Come on. The summer's going by. I miss you. I want to be with you…"

"Yeah, well. Sometimes in life you don't get what you want."

"What is that supposed to mean?"

Dead silence from her.

"Sarah? You still there?"

"Yeah. And I just need a little time, Maddox. That's all."

"Time for what?"

"To…get adjusted to my new schedule."

Okay, that did it. He'd had about enough. "What the hell is going on?"

"You don't really want to know."

"What is this passive-aggressive routine? I don't understand. What did I do?"

"Would you believe me if I said it's not you, it's me?"

"I don't know what to think. At least you can talk to me, can't you? Explain to me what the matter is."

"Talk," she said, the word itself a dismissal. "I don't think talking is what you're after."

Okay, maybe it wasn't. But he did care for her. He wanted to know what had happened, why everything had gone wrong between them all of a sudden. "Try me."

"All right. Face-to-face, though."

Dread twisted his gut. "Come to the house. Or I'll come there."

"I'll come to you, Maddox. Ten tonight?"

"I'll be waiting…"

He was standing on the front steps when she pulled up.

She got out of the car and shut the door, the sound echoing in the quiet night. He watched her come toward him through the pools of darkness and light created by the landscape lanterns and the porch lamps behind him. She wore old jeans and a blue tank top. Her hair was loose, her skin glowing, begging for his touch.

She had a canvas pack hooked on one smooth shoulder. "Brought my suit. Just in case you might be in the mood for a swim…"

His hands ached to reach for her. He kept them at his sides. "Thought we were going to talk."

She gave him a crooked little smile. "We used to do our all best talking by the pool on nights like tonight—after ten, when everybody else in the house was in bed."

He remembered those nights. When he went home to New York and she was off somewhere halfway around the world providing medical care to people in need, he was sure he would think of those nights, of her in her red swimsuit, rising from the shallows of his fancy swimming pool, smoothing her long, wet hair back from her forehead, water sheeting off her slender form.

It made him ache, to remember those nights. As though they'd happened years ago.

"All right," he said. "Let's go to the pool."

He ushered her in ahead of him. She knew the way to the back of the house and the wide hallway that led to the pool area.

They took the entrance into the pool house. He grabbed a pair of board shorts from one of the shelves along the wall by the door and ducked into a cubicle to change.

She did the same—as though, already, they had stopped being lovers and become two people who needed privacy to change clothes.

They emerged simultaneously. He smiled when he saw she was wearing the red suit.

"What's so funny?" she asked, but gently, and with a tiny smile of her own.

"That suit. It's my favorite."

The words brought a soft, sweet laugh from her. "They're all the same, Maddox, just different colors."

"Okay, then. They are *all* my favorite. But I like this red one the best."

They regarded each other in the space between their two cubicles. "So," she said. "Talk first? Or swim?"

He dreaded the talking. And he had a bad feeling that when the talking was over, she would simply leave. "I've missed you so damn much."

Her mouth quivered. She bit her lower lip to make the quivering stop. And then she tipped her head back and let out a groan. "Damn you, Maddox."

For some reason, that sounded like an invitation to him. He stepped forward.

Miracle of miracles, so did she.

When he reached for her, she melted right into his arms.

There was nothing like it—the feel of her under his hands. He lowered his mouth. She lifted hers.

The kiss was wild and sweet and endless. He was a condemned man given a sudden reprieve, offered one last chance to know the taste of joy and happiness.

He ran his hungry hands over the slim shape of her back, down to where her waist curved in and then lower, to where her back met the outward swell of her hips. Grabbing the perfect globes of her ass, he hauled her in nice and close.

She felt like heaven, with his aching length pressed into the soft, giving curve of her belly. All he wanted was never to have to let her go.

But then she pulled her mouth away.

"Don't..." he begged.

She caught his face between her hands. "I was only going to say that we should lock the doors."

Suddenly he could breathe again. "That's all?"

"That's all."

He laughed and she laughed with him. Then she turned and locked the door to the hallway. He locked the one that led to the pool.

They met up again in the small seating area between the cubicles. He reached for her and she reached back, taking him by the shoulders and then pushing him into one of the two club chairs.

He stared up at her, mesmerized by those eyes of hers, hardly daring to believe that this was going where he'd desperately hoped it might. She bent over him and gave him her mouth as she climbed into his lap, straddling him, lifting those long, smooth legs to rest them on the chair arms.

She felt so good—the weight of her in his lap, the heat of her against his aching erection. He let his head fall back against the chair. She chased him with those soft lips of hers. Her mouth devoured his. Pleasure shot out along every nerve ending he possessed as she kissed him endlessly.

This chair? He loved it. He never wanted to climb out of it.

They could simply sit here forever, making out like a couple of oversexed high schoolers.

"I didn't think…" he whispered.

"Good," she replied. "Don't think. Just kiss me. Kiss me again."

A terrible thought occurred to him. "Condom?" He should have planned for this. But he'd given up ahead of time, been grimly certain that he'd never get this chance again.

Some men are fools, and he was one of them.

"In. My. Pack." She made each word a separate statement, pressing kisses like periods between them.

"Where is it?" he asked. She pointed toward the cubicle she'd used to change in. He got his feet under him. "Wrap your legs around me."

She let out a little "whoops" against his mouth as he rose and she almost slid to the floor. But then, laughing, she caught hold of his shoulders and hooked her feet at the base of his spine. He carried her to the cubicle in question. And then, banding one arm tightly around her, he carefully dropped to his knees on the fluffy white throw rug. "Hold on." When she wrapped her arms around his neck, he rolled to his back.

As soon as he was flat on the floor, she rose on her knees

above him and reached for the pack. He stared up at her, amazed. "God. You are gorgeous," he whispered in a tone of great reverence.

She pulled the condom from a front pocket of the pack. "I can't believe this is happening. I told myself I wasn't coming over here to get naked with you." She held up the condom and shook it at him. "But this kind of calls me a liar, wouldn't you say?"

"Hell, no. Being prepared doesn't make you a liar."

She laughed again, low and sweet. "Liar."

He closed his eyes and begged, "Please, Sarah. Don't change your mind now…"

Still up on her knees, she bent over him, her hair falling all around them, smelling of lemons and some tropical flower the name of which escaped him. "Stop worrying. Yes, I came here to talk. But then I pulled in out front and you were standing there on the step and I just thought, *What the hell, life's too short.*" She gave a little lift of one shoulder. "And this past week without you, I've missed you, too. So much."

He didn't know what to say to that. Really, screw all the talking. He had her in his arms and he was pretty sure she'd just said she wanted to be here.

Reaching between them, he undid the tie at the waistband of his board shorts. She helped him ease the shorts over his eager hardness and then shoved at them until they were halfway down his thighs.

"Give me that condom," he said.

She handed it over. He kicked the board shorts off completely as he took the wrapper off the condom and rolled it on, snugging it carefully into place as she guided the straps of her suit off her shoulders. Those beautiful breasts popped free.

He groaned and lifted both hands to cradle them. In the last several days, without her to hold in the hours between darkness and dawn, he'd imagined his future once this thing between them came to its natural end.

The days ahead didn't look all that bright, even though they were what he'd chosen. They were the life he had no plans to change. He'd done his duty as a man, married, had children to carry on the family name. He had no need for anything like that again. The price of love was too damn high and he had no intention of paying it.

Still up on her knees above him, she bent her head close. "I can't wait to feel you…" She breathed the words into his ear.

That did it. He hooked two fingers under the gusset of her suit, finding her hot and wet and very ready. Easing the suit out of his way, he rubbed at her wetness. She moaned.

He whispered, "Come on, then."

Reaching down, she wrapped her hand around him and guided him where he couldn't wait to be. "Maddox…"

He took her by the hips then and surged up into her. Everything vanished except the feel of her, the heat, the wetness, the absolute perfection.

She rocked on him, her face a portrait of pleasure, her head falling back, the tangled waves of her hair sliding down her shoulders, along her back, tickling his fingers where he held on to her. He wanted it to go on and on— except it was too good, too perfect.

Too completely overwhelming.

He pulled her down against him so her body pressed all along the front of him, her soft bared breasts against his chest, her face so close. "You are perfect," he said on a growl as he took her mouth again.

She tasted of heaven, sweet and tart and a little bit salty.

And that kiss? It lasted for the longest time, their tongues meeting, dancing, twining. She moaned against his lips. He answered in kind.

And as each shining second spun by, he knew he was losing it, felt certain that he wouldn't be able to hold on one second longer.

She knew, too. "Wait," she instructed into the endless kiss. "Not yet..."

"But I—"

"Maddox, don't you dare come yet."

"I can't—"

"You can. You will."

He held out, held on. They moved together, slow and so good.

But he could not wait. He reached up, wrapped his arms around her and rolled them.

Now he was on top.

She blinked up at him through daze eyes. "Oh my..." She had her legs good and tight around him. He pushed in deeper still.

"Now," he said on a gruff husk of breath. "Sarah, now..."

She was shaking her head, but her body heard him, and it obeyed.

He felt her contracting around him. With a sharp cry, she slipped over the edge at last. He kissed that cry off her open mouth.

And then he couldn't hold on one moment longer. Wrapping her tight in his arms, he joined her in free fall.

When he opened his eyes, she was staring up at him.

And then she blinked.

And then, out of nowhere, they were both laughing.

Carefully, he wrapped a leg around her and rolled them so they were on their sides facing each other. "You okay?" He kissed the tip of her nose.

She nuzzled his cheek. "Never better."

He smoothed her wildly tangled hair, guiding the unruly strands out of her eyes and back off her sweet face. "I have missed you so much this past week…"

She tucked her head under his chin. For a while, they just held each other on that fluffy white rug on the floor of the pool house.

Finally, regretfully, he let her go. Easing the condom off, he tied the end and carried it to the pool house bathroom.

When he returned to her, she was sitting up cross-legged. She'd pulled the top of her suit back in place. Now it covered those sweet, high breasts.

"So…?" he asked, waiting for her to tell him what would happen next.

"Let's swim, why don't we?"

Were they putting off the talking—or forgoing it?

He decided not to ask. "A swim would be great." He held down his hand.

She took it and laced her fingers with his.

Grabbing a cap, goggles and a couple of towels from the cubbies by the door to the pool, he led her out there, dropped the towels on a lounge chair and pulled her to the deep end.

She eased her fingers from his grip. "Go for it," she said.

He put on the cap and goggles and dove in. The water took him. He let time fade away, lost himself in the soothing magic of each long, steady stroke.

When he finally let his feet touch bottom in the shallow end and pushed up his goggles, she was sitting on the edge down at the deep end, water beading on her skin, her wet hair slicked back. He glanced at the big clock on the rough rock wall in the sitting area behind her. He'd been doing laps for thirty-two minutes.

When she crooked a finger at him, he swam to her. She rose as he got out of the water. Together, they went to the lounge chairs where they'd left the towels.

After drying off a little, they stretched out side by side the way they used to do on those first nights. He shut his eyes. For a while, there was only the faint hum of the pool filter and the gentle lapping of the water.

Finally, she said, "I want to be with you for more than this summer, Maddox." He turned his head, opened his eyes and met her solemn gaze. She went on, "I want us to try to find a way to be together after summer's over."

"That's not going to work." He hated the words as he said them. But he needed to say them and she needed to hear them. "Nothing has changed for me."

"So then," she said, "as far as you're concerned, after Labor Day, we're done?"

"That's right." He was absolutely certain she would get up and go. He ached at the thought.

But she didn't move. She looked directly at him as she asked, "Exactly what do you want from me?"

He studied the details of her face, the beauty of her soft lips and delicate jawline, the way she looked at him, so steadily, never wavering. He thought how he wouldn't mind at all if they could lie here like this forever, talking softly together deep into the night. "I want your time, your kisses, the feel of your skin..."

"Sex, you mean?"

"Yes, sex. But if that's not happening, I would still like to see you, to spend time with you…"

She drew a slow breath. "When?"

"When you're not working, whenever you can."

She turned her head toward the skylights and closed her eyes. "Listen to yourself. You want us to be lovers, but if we can't, let's be friends until the summer ends…"

"That sounds perfectly reasonable to me."

"And that's because you're lying to yourself. There's more going on between us than you're willing to let yourself acknowledge and I can't pretend anymore that you're not the one I—"

"Don't." He cut her off. "Please." This conversation needed to stop now. He should simply get up and say goodnight.

But he couldn't. Because he was hooked on her. For now. But his need for her would pass. He knew with absolute certainty that what they had wouldn't last.

He reminded her, "Sarah. It's just for now with us. You know that."

"No. I don't. But since *you* do, tell me why." She looked at him again. Her eyes were guarded, her soft lips pressed together.

"Oh, come on. I think we've been through all this."

"Tell me again, anyway. Tell me why it can never work for us."

"Fine. I live in Manhattan. You don't. I spend my days buying and selling and working every angle until the best deal is made. You want to save the lives of the people guys like me have long ago forgotten even exist. I have two children already and that's all I plan to have. Someday, you will want to have kids, too. I won't be the one they call Dad. I'm forty and you're twenty-five."

"All of that is surmountable."

"We might wish it was. But it's not. Look at the facts, Sarah. Fifty percent of first marriages end in divorce. The numbers are even worse for second marriages. Those fail at a rate of sixty-five percent. And you and me, well, the odds are bound to be no better given all the reasons I just listed. We are what we are, here for the summer and then moving on, going our separate ways. When Christmas comes—"

"Enough," she said softly, her gaze still holding his. "I don't need to hear that again. And I don't want to do this with you anymore."

Everything stopped. He had to remember to breathe. He reminded himself that this had been coming all along. They were bound to end.

Yeah, he'd hoped to make it last until Labor Day. But she'd just laid down her terms and he had rejected them.

"All right." What else could he say? She wanted more. And he wasn't going there. They really were done.

She sat up. "I'm going to go home now."

They both rose. He said, "I'll walk you out."

She didn't argue. He followed her back into the pool house where they entered their separate cubicles and came out in dry clothes. She stuffed her wet suit into her pack and hooked the pack on her shoulder.

He led the way along the hallway to the main house and on to the front door.

Outside on the wide front porch, the night felt thick. Humid. Clouds obscured the stars.

She turned to him. "I do have another question…"

He almost smiled. Really, there was no more to say.

But another question meant she might stay a few minutes longer. He would take every last second he could get with her. "Fire away."

"You said you'll never get married again."

"And I meant that."

"Okay, then. What about love?"

"What about it?"

"Well, not everybody wants to get married, Maddox. But that doesn't mean there can't be love and commitment. That doesn't mean two people can't be together on their own terms. Let me give you a hypothetical."

"Why?"

"Why not? Just bear with me. Imagine you met a woman. A very special woman. Imagine that you loved her deeply. Don't get that cynical glint in your eye—I'm not talking about me. This imaginary woman I'm talking about, she's your age. And she doesn't care all that much about marriage. She just wants your love, just wants to be with you. Let's say she's someone in your circle in New York, someone with kids already and no plans to have more. Maybe she's even someone in international real estate just like you..."

"That's never going to happen, Sarah."

"Because you don't believe such a woman exists?"

"Because I'm not looking. I'm not cut out for all that." He ached to touch her—one last time. To trace his finger over the soft curve of her cheek, to guide a coffee-colored curl of hair behind the shell of her ear. With a supreme effort of will, he kept his grasping hands to himself.

"What do you mean, *all that*?" she asked. "I just don't get it."

"I mean, I'm not cut out to go the distance with another

person. My birth father killed my birth mother—and then offed himself. I have no memory of either of them, but what he did, the way they died, it sticks with me. It shows me how dangerous love can be—how violent and destructive. And even when love is sweet and wonderful, it can still be devastating. My dad—meaning Fergus—almost died when he lost my mom. He really didn't know how to live without her. What good is true love if your love dies on you, leaves you alone to try to keep going without the one you've built your whole life around? That could happen to you if you ended up with me. And then look at my own history. Alexis loved me when we got married, but I wasn't able to make her happy.

"The way I see it, Sarah, even if I wasn't pretty much guaranteed to die before you do and leave you alone to pick up the pieces, I'm not a guy anyone ought to fall in love with. To me, love is just an invitation to disappointment and disaster."

She was shaking her head. "You're such a smart man. I don't understand how your reasoning has gotten so completely skewed on this particular subject. Love is not at fault for all the rotten things people sometimes do to each other—and it's wrong to blame love because Fergus suffered so terribly when he lost your mom. Yes, he loved her. He had a happy marriage with her and he grieved when he lost her. It's not surprising that it took him a long time to move on. But I will bet you that if you asked him, he would say that all the great years he had with her more than made up for the horrible pain of losing her. And as for you and Alexis, well, you're the one who messed that up by choosing her for reasons other than love. I think you can do better if you'll only try."

He didn't agree with a single thing she said—and yet he wished she would just keep on talking. He could stand here all night listening to her lecture him about a subject on which they would never find common ground. "You are something special, Sarah Bravo."

She gave a slow, regal nod in acknowledgement. "Too bad you're the fool who's letting me go."

Chapter Thirteen

"We have to talk." Fergus, on crutches, his healing leg now in a short cast, stood in the open doorway to Maddox's office.

"I'm just in the middle of—"

"Too bad," said the old man as he crossed the threshold into Maddox's workspace. Pausing, he turned and shoved the door shut. "You're not supposed to be working anyway, remember? In an hour, you're taking the kids riding. Right now, as we speak, Alma is fixing your picnic lunch."

"Look, Dad. I just need to answer these few queries before—"

"No, you don't." Fergus took one of the guest chairs. Lowering himself carefully on his good leg, he sat down, then bent to lay his crutches beside him on the floor. "I've been trying to get a few private minutes with you for days now. You've been dodging me. And I know why."

"What are you going on about?"

"Sarah, son. I am going on about Sarah."

It had been a full week since the night Sarah left Maddox on the front step. Plus, for a week or so before that, she hadn't been to the house to visit the family. Guilt jabbed at him. His dad, the kids, Alma… They all loved Sarah. And because of him, she had vanished from their lives.

"Where is she?" Fergus demanded. "I haven't set eyes on her in a couple of weeks. I called her a few days ago. She was just as sweet as always, promised she'd be coming over sometime soon, but I haven't heard from her since."

"Dad, I'm sure she's—"

"I wasn't finished." Fergus talked right over him. "Don't interrupt me. Now, where was I? Right. My guess is that something's gone wrong between the two of you." His dad leaned forward in the chair and squinted as though summoning the power to see inside Maddox's brain. "What happened? Talk to me, son."

He debated pretending he had no idea what the old man was talking about. But that wouldn't work. Fergus was on to him. "Look, Dad. It was Sarah's choice. She doesn't want to be around me anymore."

"What did you *do*?"

"Nothing."

"I don't believe that. Tell me what you did."

"I'll say it again. Nothing. In fact, I would say the problem is more what I'm not willing to do."

"Which is…?"

"Dad. Come on. Let it be. I don't want to talk about it. There's really nothing to say. We want different things, me and Sarah. It's just better for both of us if we stay away from each other." That was only half the truth. It wasn't better for him. If she would have let him, he would have hung on to this thing between them, spent every minute he could steal in her arms until he boarded the jet for New York ten days from now. "It was a summer thing, Dad. And it ended. Can we leave it at that?"

"No, we can't. Because it makes no damn sense. I'm not her patient anymore. There's no longer a problem if she gets close to you. You're both single. The road ahead for the two of you is wide open."

Maddox wanted to pick up his laptop and throw it at the file cabinet across the room. "Dad. This is really none of your business."

"So what? Talk to me anyway. Who knows you better than your dear old dad?"

"Let it go."

"Sometimes you remind me way too much of your mother—stubbornest person I've ever known. When Mary got an idea in her head, she would not let it go. One time, she got mad at your aunt Florence..." Aunt Florence, who now lived in California with her husband, George, was Mary Hale's younger sister. Fergus went on, "...because Florence told your uncle George some secret Mary had shared with her. Mary was mad enough to spit nails when she found out. She didn't speak to her own sister for two years."

Maddox knew he shouldn't ask. "What was the secret?"

"Hell if I know. Mary never told me."

"Mom kept secrets from you?"

"Just that one..." Fergus frowned. "As far as I know, anyway. And don't go trying to change the subject on me. This is about you and Sarah and how you need to work out whatever is wrong between you."

"Sarah doesn't want to see me anymore, Dad. I'm respecting her wishes. That's all that's going on here."

"Now, see how you did that? You give me the downstroke, but you leave out the whole rest of the story. What I want to know is *why* Sarah doesn't want to see you anymore."

"Let it go, Dad."

"Plus, I happen to think you're wrong. Because, of course, Sarah wants to see you again. Just like you want to see her. That's why I called her this morning and asked her to join you and the kids for your ride up to Cloud Pass Ridge. She said she'd love to come."

His heart literally leaped. For a second, it almost seemed to get stuck in his throat. He gulped and took a deep, slow breath. "You are yanking my chain, Dad."

"Nope. Sarah said she'd love to head up to the ridge with you and RJ and Stevie—and I know, I know. You got those *queries* to answer before you go." He picked up his crutches. "I'll leave you to it."

Sarah appeared on a bay mare just as Maddox and the kids finished tacking up their mounts. She was the most gorgeous thing he'd ever seen dressed in old jeans, a faded plaid shirt, well-worn boots—and a helmet.

When she saw him staring, she grinned like there was nothing wrong between them. "Good to see you, too, Maddox."

"Nice helmet," he remarked.

She sat straighter in the saddle. "Yes, I do wear a helmet," she announced defiantly. "I get attitude from a few hard-core cowboys I know. But hey, I'm a nurse. I've seen too many head injuries to get on a horse without proper protection."

"I was more admiring all the stickers." The black helmet was covered with them—mostly hearts and flowers, a few butterflies, too.

"You like them? Courtesy of my niece. Emmy's a firm believer in stickering everything she can get her little hands on."

Stevie giggled. Her braces glinted in the sunlight. She patted her own helmet. "Dad makes us wear them, too."

RJ said nothing, though he might have rolled his eyes. He made no secret of his opinion that helmets were completely and irredeemably uncool. But he was wearing one anyway. Because Stevie was right. Maddox's son and daughter wore helmets or they didn't ride.

And he couldn't stand here forever staring at the woman he'd yet to stop wanting.

"Mount up," he said. "Let's get on the trail."

It was a two-hour trip on horseback up to Cloud Pass Ridge. The trail was an easy one and also well-marked. Maddox took the lead. Stevie, on a sweet-natured mare named Pretty Girl, was right behind him. RJ fell in behind his sister and Sarah took the drag.

They stopped to rest once on the way, dismounting and relaxing in the shade of a tall cottonwood tree. Maddox had to put a lot of effort into not letting his gaze stray toward the woman who had told him clearly last Saturday that the two of them were done.

Had she changed her mind, then? His blood pumped faster at the thought.

They didn't have much time left. But he would take whatever she was willing to give.

Then again, he couldn't make sense out of this apparent change of heart. It was driving him a little nuts not knowing what she was up to. One of the many things he'd always admired about her was her straightforwardness.

Had she suddenly decided to play games with him now?

He didn't know whether to be pissed off at her for giving him mixed signals—or to simply enjoy having her near again.

They made good time and reached the ridge at a little after one. RJ and Sarah decided to climb the rock formation that had given the spot its name. It was a quick climb. When they stood on top, they waved their helmets and shouted, "We made it!" their voices echoing out across the rolling land below.

After they'd scrambled back down, the four of them sat under the spreading branches of a bur oak and ate the lunch Alma had packed for them.

The ride back was uneventful. The kids were quiet and the day was hot.

When they reached the ranch, Sarah said what a great time she'd had. "Thanks for letting me tag along."

Stevie and RJ had already dismounted. They both grinned up at her.

"Come over again." Stevie urged. "We leave in a week and a half."

"A week and a half," Sarah repeated. "I'll try to stop by before you go..." She waved and turned her horse for home. The kids set to work untacking their mounts the way Maddox and Caleb had shown them.

Maddox tried not to watch Sarah riding away. He knew he should just let her go.

But he called after her anyway. "Sarah!" She reined in her mare and looked back over her shoulder. Their eyes met and locked. Hurt and anger spiked inside him—that she'd shown up here today and yet refused to give him the little time they still had left.

Her big eyes were so sad...

In an instant, his frustration turned to self-reproach. He was way out of line, behaving like too many men he knew— entitled men who focused on their own needs and expected the rest of the world to fall in line with their wishes.

He should let her go.

But he opened his mouth and asked, "Got a minute?"

She took her sweet time answering. Finally, she nodded. "Sure."

He wrapped his reins around the nearest fence rail and jogged over to catch up with her.

She dismounted and faced him. "Yeah?"

Now he felt awkward as a kid with a first crush. He had no idea where to even begin. "I thought you said you didn't want to see me anymore." He was careful to speak softly so RJ and Stevie wouldn't hear.

She swiped off her sticker-covered helmet and ran her fingers back through all that glorious hair. "Yeah. What I meant was I couldn't be with you anymore. That's all."

"*With me* meaning…?"

"The, uh, affair, or whatever you want to call it—but you're right. I wasn't clear. And then when your dad called about a picnic out at the ridge today, well, maybe I should have thought twice before saying yes. But I do feel bad, you know, about disappearing on Fergus and Stevie and RJ and Alma."

What about me? he thought and despised himself even more. Hadn't she just said that she wasn't here today for him?

He should look on the bright side. He might never get to hold her naked in his arms again—but if he acted like a grownup, she could still decide to spend more time with him and the family before they boarded the jet back to New York.

"I get it. And honestly, we all miss you," he said gently. "It just threw me, you know? I wasn't sure what was happening. I started hoping that maybe…"

She gave him zero indication that she was buying what

he was trying to sell her. Her soft mouth fixed in a grim line, she waited for him to finish.

And where was he going with this, anyway? She'd explained why she joined them today and it had nothing to do with sharing more nights with him.

He needed to quit. "Sorry. I'm an ass."

She lifted a slim shoulder in a half shrug. "Maybe. A little..." A faint smile pulled on one corner of her mouth.

"Come by the house anytime," he said. "Everyone will be so glad to see you. As for me, I swear to you that I'll keep my hands to myself."

"Thank you." Her eyes gleamed with wetness. Was she going to cry?

Was *he*? Irreconcilable urges had hold of him. To reach for her, haul her close and never let her go—or to turn tail, start running and never look back.

"I should go," she said quietly as she put her helmet back on.

He stood staring after her as she rode away.

Finally, Stevie called, "Dad!"

He turned then. "Right here!" And he jogged back to unsaddle his horse.

At least ten times a day in the week that followed, Maddox had to talk himself out of contacting her. He vacillated between calling, texting, jumping in the nearest vehicle, flooring it and kicking up dust all the way to that trailer she stayed in.

He had no idea what he would do when he reached her— beg her for another chance? Promise her anything? Ask her to marry him?

His mind spun with wild, impossible choices. The kinds

of choices he would never even consider if not for the nurse next door.

They were choices that weren't like him at all, choices he knew he would only end up regretting.

Somehow, he managed not to reach out. There was no point. They knew where they stood.

But damn, he did want to. He wanted to so bad.

When Friday came around again, he still had that longing under control. Barely.

And then, that evening in the living room as they got out the Monopoly board and gathered around it, the doorbell chimed.

"I'll get it!" cried Stevie. "It's Sarah! I texted her that we were playing Monopoly and she should at least play with us one more time before we go home..." She bounced to her feet and headed for the front door.

"Well, isn't that nice?" remarked Alma. "It's been too long since we've seen Sarah."

"She's a sweetheart," agreed Earlene.

"About damn time she came by again," grumbled Fergus.

A moment later, Stevie reappeared. Sarah, still in scrubs from the Friday shift at the hospital, was right behind her. "Here she is!" his daughter announced.

"Hey, guys..." Sarah gave them all her glowing smile.

Alma scooted over on one of the two big sofas and patted the empty cushion beside her. Sarah slid in behind the coffee table and sat down directly across from Maddox.

Everybody started talking at once, asking Sarah how she'd been, how her job up at the hospital was going. She said there was never a dull moment in the ER and then that she was glad for the paycheck and the experience.

"You get all kinds of situations in the ER," she said. "Really keeps you on your toes."

Earlene, who was now completely at home on the ranch, got up, disappeared into the kitchen and returned with a tray of snacks, which she set on a side table. Alma got up, too, and brought them all their cold drinks of choice.

Fergus showed Sarah his air cast, a special boot he'd graduated to a few days ago. Now he was practicing walking without the use of his crutches. "I'll be good as new in no time," he bragged.

"As long as you don't go falling out of any more windows," Earlene teased.

"Never again," he promised. The two shared a private smile and then a quick, affectionate kiss.

Maddox watched them, happy for them, wishing...

He cut off that dangerous thought before it could get its teeth in him. He knew who he was, what he was capable of. He needed not to get ideas above his emotional pay grade.

Eventually, they settled in to play.

Mostly, Maddox tried not stare at the vision in scrubs sitting on the sofa across from him. He was so glad to see her. She wore no makeup and her hair was pulled back in a low ponytail. To him, everything about her seemed to glow.

Yeah. He had it bad for her, all right.

Good thing he was out of here on Tuesday.

Some years, he brought the kids home to the ranch for Christmas. Not this year, though. They were going to have Christmas Eve at the penthouse and Christmas day with their mom and Teddy.

With his dad almost good as new and happy with Earlene, it was doubtful Maddox would return to Medicine Creek until sometime next year. By then, Sarah Bravo would be long gone—off somewhere getting her master's degree in nursing. Or maybe halfway around the world risking her life to provide medical care to people who rarely had access to it.

They probably wouldn't see each other again for years. And by then, she would have found someone special. She might even have children at that point—children by some guy he'd never met, some guy who wasn't him...

And damn.

He needed to get a grip here. So what if he still wanted her? It was over between them. His job now was to leave her the hell alone.

Three hours later, Earlene won the game. They all razzed Maddox for losing his Monopoly mojo.

He took the kidding with a smile. So, shoot him. His heart wasn't in it. Not tonight.

By then, it was after ten. The kids went off to their rooms. Fergus and Earlene disappeared in the direction of the grandpa suite. Maddox, Sarah and Alma took the trays of empty bowls and cups to the kitchen.

"Just leave it all on the island," Alma instructed. "I'm up early. I'll deal with it then." She covered a yawn with the back of her hand. "Night, you two."

And all of a sudden, it was just him and Sarah alone in the kitchen standing at the island, staring at each other.

"Well," she said. "I guess I should get going..."

He reminded himself not to touch her. And he didn't.

What he did do was to place his hand flat on the island and then ease it over in her direction. She did the same. Their fingers touched. It took all the will he had not to grab her hand. They stared at each other for the longest time.

Finally, the impossible happened. She covered his hand with her smaller one and grabbed hold.

"You sure?" he asked.

She nodded. And then, still holding on, she moved forward into his arms. He cradled her close. When she didn't resist he dared to press his lips into her hair. "This okay?"

She lifted that unforgettable face and their eyes met. "Yes." Her smile broke wide. "Hell, yes."

He stroked his fingers down that warm, silky hair, all the way to the scrunchie that held it in place. "I want to..."

She nodded. "Yes. Me too."

He took that scrunchie and pulled it off. She chuckled softly when he stuck it in his pocket. Carefully, he combed his fingers through her loosened hair. "One more time?"

Her eyes were so dark, full of heat and promise. "Yes."

"You're absolutely sure?"

"Maddox. Damn you. Yes!" And then, with a sweet, fierce laugh, she slid her arms up over his chest, wrapped them around his neck and surged up to crush her mouth to his.

That kiss. He never wanted it to end—and for right now, he let himself pretend it never would.

He kissed her as he scooped her high against his chest, kissed her some more as he turned and started walking out of the kitchen, through the massive living room and up the stairs to the open door of his bedroom.

He was still kissing her when he kicked the door shut with his foot. She reached out a hand to turn the lock. He carried her to his bed.

Only then, as he laid her down, did he allow his mouth to lose the taste of hers. He had to in order to undress her quickly. When he got down to her pink panties, he stuck them in his pocket along with the scrunchie he'd stolen.

Then at last, she was naked—except for the peridot necklace he'd given her. It got to him somewhere deep—that she'd worn it. He hoped she wore it every day, though he had no right to hope for any such thing.

Her mouth was pressed to his again, opening to let him in. She was everything he didn't dare hope for. She tasted of all the passion and sweetness he was going to be missing for the rest of his life.

She was also in a hurry to get him as naked as he'd just made her. His shirt went flying. He kicked off his shoes. She took his shoulders and pulled him onto the bed with her.

Pushing him flat on his back, she climbed on top of him and stripped off the rest his clothes. Finally, it was done. They were both naked.

She rolled and he went with her. They faced each other on their sides.

He stroked his hands along her skin, memorizing every smooth inch, every perfect, silky curve. He tasted her, running his tongue down the middle of her, spreading her wide, burying his face in the hot, wet center of her.

She cried out his name as he kissed her there. Another cry escaped her moments later. She had her hands in his hair, pulling on it, muttering, "Yes, please. Like that. Oh, Maddox, just like that."

When she came, he tasted every sweet, hot pulse. He stayed there with her, kissing her, wanting that moment to last and last.

But then she was grabbing his shoulders, urging him up her body.

He cupped her breast and covered it with his mouth, drawing on the nipple till it was a tight, hard bud.

She yanked the nightstand drawer wide as he lavished attention on her other breast. "Got it," she said.

He lifted up enough to look at her, flushed and triumphant, a condom in her hand. "Give it here..."

She handed it over. He went to his knees and did the honors.

Once he was covered, he looked down into her eyes. They were enormous, dark and shining, the pupils blown wide with pleasure.

"Oh, Maddox," she whispered, reaching up, pulling him down.

He entered her slowly, savoring the sweet agony, wanting to remember every moment of this night, to save it up and treasure it in all the long, lonely nights to come.

She grabbed him, her strong, small hands pulling him in good and tight. "Yes," she whispered. "Just like that. Just like that..."

He withdrew—but only to return. She groaned against his mouth as he kissed her, as he moved within her. He wanted it to last, but he knew that it wouldn't.

She wrapped those fine, strong legs around him. Her mouth was his to plunder, to own.

"Sarah..."

She pressed her hand to the side of his face. "It's okay. It really is..."

"I want..."

"I know..."

"But I can't..."

"I know..." She gasped then.

He commanded, "Let it happen."

She shook her head. "I don't…"

"Come *now*, Sarah. Right now."

And then she cried out, some wordless, lost, ecstatic sound.

He was lost, too. He surged into her.

She grabbed him close.

He whispered her name as the pleasure crested and swept him away.

Chapter Fourteen

They must have drifted off to sleep.

It was after two in the morning when she slipped from the bed. He was silent, watching her through the shadows as she put on her clothes.

He said nothing when she turned for the door.

"Goodbye, Maddox," she whispered as she left him. "Take care of yourself…"

He kept his mouth shut. If he said a word, he would say all the things he shouldn't—all the things that he couldn't.

A moment later, the door clicked softly shut behind her. He held himself in the bed with the force of his will alone. She knew the code to the front door. She could leave him without making a sound. She didn't need him there just to slip away.

And he couldn't afford to follow her out, couldn't bear to watch her go. He might do something foolish at the last minute, like make promises he couldn't keep. He wasn't the man for her. He never had been and he knew that all too well.

At breakfast that morning, his dad looked at him funny, kind of squinty-eyed and disapproving. Maddox pretended not to notice. The last thing he needed was a lecture from Fergus.

He got one anyway. That afternoon, the kids were out at the stables. Maddox had gone to his office because anytime he had a minute to himself, there was always plenty of work he really ought to catch up on.

Fergus found him there. The old man loomed in the doorway, standing tall in the air boot, no crutches. "I don't know where to start with you," he said.

"Then, don't," Maddox suggested hopefully.

Closing the door behind him, Fergus came slowly into the room. He took one of the chairs on the far side of the desk. "Sarah stayed half the night, didn't she?" Maddox didn't answer. His father went on anyway. "She stayed half the night and then you let her go, didn't you?"

Why lie? "Yes, Dad. We said goodbye." Okay, that *was* kind of a lie. But the words didn't really matter. They were on the same page, him and Sarah. He wasn't going there and she understood that.

"That's it, then? The end for you two?"

"Yeah, Dad. It's the end."

Fergus let out a low, disgusted sound. "She's the one for you. I know you can see that. You just pretend that you can't. That's a fool's game. It didn't work for me with Earlene. And son, it's not going to work for you, either."

"I'm not you, Dad."

"Then, why are you making the same mistake I made? Hurting Sarah, hurting yourself? You'll only be miserable until you wake up and admit how you really feel."

"Dad. Stop."

Fergus slapped the desk with the flat of his hand. "Wise up. Get out of your own way—and I don't know why I can't seem to get through to you."

"Because you and I disagree on this. And you're not going to change my mind."

Fergus's shoulders drooped. When he spoke again, his voice was gentle. "There's always been some part of you that's locked up so tight nobody's ever getting through. I don't know where that comes from. I suspect it's from way back at a time you don't even remember."

"Dad. I love you. And you don't know what you're talking about."

"Maybe not. But I do know you are throwing away your chance at happiness."

"Please, Dad." Maddox kept his tone mild. "You need to leave it. You need to let it be."

"A woman like Sarah, she's not going to wait forever."

"She's not waiting at all. She knows we won't be seeing each other again. That's just how it is."

"You're a damn fool, you know that?"

"No, Dad. I'm not. I know myself, that's all. Can we please let it go at that?"

Carefully, shaking his head, Fergus pushed himself up from the chair. "I give up. And now I'd better get out of here before I say something I can't take back." Head high, one cautious step at a time, he walked out the door.

The next day was Labor Day. Maddox and the kids hung around the house. They spent hours by the pool. It was a great day. The only hard part was trying not to wonder what Sarah might be up to.

On Tuesday morning, he hugged his dad, Earlene and Alma goodbye.

Stevie cried when her turn for hugs came. "We'll be back in the spring, Grandpa."

"I know you will, sweetheart."

She moved on to Earlene. "I will miss you so much."

Earlene hugged her tight. "We'll be thinking of you, looking forward to seeing you soon…"

Alma handed Stevie a tissue. "It won't be that long."

Stevie threw her arms around Alma's neck and sobbed. "It's not till spring and that *is* too long. Way too long. I don't know how I'm going to stand it…"

Even Caleb had appeared from the stables to see them off.

Stevie hugged him, too. "You take care of Pretty Girl for me."

"I will, honey. You can count on that."

RJ's goodbye was more dignified. He didn't say much, but he gave as many hugs as Stevie had, and he might have swiped moisture from his eyes once or twice.

They enjoyed an uneventful flight home. Both kids were quieter than usual. They'd barely arrived at the penthouse before Alexis and Teddy showed up. Alexis said she just couldn't wait to see her babies. Plus, they had a long to-do list to tackle in order to be ready for school, which started again on Thursday. Maddox hugged his children and sent them home with their mother.

It was too damn quiet after everyone left, just Maddox and Evan in the penthouse that seemed to echo with emptiness.

He couldn't take it. He called a buddy, Ryan, from the office. They met up at a bar midway between their apartments. Newly divorced and looking to blow off some steam, Ryan quickly got cozy with a woman who'd come in for happy hour with a few of her girlfriends. She and Ryan left together.

Maddox bought a round for the girlfriends. He knew

one of them. Her firm had done business with his in the past. She struck up a conversation with him and they talked for a while. She was pretty and bright and friendly, in her midthirties.

He didn't make a move, though. What was the point? He looked in her eyes and all he saw was Sarah, so he went home by himself.

This is bad, he thought, as he stood out on the terrace alone, staring out at the city lights, just him and a nightcap of excellent scotch. He couldn't stop thinking about big, dark eyes, about tangling his fingers in long brown hair.

But then he reminded himself that it hadn't even been seventy-two hours since he let her walk out of his life. He just needed to give it time. She'd really gotten to him in a way no other woman ever had. He had to accept that it would take a while to get over her.

He set his sights on enduring the loneliness without her. Eventually, this weird sense of desolation would fade. In a month or two—at least by Christmas—he would be his old self again.

September went on forever. At the office, he buried himself in work. It helped. But then, eventually, he had to go home and face the emptiness there, an emptiness that should have been no different than it used to be. After all, for years now he'd lived alone more than half the time. Nothing had changed, he constantly reminded himself.

At least he had the kids most weekends. That helped. Stevie was her usual happy, bouncy self. And he and RJ went to see a family therapist together once a week. It seemed to Maddox that his son was changing in good ways—becoming more open, more confident. RJ was on the soccer team and he'd signed up for track and field in the spring. His grades were excellent, as always.

By mid-October, Maddox had nothing but good to report. Business had never been better and his family was thriving. He talked to his dad every week or so. Fergus was happy, spending quite a bit of time up at Sylvan Acres and the rest of it at the ranch with Earlene at his side.

When Maddox ribbed him about the possibility of wedding bells in his future, his dad said no way.

"I will be with Earlene for as long as she'll have me," Fergus said. "But she lost her husband and I lost my wife. Neither of us wants to get married again. We're just happy we've found each other. And I'm damn grateful she forgave me for all the crap I pulled there at the first. Now we've gotten past all the trouble I made, we are a team. We're thankful to have what we have together at this time in our lives."

"Wow, Dad. What can I say? I'm happy for you."

"Thank you, son."

Not only had Fergus and Earlene become inseparable, but Earlene had given Fergus an Australian shepherd pup. He'd named the dog Atlas. From the way both of them talked, that dog was their baby. Sylvan Acres was pet-friendly, so wherever the love birds were staying, Atlas stayed with them.

Twice since Maddox had returned to Manhattan, Fergus had broached the subject of Sarah. Maddox never let him get going. He said he didn't want to talk about that. Both times, Fergus reluctantly let it go and Maddox went on waiting for the longing inside him to fade.

In the first week of November, he got a call from Tory Obermier, a lawyer he'd known since they were both at

Harvard. Like him, Tory had been married and was now divorced.

He and Tory met for dinner now and then. He always enjoyed catching up with her. She was funny and perceptive—great in bed, too.

When she called him this time, they agreed to meet at that terrific Indian restaurant at the Thompson Central Park. That way they could just get a room upstairs after dinner. He booked the room when he made the dinner reservation.

Before he headed for the hotel, he gave himself a pep talk, reminding himself that he'd always liked Tory and he hadn't had sex with a woman since that last time with Sarah.

He really should be over Sarah by now. And yet he dreamed of her almost nightly, sexy dreams that had him taking himself in hand afterward. He missed her every day—and if his dreams were any indication, all through the night, as well.

The evening did not go as planned. The minute he grabbed Tory in a hug at the table, he knew he couldn't do it.

She knew, too. She looked at him sideways and asked, "What's going on?"

He couldn't get the lie out. "Long story…"

"Oh, really? So what's her name?"

He just shook his head. They had dinner anyway and they talked about old times, about how their kids were doing, about the house Tory was building upstate.

Before they said good-night, she wished him luck. "…with whoever she is. I figure she's got to be someone special if she's gotten through to you."

"What? I'm that bad?"

"I did not use the word *bad*."

"But you thought it."

She laughed then, that big, rolling laugh that always made him want to grab her and hug her again. And then she said, "Give in, why don't you? How hard can it be?"

"I have no idea what you're talking about."

She went on tiptoe to whisper, "Liar," in his ear. And then, with a last wave over her shoulder, her full hips swaying, she headed for the door.

November crawled by. The kids had Thanksgiving at their mom's place. Alexis invited Maddox. He went because it seemed wrong to turn down Thanksgiving with his children. Teddy's brother and his family came, too.

It was nice, overall. The hardest part, strangely enough, was seeing Alexis and Teddy together. They were happy, the two of them. And for the first time, he envied them.

Why, he wondered as he walked home in the rain. Why did he suddenly envy his ex-wife her happiness? He'd known she was happy since she and Teddy got together. It had never been more than a fact to him before. His ex-wife's happiness with her second husband had nothing at all to do with him. He'd always been happy *for* her.

And he was still happy for Alexis. But now he was envious of her, too.

He needed to knock off the melancholy. It was Thanksgiving. He was supposed to be grateful, not envious and sad.

He got back to the penthouse around eight and called his dad at the ranch to wish him a happy Thanksgiving. Fergus was in great spirits. Alma and Earlene had prepared a feast. They'd invited several friends from Sylvan Acres.

In the background, he could hear laughter. The old folks were having a fine time.

His dad said, "Love you, son. Happy Thanksgiving."

"Happy Thanksgiving, Dad."

They said goodbye and Maddox stood there staring down at the phone in his hand. Before he could remind himself not to be a fool, he scrolled his contacts to Sarah's number—which he'd never managed to make himself delete—and sent her a text.

Happy Thanksgiving.

The text was barely gone before he considered unsending it.

Too late. It had been read.

Thanks, she replied. Happy Thanksgiving to you.

He hit the phone icon because he somehow couldn't stop himself. It rang once.

"Hello, Maddox." Her soft voice in his ear just about broke him. "What's up?"

"It's good to hear your voice." In the background on her end, music played. Other people talked and laughed. "Where are you?"

"Out with friends."

"Arlington's?" The steakhouse and bar was a Medicine Creek landmark.

"No. I'm not in Wyoming anymore. The job up in Sheridan was only for twelve weeks. Now I have another job, one I really like, at a family clinic. And I start school again in January."

"Great." He had a million questions and no business asking any of them. "So things are…moving along, huh?"

"Yes, they are—hold on." She said something to some-one on her end. And then she spoke to him again. "I have to go now."

"Right. Yeah. I…" He fumbled for the words and didn't find them.

"Maddox. Just say what you need to say."

"Is it all right if I call you again?" Where the hell did that come from? He closed his eyes and stifled a groan.

"Why?"

"I…" He felt like a kid again, and not in a good way. "I miss you. It's bad. I don't know how to stop."

"I miss you, too. All the time. What else do you want to know?"

He struggled for words.

And she got tired of waiting. "Goodbye, Maddox."

That was it. She ended the call.

He put the phone down and silently vowed never to try to contact her again.

And he kept that vow—though it wasn't easy. November became December. He helped the kids and Evan put up a tree at the penthouse.

The whole of New York got festive, as well. The tree went up at Rockefeller Center, where the ice rink was now open for business. Saks Fifth Avenue dazzled with their Christmas window displays. The Hudson Yards was a sea of golden light crowned with a giant, glittery hot-air balloon.

On the second Thursday in December, his dad called. "I'm coming to see you. I'll arrive at LaGuardia at seven thirty tomorrow night."

Maddox was flummoxed. "Why?"

"What, I can't come visit my own son?"

"Well, yeah. Sure you can. Sorry, Dad. You caught me by surprise. Listen, cancel that flight. I'll send the jet."

"Thanks, son. But I'm already booked on United."

"Is Earlene coming—and what about the dog?"

"Nope. They're staying home. It's just me. And it's only for two nights. I fly back Sunday morning."

This was definitely out of the ordinary. Should he be worried? "Is everything okay?"

"Better than ever. I just want a little *us* time, you and me."

"*Us* time?"

"Yeah. Got a problem with that?"

"Of course not." He was thinking of Alexis, flying to Wyoming last summer for a sit-down about RJ. What was so important that his dad had to fly here to see him now? "But why?"

"How many ways do I have to say it? I miss you. I want to see you and I'll be there tomorrow night."

"Well, great. I miss you, too, Dad. And just so you know, we won't be alone. RJ and Stevie will be coming over first thing Saturday morning."

"I can't wait to see 'em. You and me, we can talk alone when I get there Friday night."

"Talk alone about…?"

"Tomorrow, son. I'll tell you everything. Send a car to pick me up?" He rattled off the flight number.

"You got it. But Dad, I'm still a little confused as to why—"

"Whoops! Gotta go. Atlas wants out. And believe me, when Atlas wants out, it's better to let him out quick before he piddles all over the floor."

"Dad—"

"See you tomorrow, then."

"But Dad… Dad?"

It was too late. Fergus was already gone. Maddox started to call him back to try to get a straight answer as to what was really going on.

But he hung up without dialing. The old man was too cagey by half. If he'd wanted Maddox to know why he was coming, he would have told him already.

Maybe he and Earlene had decided to tie the knot, after all.

Fergus arrived at the penthouse at little after nine Friday night. He came striding in on both strong legs wearing a sheepskin coat and carrying a canvas duffel bag, looking straight out of *Yellowstone*. "Evan gone for the night?" he asked as he hung his hat and coat in the foyer and dropped the duffel beneath them.

"Yeah." Maddox stepped close. They shared a quick hug. "Dad, it really is great to see you. You look good."

"Thank you. I'm feeling good, too. Now put the coffee on, son. We need to talk."

They sat in the living room. Fergus took a sip of coffee and started right in. "I called Sarah last week, just to check in, see how she's doing."

Sarah?

Maddox jerked up straight in his chair. So then, this was not about marrying Earlene, after all? He demanded, "Are you telling me that you came all the way here to talk about Sarah?"

His dad gave a single firm nod. "Damn right I am—or mostly, anyway. She said you called her on Thanksgiving."

"It was a mistake…"

"No, son." His father's voice was softer now, full of tenderness and weighted with real sympathy. "This other thing you're doing, denying what you feel in your heart—that's the mistake. Calling Sarah is exactly the opposite of a mistake."

Now his throat felt thick with emotions he didn't want to own. He opened his mouth—and somehow, the truth fell out. "I try not to think about her."

"How's that going for you?"

He swallowed. Hard. And admitted the truth. "Not so good."

Fergus spread his knees, braced his forearms on them, clasped his hands together between them and narrowed his eyes. "Talk to me, son. Tell me. What are you afraid of?"

He intended to deny everything. But he was getting pretty fed up with denial. It wasn't working and every day he felt lower than the day before. So this time he tried a little honesty. "I'm not sure, Dad."

"Is it because she's so much younger, or because you don't want people saying you married your dad's nurse?"

"No—I mean, yeah, people would probably think those things if Sarah and I were together, but I'm past giving a damn what people think. As for what they might actually say, I'm forty years old and a senior VP at Hightower Property Trust. If they did say that garbage, I would never know. Because nobody would dare say crap like that to my face."

"Well, all right, then. If you're not afraid of what some damn fools might say, then what *are* you scared of?"

"Good question. It's…about the past. The distant past." He almost stopped there. But more words came to him and he went ahead and said them. "You and Mom and that nice therapist I had way back when, you did everything you could. But sometimes I think a part of me is still stuck in that crib on the day my birth parents died—afraid to move, scared to make a single sound."

Fergus shut his eyes and shook his head. "They told us you wouldn't remember any of it, that you were too young."

"And I *don't* remember it, Dad. But that's how I picture it. And I still feel it holding me back, you know? It's true that I did learn to trust you and Mom. But it wasn't by choice. You were just there and you wouldn't go away and you were good to me. There was no yelling. There were hugs. Gentle words. Slowly, against my will, I started to know that you weren't dangerous to me. That I could rely on you…"

"You can trust Sarah, too. She's got a big heart, that one. And she's wise beyond her years."

"I know, Dad. You're right. There's no one like Sarah. Not for me anyway."

"Well, then. If that's really how you feel…"

"Yeah. It is. It's really how I feel."

"Then, if something's still holding you back, you might consider just acting like you trust her."

"*Acting* like it?"

"That's right. Just go through the motions of trusting her. It's safe, because deep down you know that she deserves your trust. Eventually, you'll start believing what you already know."

"Dad, I know *nothing*. I don't even know where she is now. I don't even know where to start."

"She wouldn't tell you when you called her?"

"Well, she said she'd moved, that she was going back to school in January. She has a job at a clinic and she likes it. But she never said what town she was living in or what school she would be going to."

"She's here, son."

"Here?" The world seemed to tip on its axis. "What do you mean, here?"

"Here, in New York City. She's got a job at a family clinic on East Fifty-Fourth Street, just a few blocks from this apartment. She told me she's living in a dinky place, three hundred square feet down in the East Village. She's enrolled at New York University, the Rory Meyers College of Nursing, and she's starting school at the first of the year."

Chapter Fifteen

Maddox hardly slept that night. He kept thinking that Sarah had a job just blocks away from where he tossed and turned in his bed. That seemed impossible. That she was here, in his town.

Even more unbelievable, he hadn't even known it until his dad flew in and broke the news.

The kids showed up first thing Saturday morning. They were thrilled to see their grandpa. They all four went out to breakfast and then hung around the penthouse all day and evening, just being together.

Fergus left for the airport early Sunday morning. Stevie and RJ hated to see him go, and Maddox did, too. The rest of the day was spent going over homework and then visiting a local arcade for a couple of hours of fun and games before Maddox dropped his children off at their mother's townhouse.

As soon as the kids were out of the car, he gave his driver the address his dad had given him. A few minutes later, the car cruised slowly by Midtown Family Clinic on East Fifty-Fourth Street. The clinic was on the second floor, the entry door sandwiched between a liquor store and a deli.

Back at the penthouse, he'd looked up the clinic hours. Eight to five, Monday through Friday.

He considered calling her cell again.

But now that he knew where to find her, it became imperative to see her first, to make sure she was really there. He didn't doubt what his father had told him. He just needed to see the truth for himself.

Because that she was here, in New York? He still couldn't quite wrap his mind around it.

He decided to stake out the clinic where she worked. If she spotted him, so what? The whole point was to find her, to get a little time with her to tell her...

So much.

Everything. All the things he'd been holding himself back from saying through these endless months since that last perfect night with her at the ranch.

Coffee in hand, he was waiting outside the Midtown Family Clinic at seven thirty Monday morning. By nine, he'd failed to catch so much as a glimpse of Sarah. He did get a lot of dubious looks, though. Apparently, people got suspicious when a man lurked for more than an hour between a liquor store and a deli—even if he happened to be wearing a Tom Ford suit. At ten, he signaled his driver and headed downtown to the office.

But then, at four thirty, he was back on the street in front of the clinic. A light, soggy snow was falling. He flipped up the collar of his coat and stuck his hands in his pockets. His breath came out as mist. The Christmas lights in the window of the liquor store ten feet away blinked cheerfully, framing giant bottles of Smirnoff Peppermint Twist, Baileys Salted Caramel and Benchmark Egg Nog Bourbon.

Stalking was truly boring work—and again, no sign of Sarah. At six, he gave up and went home.

He should probably just call her. But first and foremost,

he needed to see her sweet face. He needed to be looking in those big dark eyes when he said the things he planned to say.

Tuesday morning, he was back at his post, even though his hope was dwindling. But then, at just a few minutes before eight, he spotted her.

She was walking east along Fifty-Fourth Street, coming straight toward him. She wore a red coat, a thick green wool scarf and a hat to match. Beneath the hem of her coat, he saw that her scrubs were green.

It hurt, just seeing her. Because he'd been missing her for months now. Because she'd been right here all this time, and he'd been too much of a stubborn fool to call her and ask her, *Where are you? Where can I find you? This is bad without you and all I want is to see your beautiful face again...*

He tried to think of what to say as she came straight at him—and then walked right on by without meeting his eyes. She pulled open the glass door that led up to the clinic and disappeared inside.

Stunned and thoroughly pissed off at himself for standing there gaping instead of making his move, he remained rooted to the spot as he debated the wisdom of following her in.

But no. He would try again this evening, and this time he'd be ready to step up, say hi like a normal man, ask her if maybe she'd go for a drink with him.

He pulled his phone from his pocket to call his driver, but before he could, it rang in his hand. He looked down at the lit-up screen.

Sarah...

His heartbeat roaring in his ears, he took the call. "Hello?"

"Maddox." Her voice. He smiled at the sound of it. "You've got to stop stalking me."

"Uh...it was only yesterday."

"Twice yesterday. And then again, right now—you do know you're standing outside the clinic where I work?"

"I do." What he didn't know was whether to laugh or start begging. "So, you knew I was here yesterday?"

"How could I not? Dr. Belo, our two other nurses, the receptionist and our PA all noticed the hot guy in the bespoke suit and the gorgeous wool coat lurking outside the downstairs entry door."

"But I didn't see *you* yesterday."

"It was a busy day. I got here early and left late. And you should know that Fergus called me Sunday night to warn me that he'd told you I was here in town."

"He did, yes. Flew all the way here just to talk a little sense into me."

"Did it work?" Now she sounded slightly breathless— which he decided was a good sign. Wasn't it?

"Yeah," he replied, his voice sounding ragged to his own ears. "It worked. That's why I'm here on the street outside your building. I'm hoping to convince you that I'm worth a second chance."

"I...see." Now she sounded a little bit...what? Overwhelmed maybe?

"Sarah?"

"Yeah?"

"Listen, don't tell me yes or no right now. Right now, just let me offer you my congratulations on getting into NYU. I understand that Rory Meyers is a great school."

"It is, yes. Only thirteen percent of applicants get in."

"And you are one of them. Congratulations."

"Thank you—and listen, Maddox, I do have to go now…"

"I get it. Just… When can I see you?"

"Why?"

The single word stopped him cold. Was she trying to figure out how to tell him he was too late?

He decided to think positive. "I'll be right here on the street waiting for you tonight at five."

"And then what?"

"Dinner. Please?"

"You sure about this?" She sounded almost nervous now.

"God, yes. Five?"

A slow, shaky breath on the other end and then, "Yes. All right. I'll see you at five."

She came out of the glass door downstairs from the clinic at 5:03 p.m., carrying a big tote on her shoulder. It was snowing and the wind was blowing. He'd never been so happy to see anyone in his life.

Hunched in their heavy coats, they stared at each other. She was shivering. People hurried along the sidewalk swerving around them and moving on. Down at the corner, a Salvation Army Santa stood by his red kettle, ringing his bell.

"You're freezing." He signaled his driver. "Let's get you in the car." A moment later, the car swung in at the curb. Maddox opened the door and she slid in across the back seat. He got in after her and pulled the door closed on the blustery evening outside. "I got us a table at Marea on Central Park South. It's quiet and cozy. Great food…"

"It sounds wonderful…" But she was frowning.

"What? Tell me…"

"Well, I was just thinking. I would love to go to Marea—but not tonight. We do need to talk, you know? I keep thinking it should happen somewhere private. Maybe your place?"

The penthouse? That sounded good—didn't it? If she planned to tell him to forget about her, she wouldn't be asking to go to his apartment. Would she? "Evan's already gone. We'd be raiding the refrigerator."

"That sounds perfect to me."

The choice was made. The car slid out into traffic headed for home as he called the restaurant and cancelled their reservation.

At his building, they ran through the driving snow to the lobby doors. Roger, the doorman, greeted them."Mr. Hale."

"Thanks, Roger."

A minute later, they were on the elevator up to the penthouse. She was too quiet. By the time they entered the apartment, he was certain she was only trying to figure out how to let him down easy.

He helped her out of her coat and hung it in the foyer. She was wearing a red wool dress that came to midthigh, black tights and black lace-up boots. "What happened to your green scrubs?"

"I keep a change of clothes at the clinic." She hung the big tote by her coat. "When I finished my shift, I assumed we were going out to eat." The doors were wide open to the living room. She made a low, delighted sound as they approached. "The tree is beautiful."

"Yeah. The kids and Evan do a mean Christmas tree."

"I'll bet you helped."

"Maybe. Just a little…"

They stood at the big window that looked out on the terrace. Lights twinkled in a thousand other windows, some of them on Christmas trees.

He wanted to touch her, pull her to him, wrap her up in his arms.

But as of now, he didn't dare. "Are you hungry?"

She looked at him then, those dark eyes enormous. "Right now I'm too nervous to eat."

He dared to smooth a stray curl of hair back over her shoulder. "I know the feeling." This close, her scent teased at him. At the moment, all the signs were good. She did seem glad to see him.

Still, he kept wondering, was this just another goodbye?

And he realized that even if it was, at least she was here with him this one more time.

She gestured toward the sofa. "Come on. Let's sit down, okay?"

"Good idea."

They sat side-by-side.

There was silence. They stared at each other.

He almost threw up both hands and begged her to put him out of his misery.

Finally, she said, so softly, "I've missed you, Maddox. I've missed you so much."

His heart went wild in the cage of his chest. Because there was no doubt about it. This was definitely good. This was hope and hope was everything.

Because *she* was everything. "I've missed you too, every damn day since you left me that Sunday morning before Labor Day." His voice sounded gravelly to his own ears. "I can't tell you how many times I wanted to punch my own face for letting you go."

She drew a slow, careful breath and asked in a low voice, "Well, then. Why *did* you let me go?"

"Because I honestly believed that I was too messed up, too damaged, that I would only screw it up with you. That it was better for both of us if we didn't even try."

Tears gleamed in her eyes. She swiped them away. "Are you saying you were damaged by what happened when you were little?"

"Yes."

She reached out, brushed her finger lightly along the crest of his cheek. That feathery touch was everything. "What changed?"

"I've missed you so much. I started to see that I would never stop missing you. I finally began to think that I ought to get real about how much you mean to me so I could somehow learn to deal with that. Then my dad flew in to see me. He convinced me that I needed to stop standing in my own way."

"Fergus." A soft smile curved her lips. "He's the best." That smile vanished too soon. She was suddenly all seriousness. "Can you do that, then? Can you get out of your own way?"

He nodded slowly. "For you, yes I can—I mean, if you'll take a chance on me. If you'll trust me that much." He took her hand. She didn't pull away. And that made him bold enough to say the words that mattered most. "I love you, Sarah Bravo."

She drew a sharp breath. "Oh, Maddox…"

He slipped his thumb into the curve of her palm and stroked it gently. "But let's face it," he confessed. "I'm new at this. I've never been in love before. And I'm terrified I'll screw it up. But I promise you, it's real, what I feel for you. And all I want is to find the ways to show you every day that you are everything to me."

Her soft lips were trembling. "I love you, too."

He closed his eyes. "Say that again."

"I love you, Maddox Hale. So much." She leaned even closer.

He couldn't hold back any longer. He wrapped his arms around her and kissed her.

The miracle happened. She kissed him back.

For a while, they just sat there on the sofa in the soft glow of the Christmas tree lights, holding each other, sharing one kiss after another.

In time, with a sigh, she leaned her head on his shoulder.

He said, "I know you've got plans. I know you won't always be here at my side. That you'll be heading off to help the people who need you the most, that I'm going to have to show some serious self-restraint and trust. I'll probably screw up a lot. But I swear, if you'll bear with me, I will keep trying. I mean, if you say yes…"

She blinked at him. "Wait. You're proposing right now?"

"Well, I don't want to freak you out, but I do want to marry you, Sarah."

"So…not a proposal. More of a warning?"

They both laughed at that.

He said, "Call it whatever you'd like. I would be on my knees right now if I didn't have the feeling that might be pushing you too fast."

She was nodding. "You're right. Let's just be together for a few months. Let's take it one step at a time."

"Agreed. And about children…"

She gave him a teasing smile. "You mean RJ and Stevie? They're not a problem for me. I already love them both."

"I'm glad. But what I'm getting at here is that if you want babies of your own, I'm onboard with that."

"Whoa. That's a lot. We don't have to decide all that now, do we?"

"No, we do not. But you should know that I've thought it over and I'm up for more kids when the time is right, if that's what you want."

"Are you sure?"

"I am."

"Well, then, yes. I will want to try for a baby. Not for a while. But at some point." She squeezed his fingers. "Right now, though, we do need to think about Stevie and RJ. We have to talk to them about this, about you and me, about our future as a family. It's important that they feel included, that they know they come first."

"Sarah. I'm not worried. They love you already."

"Still. They have to be consulted. We can't get too far ahead of ourselves, you know?"

He chuckled. "Suddenly cautious, are we?"

"Well, you have to admit you've had a giant change of heart."

"I have, yes." He tried a slow breath. "Sorry if I'm rushing you. It's as if I finally woke up and there's so much to do…"

"I get that. And if you really mean all this…"

"Sarah. I do. Absolutely."

"Then, you *will* have to talk to your children."

"I know. They're with me on the weekends. Saturday, I'll—"

She put her hand against his chest. "Hold on. Maybe wait till after Christmas?"

He chuckled. "Hurry up, but not yet?"

"Kind of. I don't want to push them too fast."

"I hear you. We'll talk about it more. We can't decide everything right this minute…"

She sighed. "Yeah. We need to take this one step at a time." She leaned her head on his shoulder. "I have to confess…" Her voice trailed off.

"What? Just say it."

"Well, I applied at NYU in part because it's one of the best nursing programs in the country. But that wasn't the only reason. I was still hoping that maybe someday, you might come looking for me." She glanced up at him then. Her glowing smile was just the slightest bit devious. "I didn't want to make it *too* hard for you to find me."

He eased a hand under the soft waves of her hair and turned enough to press his forehead to hers. "I can't believe you were right here in Manhattan when I called you at Thanksgiving. And I have a confession, too…"

"Tell me. Please."

"Wherever you finally decided to get your master's degree, eventually I would have shown up there to beg you to give me one more chance."

"I think you really mean that." Her voice was reverent now.

"I absolutely do." He kissed her then. That kiss started out tender and sweet but slowly turned hungry and deep. When he scooped her up to carry her to his bedroom, she wrapped her arms around his neck and whispered his name against his parted lips.

An hour later, they headed for the kitchen to raid the refrigerator and continue the ongoing discussion of the rest of their lives.

On their way back to bed, she paused at the row of windows that looked out on the terrace. He stepped behind her and wrapped her up in his arms.

"It's so beautiful…" she said. The snow was coming down steadily, a glittery curtain of white. "Suddenly, it's almost Christmas."

He pressed his lips into her hair. "And I know what you're thinking…"

She tipped her head back to meet his eyes. "Last summer, you said that when Christmas comes—"

"I remember. I said we'd be miles and miles apart, living our completely separate lives."

"Well, Maddox, it looks like you might have been wrong." She turned in his arms and grinned up at him.

He didn't think he'd ever been happier than at this exact moment. "I *was* wrong. So wrong."

"But look. It all worked out."

"Yes, it did. And now here we are, together. There is no place on Earth that I would rather be."

"Merry Christmas, my love," she whispered as he lowered his mouth to hers.

They were married the following summer, an outdoor wedding on the Double-K. Fergus stood up as Maddox's best man and RJ was his groomsman. Piper Bravo was Sarah's maid of honor with Stevie as her only other bridesmaid. Emmy proudly took part as the flower girl.

After the vows had been spoken, Maddox took Sarah into his arms. He stared down into her big brown eyes and marveled at how his life had changed in the course of a single year.

"I love you, Maddox Hale," she whispered, smiling up at him.

"And I love you," he replied in wonderment. "I never thought this could happen."

"But it has," she said. "Now kiss me."

* * * * *

Watch for Ethan Bravo's story,
coming in April 2025
only from Harlequin Special Edition.